HOW
WE
FALL

Kate Brauning

MeritPress | fw

Published by
Merit Press
an imprint of F+W Media, Inc.
10151 Carver Road, Suite 200
Blue Ash, OH 45242. U.S.A.
www.meritpressbooks.com

ISBN 10: 1-4405-8179-7
ISBN 13: 978-1-4405-8179-3
eISBN 10: 1-4405-8180-0
eISBN 13: 978-1-4405-8180-9

Printed in the United States of America.

10 9 8 7 6 5 4 3 2 1

Library of Congress Cataloging-in-Publication Data
Brauning, Kate.
How we fall / Kate Brauning.
  pages cm
  Summary: As first cousins, seventeen-year-olds Jackie and Marcus know their love is taboo, but
living in the same house, working at the family's vegetable stand, and seeking Jackie's missing
best friend, Ellie, draws them together.
  ISBN 978-1-4405-8179-3 (hc) -- ISBN 1-4405-8179-7 (hc) -- ISBN 978-1-4405-8180-9 (ebook)
-- ISBN 1-4405-8180-0 (ebook)
  [1. Missing children--Fiction. 2. Love--Fiction. 3. Cousins--Fiction. 4. Family life--Missouri--
Fiction. 5. Missouri--Fiction. 6. Mystery and detective stories.] I. Title.
  PZ7.B73788How 2014
  [Fic]--dc23
                              2014013254

Cover design by Frank Rivera.
Cover image © iStockphoto.com/DanSchmitt.

This book is available at quantity discounts for bulk purchases.
For information, please call 1-800-289-0963.

To my mother, Lori, for telling me I could be anything, and especially for all those talks in the kitchen. And to my husband, Jesse, for everything, every day.

"I'm the last of the worst pretenders."

~Matt Nathanson, "Mission Bells"

Chapter One

Last year, Ellie used to hang out at the vegetable stand with Marcus and me on Saturdays. This year, her face fluttered on a piece of paper tacked to the park's bulletin board. Most weeks, I tried to ignore her eyes looking back at me. But today, Marcus had set the table up at a different angle, and she watched me the entire morning.

The day that photo was taken, she'd worn her *Beauty and the Beast* earrings. The teapot and the teacup were too small to see well in the grainy, blown-up photo, but that's what they were. She'd insisted sixteen wasn't too old for Disney.

The crunch of tires on gravel sounded, and a Buick slowed to a stop in front of the stand. I rearranged the bags of green beans to have something to do. Talking to people I didn't know, making pointless small talk, wasn't my thing. My breathing always sped up and I never knew what to do with my hands. It had been okay before, but now—surely people could see it on me. One look, and they'd know. Chills prickled up my arms in spite of the warm sun.

Marcus lifted a new crate of cucumbers from the truck and set it down by the table, his biceps stretching the sleeves of his T-shirt. Barely paying attention to the girl who got out of the car, he watched me instead. And not the way most people watched someone; I had his full attention. All of him, tuned toward me. He winked, the tanned skin around his eyes crinkling when he smiled. I bit my cheek to keep from grinning.

The girl walked over to the stand and I quit smiling.

Marcus looked away from me, his gaze drifting toward the girl. Each step of her strappy heels made my stomach sink a little further. Marcus tilted his head.

He didn't tilt it much, but I knew what it meant. He did that when he saw my tan line or I wore a short skirt. I narrowed my eyes.

"Hi," she said. "I'd like a zucchini and four tomatoes." Just like that. A zucchini and four tomatoes.

Marcus placed the tomatoes into a brown paper bag. "Are you from around here?"

Of course she wasn't from around here. We'd know her if she were.

"We just moved. I'm Sylvia Young." The breeze toyed with her blonde hair, tossing short wisps around her high cheekbones. Her smile seemed genuine and friendly. Of course. Pretty, friendly, and new to town, because disasters come in threes.

"Going to Manson High?" Marcus handed her the bags.

She nodded. "My dad's teaching science."

Finally, I said something. "Three bucks."

"Hmm?" Sylvia turned from Marcus. "Oh. Right." She handed me the cash and looked over the radishes. "Are you here every day?" Her eyes strayed back to Marcus.

"Three times a week," he said.

"I'll see you in a day or two, then." She waved.

I was pretty damn sure she wouldn't be coming back for the radishes.

Sylvia Young walked herself and her vegetables back to the four-door parked at the edge of the road. The tires spit gravel.

I glanced at Marcus, but he wasn't watching her leave. He was rearranging the tomatoes. In true Marcus fashion, now that four of them were gone, he'd want to make the pile neat again.

I exhaled. Maybe I was overreacting, but he hadn't done that before.

"You're going to bruise those." I grabbed a tomato that nearly tumbled off the mound. The globe-shaped Early Girls rolled too easily. "Don't we have extra crates?" I looked to the shade of the bulletin board, where we stored the refill crates. No empties.

"Nope. Too much corn." He wiped the sweat from his forehead and popped the top on his water bottle.

What amounted to a sweet corn fortress stood behind us. Stacks of milk crates—neatly stacked, because Marcus is Marcus—blocked the park and most of the town from view.

He leaned against the table and smiled at me, his brown eyes finding mine and his body turning toward me again. I felt the shift, felt the pull in my body that made me stay with him. My shoulders loosened without me even trying. He hadn't smiled at Sylvia Young that way.

He tapped my nose with a finger. "Hey, what an expression. Jealous of something, Jackie?"

"So jealous. I'd love to have my own car. What's the point to being seventeen if I can't have a car?"

His eyebrows went up. He took a drink from the water bottle and set it down, his eyes flicking from me to the ground then back to me again.

Being jealous would be silly, because Marcus and I weren't dating. That was the deal. For an entire year, our deal had worked, and there was no reason it couldn't work longer.

Whatever expression that had been vanished and his grin came back. "Whatever. You use my truck all the time." He was tall enough the edge of the table met his thigh instead of his hip.

Anytime I used his truck, he came with. Down to the river. Everyone in the county knew what those tree-lined fencerows were good for.

Marcus reached for my hand and threaded his long fingers between mine. The rough calluses on his palm made a warm, silly feeling trickle through me.

My face flushed and I glanced around. He'd started doing this lately. Reaching for my hand. Touching my shoulder as he walked past. I pulled my hand away and rubbed my palms on my shorts.

Acting like this was ridiculous. Sylvia was pretty and friendly, so of course he'd smile and say hi. And Marcus owed me nothing.

It was a cheap move, but just because I was nervous, and okay, jealous, I played with the frayed edge of my jean shorts. My legs weren't bad, and these shorts were my shortest pair.

He glanced down like I knew he would and touched my hand again. "Well, don't be too upset. She doesn't have your legs."

Something tiny thrilled inside me. "That's true. She does have her own." That was the thing about Marcus. He knew I didn't mean what I said; that when I claimed I wasn't jealous, I absolutely was.

He shouldn't know those kinds of things. And he definitely shouldn't be holding my hand to make me feel better.

An engine guttered and cut out. The door of a white pickup right in front of us opened and then slammed.

Marcus jerked his hand back like mine had stung him. I hadn't heard the truck. I hadn't noticed. How had I not noticed?

A skinny man in jeans and sunglasses walked toward us. No one we knew. Relief churned into nausea in my stomach. I turned away to restack some of the sweet corn with my heartbeat reverberating in my ears.

Nothing had happened, it was fine, but I still couldn't stop my hands from trembling. I gripped the crate harder.

The man in sunglasses talked to Marcus, but he kept glancing toward me, his head tilting just a bit when he looked my way.

He wasn't someone we knew, but he could have been. In a town this small, it was odd to have someone we didn't know come to the stand. He left after a few minutes with spinach and green onions, and the white truck rumbled away.

We'd let this go on too long. We were too comfortable. And Marcus knew it, too—he stayed away from me for the rest of the afternoon, our glances brief and casual, even when no one was around. He did not touch me again and I let the sick feeling in my stomach keep my mind where it needed to be.

By dinner time, we'd sold only a third of the sweet corn fortress. Sweet corn wasn't the smartest garden crop, because everyone around here had a patch in their yard. Two weeks from now, we'd be giving it away. A month from now, we'd be throwing it away. But grow sweet corn we did, because my parents had read too much *Little House on the Prairie*.

Of course, no one in that story smoked weed through their early twenties. My mother's pothead college days were a secret to no one, and my parents' room still sometimes smelled like weed.

Once five o'clock came, I lifted crates and combined the leftover produce without hurrying more than necessary. But like usual, Marcus seemed hell-bent on beating some personal record, stacking, shoving, lifting at twice my speed.

I picked up a crate from the shade of the bulletin board. The breeze fluttered the papers tacked to the cork—papers offering lawn-mowing services, piano lessons, babysitting. And the flyer with Ellie's junior photo and a tip line number.

The soft rasp of the paper edges scraping each other caught me like music.

Four months.

That weight in my chest—always there, now—seized up and for a moment I couldn't breathe.

I ducked my head and went back to loading the cucumbers. Ran away with some guy, everyone said. Not a chance. We'd played volleyball together, hung out at the pool on weekends, did homework together. She would have told me about a guy.

I ran my finger along the silver bracelet that always hung on my wrist. Ellie had given it to me before she moved. I hadn't taken it off since she'd gone missing, and now I never would.

Late-afternoon sun baked the park and the vegetables and my skin. If I could get to the pool still today, I could chill my body in the water, lay out on my towel, and put myself, Ellie, and Marcus out of my mind.

I rolled up the tarp and tossed it to Marcus. The pool wouldn't happen, but maybe we could watch a movie instead.

No way was I going to let the things that hurt ruin the things that didn't. Worrying about Ellie wouldn't help her, and Marcus and I were fine. A little too comfortable, maybe. But changing the topic was just as good as fixing the problem.

I grabbed his water bottle from the tailgate as he jumped down from the truck bed. Just as he turned toward me, I popped the top up and squeezed. Water shot out and soaked his shirt.

"Hey! What the—" His face colored pink, but he was half-grinning. Rattling him was too easy.

But I was in for it. Determination settled in his eyes and he took a step toward me. I ran for the truck, jerked the door open, and scrambled inside, then hit the lock button.

The tailgate slammed and he walked past the passenger door, tapping his finger along the window.

He climbed into the driver's seat and started the engine, the muscles in his forearm tightening when he turned the key. He wouldn't let me off the hook that easily, so he must have a plan for delayed revenge. I waited, but nothing. My eyebrows went up. He looked over at me and shook his head.

This was lousy payback. His nice blue T-shirt was soaked. "That's all you've got? You're going to shake your head at me like you're my mom?"

He spun the steering wheel and braced his arm behind my seat, looking out the back window as he backed the truck down the asphalt path and out onto the street. "I'm definitely not your mother."

"Thank God for that."

His mouth twitched. I shifted in the seat, turning toward him. He couldn't do much while driving, but being on my guard couldn't hurt, and my curiosity was getting the better of me.

"Hey, buckle your seatbelt."

I reached for the belt. "Now you really sound like Mom."

He ignored me and drove the few blocks to the edge of town. The welcome sign for Manson, Missouri, boasted a population of 212, but that was wishful thinking. The town was a collection of abandoned buildings and poorly insulated homes from the early 1900s. My sister, my only sibling and my extroverted, energetic opposite, bolted for the nearest city as soon as she graduated, but I didn't mind Manson so much.

Outside town, Marcus turned off the blacktop highway and onto a dirt road. Not even gravel. Dirt. Nothing was down this road except fields. "Uh—where are we going?"

He parked the truck on the side of the road under the shade of the tree-lined fencerow. The shadows from the branches swam back and forth on the road. Marcus rolled down his window and the breeze swept through the cab, smelling like summer and creek water and grass.

"You can unbuckle your seatbelt now." He grinned, no trace of embarrassment left.

My eyes narrowed. Maybe my attempts at getting him to loosen up were a little too successful. "What are you doing?"

He reached over and unbuckled me. The belt slid back over my shoulder and I moved it aside.

Marcus slid toward me on the bench. He hooked an arm around my waist and one under my knees, and pulled me toward him.

Tan arms. Sandpaper skin, because he hadn't shaved this morning. I touched the wet fabric of his shirt.

We shouldn't. Not now, not even to begin with. He knew it. I knew it. But he leaned closer, bent down, and I didn't move away. His lips touched mine. Warm. Familiar. A little desperate.

No one was here. The road was abandoned. I'd kept myself where I ought to be all afternoon. I relaxed, closed my eyes, and kissed him back. I should be watching out the window, should be glancing in the mirror, but his mouth pressed into my neck, and I exhaled, tipped my head back against the headrest, and let my mind stop spinning. When he pushed closer, our bodies touching everywhere they could, my stomach fluttered. His hands found my hair, his lips came back to my face, and I tasted the salty sheen on his skin. His eyelashes brushed my cheek. Any thoughts I'd had dissolved. Just him, yes. Us, connected.

My hands found his shoulders, feeling the clench of his muscles. That was for me. Because of me. I traced down his arm to his hand that rested on my bare leg, touching the hem of my shorts. He kissed my neck and my jaw and then came back to my lips again. He was so much but so soft and slow that it seemed like he was trying to tell me something.

I did not want him to.

I moved my hands to his chest and tangled my fingers in his shirt. Then I pushed a little, the weight of his body on my hands.

He moved back, sighing. The breeze rushed between us. "Later?" I asked.

Everyone knew his truck, and everyone knew us. He cleared his throat and nodded.

"You okay?"

He nodded again.

I bumped him with my shoe. "As far as payback goes, that wasn't exactly fair."

He raised his eyebrows. "You started it."

Sitting with him in the truck like this was tempting. Just to talk. To tease him and watch him grin like that. Here we were the most ourselves, and us together like this was where act three of a happily-ever-after would end. And much as I would love a fade to black and the end credits to roll, letting this be the point we hung on forever, we wouldn't get a fade-out, and the other half of our lives was waiting.

Chapter Two

Marcus turned left onto the blacktop. He didn't say anything, and I didn't, either. By now we'd learned there just wasn't anything to say, and trying to find something that would help never did.

We pulled up the long driveway to the house. It had a two-story brick front, but the rest was built into a hill. "Earth-sheltered," Aunt Shelly said, but my friends called it hobbit-style. I loved the stained wood and the dozen small places for hiding to read. Useful, since my parents and I shared the house with my aunt and uncle and their six kids.

I climbed out of the truck. Marcus fiddled around with something in the truck bed, so I went on ahead of him, glancing back in spite of telling myself not to. After managing to find time to ourselves, it always jarred me a bit to come home. Readjusting my personal space to not include Marcus took me a minute.

He jogged up the driveway. Like always, he caught the screen door before it banged behind me.

"Sixty bucks, Mom." I dropped the cash on the counter. People said we looked alike, but I didn't have her smile or the hair. I'd seen her college pictures—frayed jean cutoffs, a bikini top, a guy-stopping smile. The same gorgeous, blonde waist-length braid she had now.

I refused to do the braids. Braids make redheads look like Pippi Longstocking.

Her giant chef's knife snicked on the cutting board. She was slicing zucchini while Simon & Garfunkel played from the kitchen sound system. "Oh, thank you. Can you whip the egg for these? I'm in a hurry."

"Give me a second to wash my hands." I headed for the main-floor bathroom at the end of the hall.

"I should do that, too." Marcus followed me.

I turned the taps to the cool side of warm and pared the dirt from under my fingernails. Marcus hovered behind me. An inch over six feet tall, and not done growing. Aware he was watching me, I leaned back half a step to brush his chest with my shoulder. Teasing him wasn't fair, but I couldn't help myself.

"Hey." He hooked a finger in one of the belt loops on my jean shorts and pulled me back another step. His hands settled on my waist, his body close to mine.

I pulled his hands off me. "Not here," I whispered. Dad's office and my bedroom were the only rooms back here, but still. If we bent one rule, we'd break them all.

"No one's around," he said, his brown eyes meeting mine in the mirror.

His expression stopped me. His shoulders were too straight, his smile forced, his stance too casual.

I almost never did this because it fell into the category of handholding and pet names, but because I didn't want him to look like that, I stood up on my tiptoes and kissed his cheek.

For a moment, he looked stunned, then a slow grin split his face.

"What's that look for?" I asked. If it weren't so dangerous, I'd do that more often just to see him look like that.

"I mean, it's not what I was hoping for, but I guess it'll do." He shoved his hands in his pockets, still grinning.

That meant we were fine. I pulled away and continued scrubbing the dirt out of my nails, but his expression in the mirror caught me. "Later." I smiled. Marcus didn't mind me teasing him. He knew there would be later.

He leaned against the bathroom wall, looking stern. "You really like playing hard to get, don't you?"

"It's half the attraction." It wasn't. But I did enjoy it.

Something creaked in the hall. My hand slipped on the faucet and Marcus stepped toward the doorway just as his dad walked past. Hot water scalded my hand and I yelped. Uncle Ward barely glanced at us and continued down the hall.

I braced my hand on the edge of the sink and took a breath. All those sick feelings were back.

My uncle was mostly to blame for my family moving to Missouri. Uncle Ward and Aunt Shelly were into whole wheat and fresh air—ideas he picked up during his pot phase. They'd pecked away at Mom and Dad until I was fourteen. "Oh, sis, you have no idea. Missouri hardwoods. Great for handmade cabinets. And the children play in the yard all day. No kid wants video games when they can have creeks and crawdads."

Uncle Ward's opinions were a junk-drawer combination of traditional family values, generous interpretations of self-restraint and normalcy, and questionable ideas Aunt Shelly found on the Internet. He was right about one thing, though: Missouri had its benefits.

I just had to keep my two selves separate.

Marcus followed me back into the kitchen, but we both stopped in the doorway.

"Oh, gross, Dad." My dad had Mom pinned up against the counter. Her arms were around his neck, and they were full-on making out. "Ugh. Get a room."

Dad pulled away, not looking the least bit embarrassed. He grinned at us. "That's the plan."

I groaned. I had never managed to convince my parents, or my aunt and uncle for that matter, just how much their children did not want to see them Frenching.

Mom pushed him away and scooted the bowl of zucchini slices toward me. Marcus was avoiding making eye contact with anyone, still weirded out even though this happened at least once a week. Some things people just didn't adjust to.

Dad straightened the cuffs on his striped green button-up and cleared his throat. "Are Ward and Shelly ready?" The expensive black slacks were leftovers from his days of lawyering in California. He did legal consulting from home now. I'd once hoped moving to Missouri was his midlife crisis, but it now looked like a rest-of-life crisis.

"Can you tell them to hurry?" Mom peeked into the oven. "We can go as soon as I change."

Dad left the room and I set a bowl on the stone countertop and cracked three eggs.

"I need the whisk," I said to Marcus.

"Please. I need the whisk, please," my mother added for me. "And ignore your cousin when she talks like that, Marcus."

Our kitchen had hardwood floors and a huge window nearly covering the wall, separated into panes by strips of lacquered wood, to make up for the few windows in the rest of the house. A giant island commanded the center of the room. When my parents decided we should all move in together to live cheaply and reduce our environmental impact, they'd sold our place in California to build this one. That way, they could share cars, a lawnmower, and house payments. Having her dream kitchen had been one of Mom's conditions for building a house with her brother's family.

"I don't mind." Marcus handed me the whisk and leaned against the counter. "She can boss me around. I don't have anything better to do."

I raised an eyebrow at him when Mom turned away. I was plenty nice to Marcus. I dropped a stack of zucchini slices into the egg and then dipped them one at a time into the bowl of seasoned bread crumbs and Parmesan.

Dinner was usually a family sit-down thing. Part of the wholesome lifestyle goal. Mom would stir her coffee with her straw and talk about how the chickens were hiding their eggs again and we'd need to go find the new nests. Uncle Ward would rant about Sheriff Whitley getting re-elected only because he let the farmers' kids drive grain trucks underage, while my twin cousins would bang their plates with their spoons and Marcus's younger sister Candace would eventually tell them to stop it, boys, I can't hear anything. Marcus would sit across from me and try to make me turn red while my parents were watching. Usually I won.

"You kids can eat whenever you want," Mom said as Candace wandered into the kitchen. "We won't be back til late."

At nine, Candace was too young to know where the parents were going for their date night. Some kind of adults-only club in the city. I didn't want to know anything more than that, and had never wanted to find out in the first place.

Candace gave the platter of raw zucchini a sideways glance. "Since we have to eat zucchini, can we have ice cream after dinner?"

Mom flipped the zucchini with a pair of tongs. The olive oil snapped and the toasty smell of frying Parmesan rose with the steam. "That's up to Marcus and Jackie. They're babysitting."

"We can have ice cream, right?" Candace turned to Marcus. The younger kids all knew he'd let them have pretty much anything. Candace had figured that out by her second birthday.

"Hmm. What do you think, Jackie? We could make them earn it." His smile made me grin.

"The basement does need a good debugging," I said. "I think I even saw a goblin down there last week." Our basement was more of a cellar—uncarpeted and mostly for storage. But it was also cool and quiet and one of my favorite hiding places.

Candace looked at me like I should know better as she walked out of the room. "Goblins aren't real, and children shouldn't use pesticides. I'm telling the twins you said we can have ice cream."

Mom opened one of the in-wall double-oven doors. A chicken and rice casserole bubbled on the rack. "I have to go get ready. I should have gone twenty minutes ago." She set the casserole on the table. "We might be gone overnight. Ward and Shelly want to stay at that hotel they like, and we'll be at the club until late anyway."

Marcus glanced at me, grimacing, at least as uncomfortable as I was. I shook my head and pulled a stack of plates from the cupboard. Seven instead of eleven tonight, since the parents would be gone. "I know. I figured." My mother was nothing if not frank with her children.

My parents had always been semi-closeted hippies, but now that Uncle Ward had won them over, all freak flags were flying. Repression and self-restraint could damage your brain, he said. Probably another one of Aunt Shelly's ideas from the Internet. Any time I protested the public making-out, they reminded me of the importance of "fully expressive" relationships.

If only they knew.

I watched Marcus stirring his hot chocolate on the stove, thoroughly at home in this kitchen, this house, because it was his home, too. I almost wished that first kiss had never happened.

We were friends first, and this deal of ours risked that. Marcus had kept me from being bullied at school three years ago when we first moved here and I was the new girl with the weird family. He was an island of sanity in a household of anything-goes chaos. I never felt like I didn't fit in when he was around, because we were our own group. He and I. And even when he was tired—I could see it right now in his shoulders, his eyes—he was patient and did his share. More than his share.

Mom left the kitchen and I turned down the burner so the oil didn't smoke. Marcus shook his head and huffed as he rinsed out the hot chocolate pan. "Brain damage. That's what's going to happen. If I have to see our parents doing that one more time, I'm going to suffer serious mental trauma."

Grinning made my sympathetic glance unconvincing.

"Hey." He picked up a newspaper from the table. "Another neighbor talking about Ellie."

"Really?" I glanced over. Her photo, the same one on the park notice board, headed a multiple-column article. More speculation about her disappearance. News was scarce around here, and her story kept getting dragged up as the headline. I skimmed the article. The neighbor said he'd seen Ellie behaving strangely for the last several weeks before she went missing. He suspected drugs. The article digressed into hearsay about Missouri's meth labs.

Ellie would never do drugs. I touched the silver charm bracelet she'd given me. She had one that matched. At least, when she left, they had matched. She might have added to hers by now, decided it could be hers instead of ours. I hadn't changed mine. A volleyball, an Eiffel Tower for her Paris obsession, the world's clunkiest cell phone for all the hours we'd spent texting, a book, and a tiny silver computer dangled from the chain. The computer was for my blogging. She was the social media queen, so it fit for her, too. We often did homework at the picnic tables outside the dilapidated burger place in Manson, ice cream in hand. My one year of volleyball had been Ellie's last year at Manson High. Because I was clearly the worst player, and Ellie was clearly the best, she'd tried to show me some tricks, and I was actually enjoying myself by the time she transferred to Edison High School in St. Joseph.

The sixth charm on the bracelet was a bird in flight, wings outstretched. We'd sworn to stay friends even though she was leaving. The bird had come to mean a lot more than just her move to St. Joseph. She was really, truly gone now, and the part that made me sick was that we hadn't stayed close. We hadn't kept up like we'd meant to. Phone calls. E-mails. A few visits. The months before she disappeared, we'd barely been texting.

Marcus set glasses on the table and didn't say anything for a few minutes, simply stared into his hot chocolate. He'd drink hot chocolate any time of day, regardless of the season. I left him alone, since he was thinking, and started loading the dishwasher. His glance flicked over to me a few times, his jaw set but his shoulders slumped.

"I'm hurting you," he said. He said it so quietly I had to watch his lips move to tell what he was saying.

"No," I whispered. "You aren't."

"This is," he said. "We are." He set his mug in the sink and left the kitchen before I could find the words to reply.

He couldn't mean that. I braced my hands on the counter and stared out the window at the hills.

Aunt Shelly walked in and poured a glass of water from the filter pitcher in the fridge. Hair and makeup done, but still wearing jeans and a loose button-up. She smiled. "Look at you, making dinner."

I almost always either did it myself or helped, so she shouldn't be that surprised. My half-smile was all I could manage. Ever since my deal with Marcus, I'd had a hard time looking her in the eye.

"I sent Marcus to corral the kids for dinner. Gotta get dressed," she said, on her way back out of the room. I propped my elbows on the counter and rested my head in my hands.

Marcus's voice sounded in the living room. His fifteen-year-old brother, the nine-year-old and seven-year-old sisters, and then the twins completed my cousins. He was the oldest in his family, and it showed. He yelled up the stairs for Chris and herded the twins to the bathroom to help them wash their hands because Candace had forgotten. When they came out, over the white noise of the twins' toddler chatter, he told Angie to stop stuffing the head to Candace's Barbie in her mouth and to come to the kitchen for dinner.

Neither girl came. Candace started wailing, so Marcus deposited the twins in the kitchen and went back to the living room. He caught my glance as he left and shook his head.

The parents, particularly his parents, almost never disciplined the kids. They thought fresh air and a naturally instilled work ethic would keep them from pulling the heads off each other's dolls, but it didn't.

Dad wandered in and picked up a slice of the breaded zucchini. "All set for tonight?"

I had no trouble meeting my dad's eyes. "Yep. We'll be fine," I said. "You look nice." He actually looked great. His dark hair had turned gray, but it made him seem all the more sophisticated, George Clooney–style.

Uncle Ward and Aunt Shelly appeared. The two-year-old twins ran to them, jabbering incomplete sentences. "Goodbye, kids." Uncle Ward said. "Have fun tonight."

Mom's heels clicked down the stairs. How little time she took to get ready always amazed me. The peach cocktail dress and her obsidian jewelry easily made her prettier than I'd ever be. She tugged gently on my hair with a "Bye, babe," and whirled out the door with Dad.

The door had barely closed when the twins started crying. They weren't my siblings, but I'd been there when they were born, helped them take their first steps, and panicked when they swallowed their first Legos. "Hey, hey, it's okay. Come here," I said. They wailed louder. If they didn't calm down, everyone was going to be on edge and cranky. I grabbed a napkin from the counter, sat Gage on my lap and pulled Nathan onto the bench beside me. "Did you guys see the bunnies in the yard today? I saw a mom, and a dad, and two babies." I wiped at Gage's face, and he paused his sobbing, but Nathan kept right on crying.

When the parents and my sister were home, walking through the kitchen at dinner time was like wading upstream during a salmon migration.

Marcus stood back while the rest of the cousins crowded the table. He saw me watching him and smiled. Not a real smile, but enough for now.

Chris had grabbed a bowl and poured in at least a cup of ranch dressing for his zucchini. Candace's face was red from scrubbing away angry tears, and Angie still had the Barbie head, dangling it by the hair.

"Can you fill the plates?" I asked. The boys wouldn't let me go. Gage hiccupped between sobs and Nathan's face dripped tears.

I wished the parents wouldn't all four bail at once. I'd spent most of my life with one sister and my parents. There weren't enough of us to make this kind of chaos.

Marcus met my eyes, and after a moment, he nodded. He'd looked tired since we got back from the park, shadows gathering under his eyes. He stepped over to the table and took the Barbie head from Angie. "If you don't stop being mean to your sister, you're going to bed early."

Angie looked to me. "Nuh-uh. Jackie won't make me."

"Oh, yes, I will. Listen to Marcus or you don't get dessert."

"I can fill my own plate," Candace said. "I'm nine."

"No, you can't. The casserole pan is too hot." Marcus handed her a plate, but let her serve her own zucchini. "Let's go to the living room. We can watch a movie."

"But we're over our screen time limit," Candace argued.

Perfect idea. "We're babysitting. If your mom has a problem with it, we'll fix it later," I said.

The twins' wails of misery ceased the moment they heard the television static. Their family didn't watch much TV—another one of my aunt and uncle's ideas. My parents, thankfully, gave me one to put in my room when we moved from California. We didn't have cable, but I could watch the mainstays of my classic film collection after everyone else went to bed. This crowd would never sit still for Marlon Brando or Audrey Hepburn.

I carried Gage and my plate out to the living room, Nate wandering after me, bawling at not being carried too. "Marcus, can you get him?"

Marcus plunked Nate onto his lap and the toddler distracted himself with the sleeve of Marcus's shirt. "Did you guys pick a movie yet?"

Candace, Angie, and Chris were pulling DVDs out of the cabinet. Chris was arguing the supremacy of Pixar over DreamWorks while Angie argued back and Candace tossed aside the action films.

Our living room wasn't as big as the kitchen, but it comfortably fit two couches, an armchair, and a number of end tables. A narrow window had been dug out of the side of the hill, and pansies in pots rested on the outside ledge.

Marcus ate in three minutes and then leaned back in a boneless, exhausted slouch. I was nearly done with my dinner by the time Candace reached around her brother and slid in a DVD. As the logo flashed across the TV, I looked at the space between us. He sat in the middle of his cushion, and I sat in the middle of mine. Like at the park today, he didn't look at me, didn't react to me, and I kept my distance.

I wouldn't mind so much, except the distance wasn't only physical. Alone, we were us. But at home, with our families, anywhere in public, we couldn't be. We said it was a pause, but it didn't feel like one. It was more like an endless pattern of daily breakups.

Marcus glanced over at the sticky toddlers crowding me. His hand brushed my arm. "Done with your plate?" He gathered up his and mine and carried them to the kitchen. I watched him leave, not missing the way his shirt stretched tight across his shoulders.

My phone chimed. A text from Hannah.

So, apparently Anna hooked up with Eric F. He's only been single for 2 weeks.

My hand tightened around my phone. That sickening guilty feeling surged upward. Hooking up so soon after a breakup wasn't nearly as bad as hooking up with a cousin.

I'd chosen this, I didn't want to leave this, but sometimes I hated myself for it.

Marcus came back, turned off the lights, and sat next to me, an inch closer than before. He stretched out his legs and one touched mine. My lungs started to hurt so I took a deep breath and let it out slowly. I leaned back, forced my body to relax, and let my hand rest on the couch between us. Here, that was as much as I could do to reach for him.

I could have gone for ice cream at Todd's to hang out with everyone tonight; that's where Kelsey and Hannah were. Marcus would have agreed to watch the kids by himself. But every Saturday he got up before dawn to help the parents load the truck for their weekly trip to the farmers' market, then helped me get the kids up and make breakfast for them, and if it was my turn for managing the produce stand in town, helped me with that. He shouldn't have to handle dinner and the kids' bedtime routines by himself.

Marcus shifted and his hand brushed mine before he pulled away. How no one knew what we were doing was beyond me. The parents threw us together all the time, had paired us off as soon as our families moved into this house. They assigned us chores together. We babysat together. We drove to and from school together. Maybe they were simply relieved we got along well; the two kids who weren't going to fight and tear down the house if left by themselves.

Not that we were left by ourselves very often.

"I've seen *Avatar* eight times," I said.

The shadows on his face lifted a little. He glanced at my leg, which still touched his, and then looked all the way up to my face, his glance pausing on my lips. Today, for some reason, he was breaking the rules. Maybe because I was, too.

He sat up a little straighter. "Didn't you say you saw a goblin in the basement earlier?"

"I did." The cousins were paying no attention to anything besides the movie.

"We should probably check that out."

"Definitely."

Marcus winked at me and stood up. "Watch the twins, Chris? I've seen this too many times."

"Uh-huh," Chris mumbled, sprawled on the floor. Almost three years younger than Marcus, he'd never been much help with the younger kids, but at least he'd grown out of antagonizing them.

Marcus turned off the outdoor lights, I closed the kitchen curtains, and he locked the front door. I snapped the lid on the casserole pan and shoved it in the fridge. We had an hour or so until we'd need to give the twins a bath and get them in their pajamas. By the time that was done, the movie would be over and I'd have to bribe Angie to brush her teeth and then Marcus would sweet-talk her and Candace both into going to bed without a fight. Chris would be up and wandering around until midnight at least. But right now, we had an hour of freedom.

Three minutes of which had already passed.

The basement door was off the kitchen, and the absurdly creaky stair boards were a great sibling warning system. Bare bulbs dangled from the ceiling, and the cement floor was empty except for a stack of boxes and my reading corner. I'd brought down a square of leftover carpet, a reclining beach chair, and a worn but supremely comfortable quilt. I stood in the quiet, cool space, and the stress drained away.

"I know it's hard," he said.

"What?"

He stopped beside me and touched my hair, let the strands sift through his fingers. "I mean, I can tell. Going from the youngest in a small family to one of the oldest in a huge family. I get it."

But he couldn't, really. He'd been a part of this family since he was born. I'd moved in at fourteen.

No matter how hard I tried, it was still overwhelming, even after three years. I'd never be as good with the kids or as responsible as Marcus. "I wish all four parents wouldn't leave at once."

"I can pick up the slack. You don't have to."

"You shouldn't have to, either."

"I don't mind so much." He sank onto the beach chair. His voice lowered. "You said I'm not hurting you. Are you sure?"

That weight in my chest grew heavier. Marcus wasn't hurting me, exactly. It was something else. Something I couldn't look at too closely. We had our rules, and they'd keep us safe. "I'm sure." I moved closer to him, stood by the beach chair.

He looked up at me. "Promise me."

I sat down on his lap. "I promise. I won't let you hurt me." I just had to keep things in their place.

"Good." His hand touched my waist, slid down to my hip. "So this is 'later' I take it?" His brown eyes were dark in the dim light.

I didn't protest. "Actually, I was thinking I'd bring down my computer. Take a look at a few more university websites. College is important, you know." The shadows on his face were sharp. I swung my legs over his so I sat sideways. The fact that my tank top had been pulled down a bit far didn't bother either of us.

He shook his head. "Half the time I don't know what to do with you."

I could give him a suggestion if he wanted one. I leaned closer and he met me more than halfway. His lips warmed mine. I put my hands on either side of his face, the stubble on his jaw pricking my palms. He exhaled and his body relaxed. Locking his arms behind my back, still kissing me, Marcus leaned back against the beach chair and took me with him. I rested my weight against his chest.

When this whole thing started a year ago, we'd agreed we couldn't really be together. We'd made our three rules: no commitment, no labels, and no sex. Our thing, whatever it was, wasn't a big deal. But it felt like one when his hands slid down my back and gripped my waist, when he traced my cheekbone with his thumb, when his breathing sped up and mine matched his and I didn't want to stop, couldn't stop, even though I needed air.

He was my best-kept secret. When Marcus looked at me, what other people might think didn't matter. This was me, and we were us.

Here, he wasn't so reserved, so quiet. His responsibility was left upstairs with the kids and the dishes and the arguments. I ran my hand through his hair and brushed my lips against his jaw. His arm slid around my waist, holding me to him. I couldn't help but grin as I threaded my fingers through his and kissed him until his heartbeat pounded and I kept every bit of his attention.

The basement was dark. We lit it up.

Chapter Three

Sylvia Young returned to the produce stand Monday and Wednesday, both of the days Marcus and I worked the stand. First for radishes and onions, then sweet corn and green beans. Both times she lingered, talking about either moving into the house her dad was renting or senior year. She made eye contact with Marcus for thirty seconds out of every minute, and she wouldn't quit playing with her hair, twisting a dark strand of it around her index finger.

When she took her second bag of produce for the week back to her car on Wednesday morning, I crossed my arms. Marcus didn't notice. He was rearranging the bags of spinach.

He liked order. He liked consistent patterns and reliable processes. My whole family was a chaotic jumble of mixed-up parenting roles and babysitting shifts and nontraditional everything, and he was the one person who kept trying to put things back together.

When he looked up at me, he frowned. "What?"

The words got stuck in my throat so I glanced at the ground. I'd barely seen him alone since our escape to the basement when the parents had gone to the city. The start-stop intensity of it all was screwing with my brain.

He dropped the spinach and walked over to me. "What's wrong?"

I shook my head. "She's kinda weird."

"She seems pretty normal to me."

I looked up. He watched me.

This was how girlfriends should feel. I wasn't a girlfriend, and I didn't want to be one. I definitely shouldn't be feeling like one.

The line between being friends who made out and dating was muddier than I expected it to be. I played with the volleyball charm on my bracelet as the silence stretched between us.

"So, hey." Marcus shoved his hands in his pockets. "I want—I want to take you somewhere."

"You—what?"

He looked at the grass. "Someplace people don't know us. Dinner somewhere nice, maybe? We could go to St. Joseph."

Tension settled in my shoulders. A date. That was a date. We weren't dating. "Um—what? Why?"

He frowned. "We're always sneaking around. You shouldn't have to do that all the time."

I stared at him, not understanding. But then I did. This was the problem. I should have seen it.

He cleared his throat. "I should be buying you gifts and stuff and taking you out every once in a while. I mean, I know we live together and whatever, but I don't want to be a lousy—" He stopped. His face flushed.

A lousy boyfriend. That's the only thing he could have meant to say. Boyfriend.

I had no idea what to say so I just started talking. "But we aren't dating. We can't be dating. We keep saying that and I don't know why we would go out to dinner if we aren't dating."

He searched my eyes for a moment. His face turned even deeper red and he looked down at the ground. His jaw clenched, but not like he was angry. "I just—it's been a year, Jackie. I don't mean anything big. Just something we can do by ourselves."

No labels. That was one of the rules. Dates, boyfriend, anniversary. Those were labels. Anniversaries were something official couples did. Not us. I must have been in panic mode because tears stung my eyes and I didn't even know why. Horrible. This whole thing was horrible. I was hurting him and I didn't know how we'd even gotten here.

"I just—people would find out. It's hard enough to keep this a secret now."

His eyes hardened. "Don't do this, Jackie. It's bad enough without you pretending we don't matter."

We couldn't matter. He knew that.

A rusty white truck rumbled to a stop on the shoulder of the road. Marcus turned away from me. "Whatever. I'm not going to beg for it."

He never talked to me that way. Stunned, I stared at his back as the driver stepped down from the truck and came around to the produce stand.

I climbed inside Marcus's truck so neither of them would see my eyes watering. I sank back into the vinyl seat and pressed my palms to my eyes until it hurt.

Fine. I was angry at Marcus. Angry I was so obsessed with him. Angry I couldn't walk into a room where he was without wishing he'd look at me like I was special. Angry I couldn't look at his parents without so much guilt flooding me that it made me nauseated.

I pulled my hands away from my eyes and punched the dash. Pain stabbed my knuckles, bad enough that it made me want to cry instead of hit things.

We were just burning time. We were using each other, and we knew it, and neither of us was supposed to care. This was separate, completely separate, from our friendship. It had to be.

This was as far as we could go. Just fun, just for now. If people found out, they'd think we were messed up, a product of an unsupervised, abnormal childhood.

I watched him through the rearview mirror, handing a melon and a pound of green beans to the man in sunglasses. He must be visiting someone for a while, because I'd never seen him before he'd started coming to the stand, and he'd shown up several times now.

Marcus didn't look upset. His jaw was tighter than usual, but he was really good at hiding what he was thinking. If he hadn't been so good at hiding his thoughts, we probably would have started hooking up much sooner than we had. Most of the time I only knew what he was thinking because I knew him so well.

The guy drove off after a few minutes. I slid out of the truck and went to help Marcus pack up the stand, but he didn't say a word to me. In fact, he barely looked my way. We didn't talk on the way home, and when we climbed out of the truck and I put a hand on his arm in the driveway, he shrugged.

"Don't worry about it," he said. "I get it."

Someone moved by the kitchen window, so I took my hand off his arm. "Okay. Sorry."

He shook his head. "It's fine. I'm gonna get Chris to help unload the truck."

Having me around was making things worse. I went inside and watched through the kitchen window as he and his brother unloaded the crates and moved the produce to the cold cases in the garage. Chris was better at pitching in this year than he used to be. The boys were talking, but I had no idea what about. Marcus kept shaking his head and Chris kept shrugging.

I needed to blog, to read, to watch a movie that would let me forget about this for a while, but I couldn't, because the parents were nowhere to be seen and Angie had just spilled her juice all over the kitchen floor.

When the boys came inside, Marcus still wouldn't look at me. And my hand still hurt from punching the dashboard. Candace and Angie broke out into a fight in the living room, and one of the twins started wailing at the top of his lungs.

Too much. This whole day was too much. One more minute in this house might kill me. Texting as I ran down the hall, I wished my sister, Claire, was here. She'd go with me if she was.

I grabbed my swimsuit and my beach bag and ran back out the door. I hadn't heard the parents, but if they couldn't find me, they couldn't make me babysit.

It would take Kelsey a while to get here, and I needed to run. My flip-flops slapped against the grass and I kept scuffing my toes when I reached the gravel road. I stopped and shoved my sandals into my beach bag, and jogged barefoot down the asphalt highway.

Damn this whole situation. We had rules so this wouldn't happen. There was absolutely no point to me going out on a date with Marcus. It would only make things worse. He was pretty much making me hurt his feelings; if he hadn't asked, I wouldn't have had to say no.

A battered Ford crested the hill and I waved. Kelsey braked in the middle of the lane. I jogged over to the passenger side and climbed in and barely got the door closed before she pulled a U-turn that threatened to drop us into the ditch.

Her frizzy-curly blonde hair was pulled back in a tight ponytail, and she already wore her bikini top and jean cutoffs over the bottoms. "Geez. Running on this road in bare feet? You're brave."

I slumped against the seat. "I had to. Is anyone else coming?"

"Hannah's there already."

Kelsey and Hannah were fun, but they weren't Ellie. Ellie had moved away about the time Marcus and I started things, and I'd been so occupied with him I hadn't cared as much as I should have when it got to be longer and longer between e-mails and calls.

It was my fault, but he was the reason.

The pool in Harris was the closest one, and it was almost always packed. I changed into my bikini and found the girls on the beach chairs they'd probably had staked out since that morning. I tried to wipe the scowl off my face, but it wasn't working. I threw my bag on the cement by the chair the girls had saved for me. What did Marcus think he was doing, pushing things like that?

Hannah rolled over on her lounger. "Such rage. What's wrong?"

I shook my head. "Family stuff. Someone push me in."

Kelsey bounced out of her chair. "Hannah, push us both."

The lifeguard was always halfway through some Nicholas Sparks novel. She'd never notice, and if she did notice, she wouldn't care. I stood on the edge of the deep end of the pool with my back to the water. Kelsey lined up next to me while Hannah waved her arms and yelled at the kids behind us to move away. I took half a step back so my weight balanced on the balls of my feet and my heels had nothing beneath them.

The adrenaline of hanging suspended made me focus on this and only this. I closed my eyes. Hannah waited in front of us to catch us off-guard. I stretched my hands out to the side to feel the air and the emptiness around me.

I took a breath, and on my inhale, a palm pressed to my chest and shoved. The thrill of fear surged through me and I let myself fall. I hit the water arms stretched out. Cold soaked through me. I stayed under for a moment before twisting my body and kicking to the surface.

Kids around me were whooping and hollering. I swam out of the way so Hannah could push Kelsey in and watched to make sure no one swam too close.

Some guy across the pool was staring at me as I wiped the water from my face. He wasn't from my school. I stared back, and he looked away.

I was plenty brave enough for falling into the deep end, for meeting someone head-on when I knew he was checking me out. Just not brave enough for letting the whole town, my whole school, know what I'd been doing with my cousin.

Kelsey hit the water and as soon as she surfaced, Hannah jumped in. I climbed out and glanced back to see the guy watching me again. Probably staring at my butt. There was no good way to climb out of the deep end of a pool.

The hot cement warmed my feet as I walked back to my spot. I wiped my face with my towel and wrung out my hair, but paused before sinking onto my chair. Outside the pool area, the skinny man in sunglasses who had been coming by the produce stand was waiting in line at the concession stand. I frowned. "Hey, who is that?"

"Who?" Hannah asked.

"The guy in the red shirt."

"No idea." She collapsed in her chair.

I stretched out on the beach chair and flung an arm over my face to shield my eyes from the afternoon sun. Kelsey flopped down on my other side.

"Did you hear about Heather Graves?" Kelsey asked. "Her and that guy?"

Heather was in my grade, but I didn't know her very well. "What guy?"

Kelsey's lounger creaked as she stretched out. "Some college dude. They hooked up this summer and he's like, five years older than her. They're dating now, I guess."

Hannah rubbed sunblock on her nose. "I saw them at the diner. He's twenty-three. How creepy is that? I don't think it's even legal."

My skin turned cold even though the sun was still bright in the sky. Seventeen and twenty-three. That would even out with time. Being cousins would not.

Kelsey sighed. "I dunno. I wouldn't mind a college guy. Might know what the heck he's doing."

"But five years?" Hannah tossed her the sunblock. "Five years younger than us is twelve. Ew. Just ew."

They argued over whether or not it was ew, and I moved my arm more directly over my eyes so I couldn't see either of them.

This was a huge part of why I couldn't go out on a date with Marcus. One slip, one person who knew us, and Hannah and Kelsey would be talking about me, not Heather Graves. And the rest of the school would be far worse about it.

In California, I had fit in. My dad had been a lawyer and my mom a librarian, my sister was only semi-embarrassing, and my friends didn't need anything explained since they'd known me since kindergarten. But three years ago, my life had become exponentially weirder. Too hard to explain to other people. Now none of the four parents worked traditional full-time jobs, and neighbors couldn't keep straight which of us were siblings and which were cousins. Plus anything that came out of Aunt Shelly's mouth was enough to convince the county we were some weird version of conservative hippies.

Fitting in and finding friends after leaving all the ones I'd grown up with had been hard enough without enduring the nine million questions people always had about my madhouse of a family. My first day of freshman year, some kid had asked me if we were Amish.

Dating my cousin would mean any chance I had of being normal ever again would be gone.

My eyes stung, and not from the light of the sun on the water.

Aunt Shelly gave me the suspicious eye when I got back in time for dinner, but since the house was still standing, my being gone couldn't have been too much of a problem.

Mom gave me a gentle reminder to "let us know where you're going, honey." I should have texted her once I got to the pool. It hadn't even occurred to me. Once again, I was too wrapped up in my secrets to think about what was going on around me.

I pulled Candyland from the shelf after dinner. "Candace, Angie. Let's play a game." The girls ran over as I spread the game out on the living room floor.

Chris walked through and paused. "Need a fourth?"

He was probably trying to avoid helping with dinner dishes, but I waved him over. "Let's do it."

Angie grabbed a token. "I want blue."

"But I'm always blue," Candace said.

Marcus came out of the kitchen, hands shoved in his pockets. I could feel him looking at me as I set up the game. "Want to play?" I asked.

He smiled. "Well, I mean, as long as you're okay with losing."

Chris snorted. "There is zero strategy to Candyland."

Marcus sat across from me, and the clench in my chest eased up when he grabbed the green token and said, "Green is my lucky color. You better be ready for this."

We sat around the game board in a ring, while my knees pressed into the fibers of the carpet and the evening settled around us. The tink and clatter of the parents doing dishes drifted out as we leaned forward to grab cards and move our tokens. Marcus kept pretending to think Candace's or Angie's token was his and move it forward instead of his own, while they squealed and laughed and told him to move the *green* one. Chris rolled his eyes, and I didn't even try to hide my smile.

Chapter Four

Mom hovered over the gurgling coffeepot. Her blonde braid hung over her shoulder, covering up the embroidered "Julia" on her shimmery chocolate bathrobe. "Good morning, hon," she said. She stirred her coffee with the straw she used to keep the coffee from staining her teeth.

"Yeah." I dropped into a chair at the table and squinted out the window at the rising mist. It took me about twenty minutes before I could form a coherent sentence in the morning.

Mom stirred in a spoon and a half of sugar and enough cream to turn the coffee a rich chocolate color before setting the mug in front of me. I would have smiled at her if it hadn't been six-thirty. How she kept the five different coffee preferences in this house straight, I didn't know.

Even though four adults lived here, she was the only one consistently around. Aunt Shelly worked in the garden most of the day or "researched" at local greenhouses. Uncle Ward worked at the lawn and garden store in Harris, and Dad was closeted away in his office all day.

I picked up the mug. The warm ceramic made me even drowsier. "Mom."

"Hmm?" She slid up the storm window in the screen door and a breeze gusted through the kitchen. The engine of a truck growled distantly on the blacktop.

Thankfully, today wasn't my day for working the stand in town, which meant Marcus wouldn't be there, either. Which meant if Sylvia showed up, she'd have to buy her vegetables and leave like a normal person. "You dated guys besides Dad, right?" I took a sip of my coffee. The scald of the earthy liquid waking me up was almost a conditioned response by now. Thank you, Pavlov.

Her eyebrows went up. "I went on dates, yes. I loved dating. But your father was my first real relationship."

So my anything-goes mother had avoided relationships, too. "Why was he the first?"

She shrugged. "Dates are fun. Relationships are hard. They're too much stress and distraction unless it's likely to last. Besides, I was picky."

Likely to last. I swallowed a third of my coffee. "Why did you pick Dad?"

"Oh, lots of reasons. Why do you want to know?"

It was my turn to shrug. "You guys aren't really normal. I mean, most parents don't . . ."

She laughed and refilled her coffee mug. "Honey, everyone is unusual if you look closely enough. There's no such thing as normal."

I swirled the last of my coffee as she left the kitchen and went to get dressed. I pulled on my tennis shoes without untying them and stumbled outside. Pausing for a moment on the porch, I sucked in the cool air. Overwhelming as this family was, it was easy to breathe out here. Morning mist still hung in the low spots and rose like steam from the creek. Giant oaks and maples clustered along creek beds and fencerows, following the curve of the hills.

I turned on the faucet by the gardening shed and watched the sprinklers whirling streams of water. Soaker hoses ran along the ground too, but some of the plants liked water on their leaves. Water dripped off the cantaloupe leaves and ran straight into the ground.

Summer was warming up at breakneck speed. In a few weeks, the afternoon sun would scald the tomato plants and nights would be barely cooler than the days.

Marcus came out while I was heading to the henhouse. Wooden boxes circled the inside at waist height, and thirty chickens clucked and scuffled sleepily on the beams that stretched ladder-like from the floor to the ceiling.

Pulling eggs out of the nests made me nervous. Some old hen was always sitting on her eggs. Invariably, she'd stretch out her tiny head on her long neck, her eyes would widen, and she'd let loose the shriek of an unoiled door hinge. For two seconds, I'd be convinced I was going to die.

I let Marcus get the eggs and pretended to check on the duck. She was already paddling around the kiddie swimming pool we'd bought for her, happily picking bugs out of the water. Duck eggs were too oily for me, but the duck herself was much more fun than the chickens.

Marcus left the door open to let the hens outside. They always returned to roost for the night, and they wouldn't wander far enough to reach the end of our ten acres.

"Sorry about yesterday," he said.

I shrugged. "I shouldn't have freaked out like that." I ventured into the henhouse long enough to open up the steel trash can of chicken feed and pour two scoops into the feeder.

Across the yard, Chris and Angie headed out to feed the two calves, giant bottles of milk-replacer formula under their arms. Heidi, our German shepherd, trotted behind them. Angie insisted on having her own chores even though she was only seven, and since it saved me from bottle-feeding, I let her do it. Marcus and I headed back to the garden and I turned off the water. Weeding was easier when the ground was damp.

I knelt on the mulch by the green onions and yanked out clovers and grass blades. Marcus headed to the other end of the row so he could work his way toward the middle. A few times I caught him looking at me, but then he'd smile hesitantly and go back to weeding.

Before my family moved to Missouri, Marcus and I had only seen each other a handful of times—every other Christmas. Even though we barely knew each other, we'd gotten along because we were the same age. Photos of our moms holding us as infants hung in the hall, side by side, his dated three weeks after mine.

When we moved here the summer before my freshman year, I'd sulked in my room for three months, missing California and hating the Missouri humidity. But Marcus came to find me and lay on my bed every afternoon, poking fun at *Rear Window* and *Breakfast at Tiffany's*. Our evenings were ones like last night, where all of us cousins played games until late and Chris asked my sister and me a hundred questions about California.

By the fall, I'd decided Missouri wasn't so bad.

I uprooted a vining weed and cut myself on the ropelike root. "Crap." Blood seeped from the cut. "We need to go on strike."

"Can you keep going, soldier, or should I carry you back?"

He always mocked my whining. "No. Man overboard. This hurts." I kept weeding, but it pulled on the cut.

He lowered his voice. "Ilsa, I'm no good at being noble, but it doesn't take much to see that the problems of three little people don't amount to a hill of beans in this crazy world."

I halfheartedly chucked the uprooted weed at him and let him see my grin. Quoting *Casablanca* to mock me wasn't fair.

When we met in the middle of the row, we switched to the carrots. The chill had left the air, so I unzipped my jacket and tossed it to the side. Marcus reached for his water bottle. "We need to tell the parents that Chris has to start helping. He gets away with doing a lot less than we do."

"I thought our problems didn't amount to a hill of beans." Aunt Shelly worked in the garden every morning, trimming and thinning and plucking, and every once in a while we'd have a mandatory "garden day" where everyone had to help, but for the most part, Marcus and I did the weeding and took care of the animals.

"I don't mind that much." He stopped weeding and watched me. "It's nice to hang out like this with you."

A strange feeling constricted my stomach, just like yesterday morning. He sounded like he meant as friends, but he didn't. I had to get him off this topic. "If you like this so much, instead of making out next time, we can come out here and pull dandelions. Sound good?"

He laughed. "I'm not sure I'm ready for that kind of commitment." He sat back on his heels and his grin faded. "I mean it, though. I like doing things like this with you. That's all I meant yesterday. I just wanted to hang out with you someplace that wasn't home or the stand or school."

For some reason, my face flushed. After everything we'd done, I was turning red at this. "Maybe you need more guy friends."

"I have plenty of guy friends. But we don't talk about anything, really. We play video games. But you and I, we talk about stuff."

Of course, I said the dumbest thing possible. "Well, then you need more girl friends."

His eyebrows drew together. "Girl friends or a girlfriend?"

My stomach lurched. "I don't know. Whatever you want."

Irritation thinned his voice. "I like having you for a friend, Jackie. I like that you're around and that we get along. If that's a problem, if I'm not supposed to actually like hanging out with you, then whatever. I don't know how this is supposed to go anymore."

I hadn't meant to shut him down. I wasn't entirely sure why he was upset, so I didn't say anything. I really liked that he liked hanging out with me, but the lines were getting blurred. Maybe I was worrying for nothing, but it didn't feel like it.

"Yes, you do," I said. "And you keep pushing it."

He stared at me. "What is going on with you lately?"

"I'm just saying, we have to stick to our rules."

"Jackie. Come on."

I rubbed a clod of dirt between my fingers until it crumbled. "Fine. I think we should back off a little. You said you didn't want to hurt me, and you're not." I took a deep breath and steadied my hands on my dirt-streaked thighs. My voice turned into a whisper. "But I feel so guilty all the time. Like Uncle Ward and Aunt Shelly can see it on me. I hate sneaking around. I hate being angry that you're the reason for it. It's not your fault, exactly, but—"

"But what?" His voice was flat, and I couldn't look at him or I wouldn't be able to say it.

"I don't like what it does to us," I said. "All the guilt. All these things we can't do. Feeling like we break up every time we go inside. I can't keep it separate. It's making me resent you."

"Resent me." His voice dropped off on the last word.

"Not for real. It's just getting hard to keep things separate," I said. I finally looked at him, and his face was completely blank. No expression whatsoever.

He didn't answer me. After a few minutes of nothing but the pop of roots, he stood and strode to the house. He disappeared inside and let the door bang.

I sank onto the grass and stared at the laces on my shoes. Our deal would be so much easier if we weren't friends. If he was just a guy from town I barely cared about.

He shouldn't be mad. Everything I'd said was true. We needed more than our rules if we were going to keep things from getting screwed up between us.

My sister would know what to do, if I could just talk to her about it. I wanted to text her, but there wasn't a thing I could say about the situation that would make sense. If Ellie had stayed in town, I couldn't have told her, but I would have wanted to.

I should have kept up with Ellie. She'd been my only friend my first year out here, and my closest friend until she left. A little quiet, maybe, but I liked that. She'd always tried to set me up with her guy friends, because she'd said unless I had a boyfriend, I wasn't really in high school. I'd laughed it off as a joke, but sometimes I did wonder if she really meant it.

I wouldn't put it past her to run off with a guy, but she would have contacted her family by now. She wouldn't leave them wondering, grieving, like this. Something was definitely wrong, and I couldn't believe she'd run away or gone to Paris or gotten into drugs.

If Marcus hadn't taken all of my attention for those first several months, maybe I would have kept up with her. Maybe I would have known where she went.

A car pulled into the bricked driveway, so I stood up and walked down to the drive. A blue Buick four-door. I glared. I'd seen that car twice this week already. How did she even get our address?

Sylvia rolled down her window and the faint scent of lilacs drifted toward me. "Hi," she said. "You're Jackie, right?"

She couldn't want more produce. She'd come to the stand yesterday. "Yeah. Was something wrong with the tomatoes?"

Sunglasses held back her layered blonde hair. She tapped her forefinger on the steering wheel. A shade of aqua I'd been trying to find colored her nails. "No, no. I just wondered—you're Marcus's sister?" She had a put-together, cutesy look, but her back seat was heaped with trash—fast-food wrappers, shopping bags, old soda cans.

"His cousin."

"Oh. Is this your place, then?"

"It's ours. Our families share the house."

"It's a nice house." She kept looking toward the front door.

"Thanks."

"Is Marcus here?"

"I'm not sure." After he'd walked off like that, I wasn't going to go find him and let him know admirers were lining up in the driveway.

"Can you give him something for me, then?" She dug a notebook out of her purse and scribbled on it, then tore out the page and folded it over.

"Um. Okay." I took the note.

"Thanks." She rolled up her window and backed out of the driveway.

I unfolded the paper. Her number was scrawled across the top. Underneath that,

Text me sometime.
—Sylvia

Throwing it out sounded like a great idea. Or burning it. Cramming it down the garbage disposal.

The dust from her car had barely settled when another engine sounded. A truck rolled past the trees that hid our house from the road. That white truck again. The same one I'd seen at the produce stand this week. Frowning, I crumpled the note in my hand.

No one around here drove that slowly. The road was too far away for me to see his license plate, and the driver turned the corner and sped up.

I stuffed the note into my pocket. If I didn't give it to Marcus, Sylvia might mention it, and then he'd want to know why I hadn't given it to him.

He had every right to text Sylvia. I was being childish. He'd said there was nothing to worry about.

But if he couldn't back off a little, if we couldn't keep things low-key, we'd have to call it off. It wouldn't work any other way. Someone would find out, or we'd end up really hurting each other.

It was just making out, right? The other half of us was more important. Candyland. Movies. Water fights and family dinners.

I tried to work on college applications for the rest of the morning, but gave up and hit the "add new post" button on my blog. No matter how often Ellie had told me blogging was dying, I refused to quit. I started it in middle school as an outlet for my adolescent angst, but the world wasn't benefiting from such a close encounter with my twelve-year-old psyche. I'd taken my early posts down, and the blog morphed into my ramblings about my classic film hobby. Such clever titles as "My First Date with Citizen Kane," and "Here's Looking at Me, Kid," headed my posts, and surprisingly, people read them. My hits weren't high, but my readers commented and shared my posts around much more than I'd expected.

I didn't know what to title this one. *So many of the films that make it onto my top list involve nontraditional or taboo relationships,* I typed. The King and I, My Fair Lady, West Side Story, Roman Holiday, Sabrina. *Even* The Fox and the Hound *and* Beauty and the Beast. *The bravery of the characters is one of my favorite things about them. It takes so much strength to love an egotistical king who stands for everything you're against. To befriend someone people say you shouldn't because you're too different.*

Some of those relationships held up under the weight. Eliza stays with Henry Higgins. Beauty and her beast work it out. Their bravery goes past loving someone they shouldn't to actually fighting for the relationship.

I wonder if that bravery was misplaced. Selfish, maybe. Most of those relationships don't seem harmful to us; taboo then, but not really that damaging from where we sit now. Rich men can love the chauffeur's daughter. Foxes and hounds can be friends. But even if those relationships should have been allowed, they weren't. In more than half those films, we don't get a happy ending. The characters say goodbye and move on, because in their time, those relationships were grim and bloody things. Doesn't that make them harmful? Vigilante justice. Riots. Broken hearts. Does the reaction to breaking cultural norms make the act itself damaging?

I hovered my mouse over the "post" button and took a breath before clicking it. Sharing my thoughts publicly always gave me butterflies.

Roman Holiday's Princess Ann and I had something in common. I didn't know how to say goodbye, either.

Chapter Five

Marcus was gone until lunch time. About noon, I found him in the kitchen with Chris, making a sandwich at the kitchen counter. I didn't bother asking where he'd been, since he'd been avoiding me like he always did when he got upset. Mom was mixing up egg salad and listening to U2 while the twins chattered at the table. Marcus glanced up at me, and then went back to layering salami and turkey on the requisite nine-grain wheat bread.

I pulled out a slice and spooned egg salad. "Sorry," I whispered. Apologizing had never been my greatest talent. I would have said more, but Mom was eyeing me.

"It's fine."

That was so not true. "You sure?"

He put the two halves of his sandwich together. "It's fine."

Translation: I'd hurt his feelings. I'd been honest, and this was what I got. "Okay." Maybe if we acted like things were fine, things would eventually be okay.

Mom raised her eyebrows. "What's going on over there?"

"Nothing." I walked into the living room with my sandwich, hoping he'd follow me. He did. "Hey," I said. "I really wanted to explain what I said this morning. I just—"

"You pretty much said it all," he said.

"Stop it." My eyes burned. "Please just believe me. That was a very small part of what I meant."

His shoulders fell and he glanced at me and then away. "Yeah. I know."

But he didn't know. He didn't get it. If he did, he'd meet my eyes and talk to me. "Sylvia stopped by. She asked me to give you this." I handed over the note like I didn't care.

He took the paper, so clearly he did. "Her number?"

"Yeah. Score." The words came out a lot weaker than I'd wanted.

He frowned like he was thinking. "She says to text her."

"You don't think that's kinda weird?" It wasn't, but I hoped he might think so.

He glanced at me. "Girls can't give guys their number?"

I held his stare. We stood like that in the living room for a moment, me watching him, him watching me. He shrugged and entered her number on his phone.

I set my plate down on the end table and crossed my arms. "Fine. Text away, Prince Charming. She's certainly a damsel in distress." Of course he'd text her the moment he got her number.

His fingers moved over his phone. "You wanted it," he said quietly.

Oh, no, we were not doing this. I tucked my hair behind my ear and narrowed my eyes. He couldn't miss that look. "Sometimes it seems like you don't really get what we're doing here."

His eyes snapped up. "Sometimes I think I get it far more than you do."

I took a step back. My hands curled into fists and I shoved them in the pockets of my shorts. I turned around and walked through the hall and back to my bedroom, leaving him standing there with his phone and that angry hurt look he was so good at and everything that was going wrong between us.

I sat down on my bed and pulled my book off the nightstand, but instead of opening it, I threw it across the room and let it crash into the wall.

I let myself fall backward onto my mattress and stared at the ceiling. The problem with cousins was they were too much like siblings. No matter how much you loved them, you were also a little bit okay with hurting them.

The fear curdling in my stomach for months now was spreading into every bit of me. That fear and the nasty little edge of me that was angry at Marcus wanted me to call it quits, to save what was left, and get out before things got worse.

I frowned at my ceiling. I sat up, crossed my legs, and reached for my computer. When had I gotten so gutless? I was the girl who let people push her into the deep end of the pool, who blogged about dialogue-driven black-and-white movies because she didn't give a shit if people thought it wasn't cool, who kissed her cousin for no reason other than she wanted to.

My stupid little fears weren't going to get in the way of something I wanted.

After working on my college applications for a while, a notice to approve a blog post comment popped up in my e-mail. Traveler101, who was actually Travis something or other, was one of my main blog followers. He'd written on my last post something about me being a thoughtful, well-educated teenager.

I rolled my eyes but clicked "approve" anyway. People said things like that on my posts all the time, as if teenagers usually weren't either.

Late in the afternoon was when Marcus and I would normally try to sneak off. With the twins down for naps, there'd be semi-quiet for an hour or two.

If I didn't want things to get worse, I had to not let them. I slid off my bed and went upstairs. Candace and Angie were banging around in their room, but the door was swung mostly closed. The room Marcus shared with Chris was at the end of the hall.

Music thumped from behind his closed door. Deadmau5. So, he was mad. I knocked on the door, but he didn't answer. I knocked harder.

When the door opened, he stood in the space and leaned on the doorframe. "Hey," he said. His hair was standing on end. His eyes flicked over me.

"Is Chris in there?"

"He's out with Will and whoever." Chris's friends were mostly from Harris, and from what I understood, Will was their little group's ringleader.

I almost didn't have the nerve to say it. "Want to hang out?"

He barely hesitated before grabbing my hand and pulling me into the room. He kicked the door shut and flipped the lock.

"What are you doing?" I whispered and reached for the doorknob. "If someone finds us locked in your bedroom—"

"I'll say it was an accident." He looked a little wild-eyed, so I didn't point out how unbelievable that would sound.

I leaned against the closed door. "Are you mad at me?" He had no right to be mad at me. He was the one avoiding me and pushing our rules and texting some girl.

He looked away. "No."

"You seem like it." I crossed my arms.

He stepped toward me. "It's not fair for you to resent me. I haven't done anything we didn't both want."

"I don't resent you. Not really." I looked down at my socks, then forced myself to look up. "It's just a by-product. It's not the main thing."

"Then what is the main thing? I'm not sure I know." He braced a hand on the door behind me and hovered close. "I thought things were good. Then I said I should take you out, and something went wrong."

"You're the main thing," I said. I didn't know what to tell him about the rest of it. "We're good. It's just—it seems like things are getting too serious."

That look on his face was what I was afraid of. The determination in the set of his mouth, the hurt in the lines around his eyes, the shade of something just a little too dark in his eyes.

His hands went to my waist, slid around to the small of my back. "I don't know how to do this," he whispered. He hesitated with his face close to me, then his lips touched mine. Ache surged up in me. He pulled back half an inch and his hands tightened around my waist. "I get it. I'm sorry, I just—"

I hooked my fingers in his belt loops and pulled him the half step forward that would crush his hips against mine. The weight grounded me. I kissed him back and he quit talking. I drew my thumb along his jawline. After a moment, his shoulders relaxed. His hands slipped under the hem of my shirt and traced small circles on my lower back. When my tongue brushed his, he made a sound that scrambled my brain.

This was what we did. We couldn't talk things out, because there was nothing to say.

Making him kiss me this way, press into me like this, gave me a strange thrill of power. If it had just been that, maybe we would have been fine. But there was something else that made me love the feel of his hair as it slipped through my fingers, made me memorize the curve of his cheekbone and the crinkle of his laugh lines, made me want him to look me in the eye so I could really see him.

Some addictions slowly took away your self, but some addictions kept you going; they were the water and air you needed to keep on being.

His fingertips, lightly, slowly, moved from the small of my back down to the waistband of my jeans. Starting at the back, he moved his fingers along my skin around my sides and to my stomach. I shivered when they came together.

Screw it. Sylvia could not have him. "Don't go out with her," I said against his lips.

He pulled back. "All I did was text her—"

"She wants you to. Tell her no." It didn't break one of our rules because I wasn't asking for commitment. I rested my palms on his chest, stroked my thumb up and down against the soft fabric. I wasn't asking him to stay away from anyone but me—just to stay away from her.

He didn't reply. He waited, looking from one of my eyes to the other, then said, "I really want to go somewhere with you, Jackie. Not a date. I want to get out of the house with you and do something that's not chores or errands or whatever. It might take the pressure off."

Just hang out. No watching for someone to come around a corner, no clock ticking til bedtime, no feeling like we had to make out or we would have wasted the time. "Nothing fancy?"

"Some time away from the house. Where we don't have to lock doors or wait til people leave. Is that okay?"

I met his eyes so he'd know I meant it. "Let's do it. When?"

A boyish grin split his face and he hooked his hands in the front pockets of my jeans. "Tomorrow afternoon. Come up with a reason to be gone for a few hours and I'll pick you up around back. Wear whatever, and bring a book if you want."

"Deal. But we have to be more careful. Here at home, at the produce stand—we can't do this."

He nodded. "Maybe it would help for us to get away more. Keep things away from the house."

I hadn't thought about it that way. "As long as we're careful."

He unlocked the door, still smiling. "Tomorrow afternoon. Twenty-one hours." His lips touched mine one more time. "See you then."

It couldn't come fast enough. In my head, I was already there.

When I went downstairs, Uncle Ward and Mom were watching the news. "I heard it in town," Mom said.

"Awful." Uncle Ward shook his head, his ponytail swishing. "Doesn't look like she ran away, then."

A chill settled in my bones. I stood still until Mom motioned for me to come sit next to her. I moved forward, one step, then half a dozen. I sat on the arm of the couch and she rested a hand on my back. "Someone four-wheeling near St. Joseph found a backpack out in a field. It had homework in it with Ellie's name."

The TV showed jerky local news footage of a field with a clump of trees. The cameraman was having trouble with the focus, which kept switching back and forth between the field and the trees. Photos came up of a blue backpack, flattened and muddy.

The chill turned into an ache and my body physically hurt. She'd dropped that backpack on the floor of my room too many times to count. My hand went to the bird charm on my bracelet. Her backpack shouldn't be in a field. Rain had pounded dirt into the fabric, the blue was faded, and her *Beauty and the Beast* pin no longer clung to the strap.

The reporter, his eyes bright with excitement but his face appropriately grave, discussed the actions the police were taking while photos of Ellie and her family came up onscreen. Police and volunteers were searching the surrounding area for "any other signs of the missing girl."

Other signs. So, her body.

Past the twenty-four-hour mark, missing people were rarely found alive. I knew that. But the girl who'd gotten me into Disney movies and helped me through volleyball and drank more lemonade slush during the summer than anyone should couldn't be dead. "Tell me if they find anything else, okay?" I whispered.

Mom squeezed my arm. "I'm sorry, honey."

I nodded and slipped off the arm of the couch. I stumbled outside and sat down on the porch step. Heidi whined as she trotted around the corner, ears pricked. She sniffed my hand and beat her tail against the side of the steps.

I ran my hand over her fur. If Ellie was okay, there would be no reason for her backpack to be abandoned in a field.

Whatever happened to Ellie, whatever horrible thing it was, no one knew. I should have been the one who knew. If I'd been more consistent about calling her, if I'd e-mailed her more, if I'd found a way to drive to St. Joseph for a Saturday more often, maybe I would have known what happened.

But getting away was such a hassle. I didn't have my own car, Marcus's truck got really low gas mileage so we didn't drive it that far, and two of the four parents were always using the family cars. Plus, with Marcus and me perpetually on child-watching duty, just getting the time to see Kelsey and Hannah one evening a week was a headache.

Still, I should have tried harder.

Heidi licked my hand and I rubbed her ears absentmindedly. The day was cooling down; the breeze lifted wisps of my hair, my bangs. The early evening sunlight made the silver on my bracelet glow. I held up my wrist and touched the wings of the bird. It swung back and forth.

Ellie and I had called and e-mailed each other a lot those first few months. Maybe there was something in her e-mails I hadn't noticed. Some mention of a guy. A hint I'd missed because I hadn't expected her to run away or disappear. I stood up and went back inside, leaving Heidi whining at the door. I could only let her inside when the parents were gone.

I hurried back to my room and logged on to my computer. Searching my inbox for "elliebelle," pulled up every e-mail from her for the past two years.

She'd been a bit like Belle herself—quiet, smart, bookish—but she wasn't shy. It didn't surprise me that she'd found friends in St. Joseph so fast.

Belle wasn't the reason for her relentless love for the movie, though; it was the Beast. Of course, we both preferred him pre-transformation, but she'd actually get mad about it. She'd always turned off the movie before the Beast turned human, even though it left Belle crying over him while he died on the balcony. Turning him into a nicely manicured, flowing-haired human so he and Belle could have a socially acceptable relationship had ruined it for her. Using "belle" in her e-mail address was less about her identifying with the main character and more about her wanting to be the girl who got the Beast.

Still, she'd never dated the bad-boy types; she knew they were losers and hadn't bothered with them. The one guy she'd dated had turned out to be the kind of ass who smacks girls when he got angry, and she'd told him what she thought of that, and dumped him.

I clicked open the first e-mail from after she'd moved to St. Joseph. She'd been e-mailing me from class—summer classes to help her get ahead so she could spend more time on volleyball during the school year. This had been right about the time Marcus and I had started our thing. Details about her new room, a reference to photos she'd texted me of it, excitement about the volleyball team. Lots of "I miss you" and a promise to call that evening.

She probably had called. We'd spent hours on the phone last summer.

I moved on to the next e-mail from a week later. Asking how Marcus was doing, saying to tell him and the parents hello. A fantastically boring rundown of her new workout routine. Ellie had always loved the gym, but the only kind of exercise I tolerated was running. I skipped to the next one—a giant rant about her parents setting a curfew for her since they were in the city now.

Reading her words made my eyes burn and my throat close up.

I skimmed the rest of the summer e-mails. Once the dates hit September, the e-mails thinned out. She was worried she wouldn't be good enough for the team, but she liked the girls so far. They had team sleepovers and it was her turn to host in two weeks.

At least this was something I could do. Being this helpless, worrying constantly about what happened and why, made me want to tear my hair out. Rolling over on my stomach on the bed, I started reading the e-mails more thoroughly.

The sleepover was awesome. Wish you could have been there. The house was trashed, though. Mom made me clean the whole thing but I don't care. I feel like I'm actually getting to know the girls now, and this sounds bad, but I do think I'm a better player than some of them. I didn't want to be the worst player on the team, you know? Anyway, obviously Coach Stevenson didn't come because he's a guy, but several of the girls were teasing him about not being there. He got all mad and said they couldn't tease a teacher about that, but it came out kinda harsh and he made Sylvia cry. I mean, I get it, but they were just having fun.

I stopped. Sylvia had moved from St. Joseph, but it couldn't be the same Sylvia. Right? I opened a new tab and typed in a few keywords.

St. Joseph had nine high schools, it looked like. What were the chances they'd both gone to Edison?

None of her other e-mails mentioned Sylvia. She just talked about "the girls" and how Coach Stevenson had gotten a Mohawk and freaked out the whole team.

Her e-mails became shorter and less frequent, and then stopped altogether. When she'd come to visit over Christmas, mostly because her parents had family out here, it had been awkward. My secret relationship with Marcus had been taking up most of my attention, and she'd seemed distracted, too. We hadn't talked about much.

I'd always thought we could pick back up where we'd left off if we called each other more often, but then one day last semester she was gone, and I was out of chances to fix things.

I wasn't going to let that happen with anyone else. No more regrets.

Chapter Six

My relief at having gotten things figured out with Marcus was completely drowned out by Ellie's backpack. Somehow, though, that made me all the more determined to spend the afternoon with him. I waited until the next morning when Mom was the only one around before I told her I wanted to go to the pool again.

She frowned. "Didn't you just go? I have to go to the library to help out with the summer reading program. I won't be here either."

"Well, can someone else watch the kids?" Seriously. I shouldn't have to be permanently on call as a babysitter.

"I'm sure Marcus can watch them."

I turned around from loading the dishwasher. "Um, Uncle Ward has him going to town for something. Please?" Marcus definitely couldn't babysit, and her automatically going to him wasn't fair. "They're not our kids. They're not even my siblings. And Marcus never, like never, gets time to do what he wants."

Mom sighed. "Okay. I'll tell Ward and Shelly, and they can figure it out."

I had to work to not look too excited. My bag was already packed, including sunscreen and a towel to make it convincing. At two o'clock, I put my swimsuit on under my clothes; I didn't want anyone getting suspicious. Marcus had left twenty minutes earlier, saying he had to go to town to get chicken feed. We did need chicken feed, but he'd gotten it early that morning and left the bags in the back of his truck.

If I hadn't been so excited, I would have been depressed that it took this much planning for us to get a few hours to ourselves. I ran across the backyard and up the road; Marcus would be waiting around the corner.

My sandals slapped the gravel and my loose white shirt swished as I ran. Even though I wasn't fast enough for track, I loved running. To me, running meant summer. It wasn't really summer until I could pound down our gravel road and feel sweat prick my skin, feel my ponytail flicking my shoulders.

I wasn't going far this time, so I was barely breathing hard by the time I reached his truck. He hadn't seen me come up behind it because he was connecting his iPod to the stereo. I smacked the driver's window with my palm and he jumped. I grinned up at him, then ran around the truck to get to the passenger door before he could open it for me. The less this seemed like a date, the better.

"Hey." I scooted into the middle seat and pulled the seatbelt around me.

Daft Punk beat from the speakers. "Hey." He watched me, one hand resting on the steering wheel. "How long til they'll expect you back?"

"Three hours? I said I was going to the pool."

"Good." He put the truck in gear and we pulled off the shoulder onto the road.

"Did you hear they found Ellie's backpack?" He'd spent a lot of time with me and Ellie. The three of us had gone swimming in the creek and done homework in my room and hung out while Marcus and I watched the kids.

"Yeah." He shook his head. "Are you okay?"

I shrugged. "I'm more worried about her than me."

He downshifted for the hill. "Do you think—it's so strange. Do you think she's okay?" His phone vibrated, but he only glanced at it.

My gut told me she was very much not okay. "I think she might be dead." My voice sounded expressionless.

Marcus reached over and rested his hand on my knee.

I threaded my fingers through his and gripped his hand. "I read through all my e-mails from her yesterday."

He turned toward me. "Yeah? Why?"

I looked out the window at the fields and trees traveling past. "I thought there might be something, you know? She mentioned someone named Sylvia."

His eyebrows went up. "Huh. Sylvia could have gone to her school, I guess."

When I didn't say anything, he squeezed my hand a little and we didn't say much for the rest of the drive. With him, I didn't need to fill the silence. Eventually we talked about college and how Chris was looking less like a kid and more like a teenager and how we had no idea what the parents were going to do when we went to college next year.

We drove nearly thirty miles before Marcus pulled off the road and into a field that was growing wild.

"What are we doing?" I'd never been out here. We always went south to Harris or farther to St. Joseph for shopping and pretty much anything else. We almost never went north.

"We're getting out." He pulled into the field.

"Whose place is this?" We didn't know anyone out this way.

"No idea. That's the point." He reached behind his seat and grabbed a small cooler and a blanket, then opened his door and jumped out.

I pushed open my door and watched him walk around in the long grass and pick a spot. A soft breeze carrying the smell of drying grass and dust filtered through the cab of the truck.

I grabbed my book and jumped down.

Only a few wisps of clouds were scattered through the sky, leaving the day bright and hot. Marcus shook out the blanket in the shade. His phone beeped again, so he replied to the text then shoved the phone in his pocket.

He sat down on the blanket and motioned to me. "Come sit."

"Is this some kind of picnic?" We'd already eaten lunch.

"Well." He opened the cooler. "I thought we could hang out here. And I brought you something."

I sat down and tucked my legs under me. "What is it?"

He opened the cooler. "Vanilla or chocolate?"

"Chocolate. What is it?"

His mouth tilted up and those lines around his eyes came back when he smiled. "Ice cream sundaes."

No way. I laughed. "Really?"

"We have nuts, hot fudge, cherries, marshmallows, and either chocolate or vanilla ice cream."

"Definitely chocolate." This was perfect. No screaming children, he'd brought me ice cream, and we had almost no risk of being caught.

He handed me the small container of chocolate ice cream. "Do you want fudge sauce?"

I carved a trench in my ice cream. "Um, yes. Where is it?"

He held up a thermos. "I made it."

"You what?"

"I made it. I put it in a thermos to keep it hot. Mom thought I was making hot chocolate."

I grinned and reached for the thermos. "This is awesome."

He held the thermos away from me, close to his chest. "Come get it."

I rolled my eyes. "Give it to me."

"No."

"Yes. Give it." I lunged and snagged the bottom of it with my fingers. He let me have it. "You give up too easily," I said.

A vague sort of smile crossed his face. "I suppose I'll have to try harder, then."

I unscrewed the top and tipped the container. A thick ribbon of still-warm fudge drizzled onto my ice cream and filled the trench I'd made.

We could make this work. We'd be just friends at home, and then find time to get away.

I handed him the fudge, then sprinkled in nuts and added two maraschino cherries. He put everything on his. I lay down on my stomach and swirled my spoon through my ice cream. The sun warmed my bare legs and my back, the thin white shirt a cool barrier to the heat. I knew he could see through it because he kept glancing at me, his eyes flicking from my back to my shoulders and then away.

"Nice touch, wearing the swimsuit." He opened the bag of marshmallows.

I laughed and licked off my spoon. Sweet and cold. "I figured I should make it convincing."

"Well, it's not like I mind." He popped a marshmallow in his mouth.

I shook my head. He had his legs stretched out in front of him, and he wore his blue basketball shorts and one of his white T-shirts. His wasn't sheer like mine, but it did fit him nicely. "Are we really both wearing white shirts?"

He grinned. "I noticed that. I figured it would be cooler."

I kicked off my sandals while I chased the last of the fudge around my container with my spoon. "Thanks for this."

He set his ice cream down. "I wanted to do something. I mean, it's been a year now."

I sat up. No, no, no. Don't ruin this. "Marcus."

He rested his hands on the blanket behind him and leaned back. "You know, avoiding saying something doesn't make it any less true."

No. Saying things brought them out into the open and made them something to act on. The breeze toyed with my hair and blew some of my longer bangs into my eyes. But if I moved, it would break the spell of me watching Marcus, and him watching me, and me knowing it wouldn't matter if he never touched me again as long as when he looked at me, it was like this; like he knew me and he understood and it was okay anyway.

For once, I said what I was really thinking. "Do you ever feel like we must be really screwed up or that we're messing up our lives or something?"

"What? Shit, no." His eyebrows drew together and he moved closer to me. "Why would you think that?"

"You know. It's not normal. People think this kind of thing is gross." I scraped the last bit of ice cream onto my spoon but didn't feel like eating it.

"Maybe some people would, but that's their problem. There's nothing wrong with you. Don't even think that."

I watched his eyes. "What do you think your parents would do if they found out?" Aunt Shelly, with all her micromanaging, would freak out. Healthy, well-adjusted teenagers did not hook up with their cousins.

He looked down. "I know. It would be bad. They'd probably ask your family to move out and they'd put me in therapy or something." He shifted. "But look. No one knows. Maybe we should be more careful, but it's worked so far. And maybe we can't do anything long-term. But I don't want to go back to being just cousins. As long as it works, there's nothing to stop us, right?"

But he'd be branded a pervert. And since he was the guy, I'd look like a victim when I was the one who'd started it. "Do you ever wonder how this happened? Why us?"

He shook his head. "I don't care. Lots of people crush on a cousin. And a lot of cousins have a relationship and even get married. People just don't talk about it. Come here?" He held out an arm and I moved over.

He played with the end of my ponytail. "Don't worry about it. Right now, there's no problem and we don't need to worry about it until there is one. Did you bring a book?"

I nodded. I wanted to finish *Pygmalion*. The film *My Fair Lady* was an adaptation of George Bernard Shaw's play, but with an important difference in the ending. In one, Eliza Doolittle and Henry Higgins stayed together, and in the other, she left him and married someone else. I couldn't yet tell if the difference in the ending was due to one of the Elizas or one of the Henrys.

Marcus lay down on the blanket. I dug the book out of my bag and lay back on his chest. He held still for a minute, then exhaled and played with my hair again.

He liked it when I did things like that without asking.

While I read, he messed around on his phone, texting. The shade shifted and before long we were in patchy sun. "Did you bring any water?" I asked.

Marcus reached over his head and fumbled around in the cooler before handing me a bottle of ice water. The condensation dripped on my shirt. "Wow. You planned everything."

He didn't reply, just sent a text and gently tugged out my ponytail holder. "I love your hair."

Definitely not a conversation I should keep going, but I didn't move. His chest was warm and solid, and his hands kept moving through my hair, running down the lengths. Falling asleep was tempting, but I kept reading because I was nearly done.

When I closed the book twenty minutes later, I rolled on my shoulder toward him. He was still messing with his phone. "Who are you texting?"

He glanced at me. "Hey. How was the book?"

"Good. Not as happily-ever-after as the movie." I poked his side. "Are you texting someone secret?"

He gave me a look. "It's just Sylvia."

Just Sylvia. "This whole time?" He could text her. It wasn't like there was a reason he shouldn't be texting her, because this wasn't a date and we weren't together. Still, I sat up. I reached for the water and took a drink.

"She wants to hang out some time."

"I'll bet she does."

"Hey." He touched my arm, grinning. "You're jealous again."

"I am not."

"Bullshit. You totally are. Come here." He pulled me down on top of him. My hair fell around my face so I tucked it behind my ear.

"Listen," he said. "Don't be jealous." He kissed my nose, then pressed his lips to mine.

I was still jealous, but Sylvia wasn't the one kissing him on a blanket in the middle of the afternoon. I settled more fully on top of him, stretching out until I could feel his foot with mine. My bare leg touched his, rough against my smooth skin. His hands were in my hair, his tongue brushed my lower lip. One hand moved and slid into the back pocket of my jean shorts.

I slipped my hands behind his neck and when my hair fell forward around us again, I let it stay there. His other hand moved up and down my back. His fingers found the straps of my bikini top and traced the lines across my back. Not unsnapping it, just touching. I leaned my forehead against his, watching him watch me. His eyes moved over my face and down my shirt. He wound my hair around his finger and tugged.

Sylvia could text him all she wanted. I moved my mouth to the skin below his ear, and he smelled so good I instantly forgot what I should and shouldn't want. I touched his arms, his shoulders, his chest. His hands warmed my whole body, and not just because he made these lazy, light circles with his fingertips. Because he treated every part of me like it mattered. My hands. The sensitive skin on the undersides of my wrists. My collarbone. I couldn't think about anything else while he touched me.

My hands closed around his biceps. This past year, he'd put on a lot of muscle. His shoulders had broadened, giving his upper body a slight triangle down to his waist. I saw him every day, and I still couldn't get over it. I kissed him with my mouth open, brushing his tongue with mine. He tasted like his vanilla ice cream. I slid my hand down his side and paused at his waist, playing with the elastic band of his shorts.

His breathing changed. His hands touched my bare skin under the hem of my shirt. My heart thudded right along with his. I shifted up and he found my eyes before pulling the shirt over my head. I was wearing a bikini, so it didn't matter. I tugged on his shirt and he sat up a little so I could pull it off.

I moved my mouth down his neck. His skin was hot on my lips; his face was flushed. I loved that I could do this to him, but I loved even more that with my hands and lips and body, I could tell him things I couldn't say.

I didn't want him to leave. Whatever that meant, I didn't want it to happen. He rolled to his side and I slid off him, him leaning half over me on my back on the warm blanket. This time his lips moved across my shoulder. His fingers played with the strap of my black-and-white checkered bikini top.

This was why he held my hand sometimes. This was why he touched my shoulder when I was upset and why he looked at me the way he did. My skin tingled as his hand found my stomach. We'd been telling each other things for a year now, just with our bodies instead of words. His hands said he wanted me. Mine pulled him closer.

He was so handsome sometimes it hurt. I didn't think other girls saw him this way. Cute, they said. Hot, even. But when I looked at him, I didn't just see his jawline and dark eyelashes and the slight definition in his stomach muscles. I saw Marcus. I saw his years of raising his family and trying to bring some kind of order and consistency to the house and him always lifting the heavy crates when we worked and winking at me and pulling over on the side of the road to kiss me where no one else would see us.

I didn't care. I was so sick of caring who saw and when I could see him next and what would happen later on and what people would think. I didn't care, I didn't care. All the way out here, the only thing to stop us was ourselves. He came back to my mouth and kissed me until I had no air left at all.

He was mine. I wasn't using him, he wasn't using me. I wanted this to be real and he did too. We were desperate hands and sun-warmed skin and his chest on mine.

His hand slid up my thigh. Mine found his chest and trailed down his stomach. Blood pounded through my entire body. He closed his eyes while my hands wandered around the top of his shorts again. Being this close fixed everything. Everywhere our skin touched burned me. Everything from my bare feet touching his legs to his body pressing mine into the blanket and the grass to his hair brushing my neck as he kissed my collarbone hummed with energy. Skin, hands, heat. Light fingers trailing up and down, hands finding small places.

His eyes were dark, his breathing harsh. He tugged on my shorts, fiddled with the button.

I closed my hand around his wrist. "Wait. Hang on." I couldn't think what to say. I wanted him with me, like this. But I also didn't. I wanted us to be real, but we couldn't.

We watched each other for a minute. His chest rose and fell.

I could fool myself into thinking we could undo a year of hooking up, making out, being more than friends. We could adjust and go on with our lives after all this. But we couldn't undo sex.

He moved his hand and sat up.

I took a deep breath. "We just can't."

"Yeah. I know." He reached for the water bottle.

"That would change everything. We live in the same house. We'd see each other every day."

"We already see each other every day." He took a drink.

"I mean, if we did . . . this. Later on, we'd have that history, always there. It would make things that much worse once we—"

His eyes darted to mine. I didn't want to say it out loud, but he knew what I meant and I saw on his face it hurt him, too.

It would make things that much worse once we quit, moved on, stopped messing around. Once we broke up.

For once, he didn't go silent and avoid the issue. He moved close to me and his eyes burned into me so intensely I looked away. He put his hand on my cheek and turned my face toward his. His voice went lower than usual. "Listen. I want you, Jackie. I want all of you."

I pushed his hand away. "We said no sex, and I don't—"

"Not sex. You."

My brain stuttered. "What?"

"I like you. For real. I have for a long time." He leaned closer. "When I look at you, sure, I see my cousin, but I also see a girl who's smart and beautiful and will yell at me when I do stupid things. There are a hundred wonderful things about us together, and none of them make me think it's a bad thing. I want it to be okay for me to like you this way."

"But it's not," I whispered.

He shook his head. "This is why we're not working. We set these limits on how much we can care about each other, and it's just—I'm so far past them, every time you won't let me show it—" He took a deep breath. "Caring about you isn't something I want to change. If you want it too, then why can't we really be together?"

I touched his hand. My throat was so tight it hurt. "But I shouldn't and we can't."

Something sparked in his eyes. "But you do want to be with me?" His hand closed around mine.

He'd focused on the wrong part of that. Something wet streaked down my face. Another. "What I want is to not want this." Something was wrong with me. Me sitting here, thinking these things about my cousin and doing these things with him and wanting to tell him I wanted him too.

It was a minute before he said anything. His eyebrows drew together and the lines on his face deepened. "I'd thought maybe you'd changed your mind." His hand came back to my face and his thumb stroked my cheek. "So you—you like me, but don't want to?"

"Right." I put my hand over his and pulled it away from my face, but kept his hand in my lap.

"I guess it helps to know that." He laughed, but somehow it still sounded sad. "I don't know what to do. I'd been planning on telling you this today for like, weeks now. I was so afraid I'd been misreading things and this was just friends with benefits to you, like we said. But if we can't do anything about it, if you don't want to, then . . . it comes out the same." His eyes flicked over my face. "I still don't have you."

"I'm sorry," I whispered. I so desperately was. Every cell of my body wanted this to not be happening.

Marcus moved beside me, stretching his legs out behind me into the grass. "Close your eyes," he said. "Don't kiss me back."

I closed my eyes, blocking out the trees and the blanket and Marcus, but not the summer light. My hearing sharpened, my skin noticed the breeze and the prickles of the grass under the blanket.

I felt his warmth, heard his breathing. I waited. His fingers touched my hair, brushing it aside, and then his hand moved to the back of my neck. His breath warmed my skin before he touched his lips to my eyebrow, my cheekbone, my jaw line. Each one hurt. His thumb traced my lip. And then his lips replaced his thumb, parting mine. I leaned in, but he shook his head just the slightest amount.

He'd never kissed me so slowly. The soft curve of his lower lip teased mine. I couldn't see him, but I felt him more than I ever had before. The light pressure of his mouth and the gentle clasp of his hands. His cheekbone, his jaw, his skin against mine.

He didn't want me to, but I couldn't help it. I kissed him back.

Chapter Seven

Saturday morning I usually slept in, and this Saturday I wasn't getting out of bed if I didn't have to. The parents always left at four A.M. to take produce to the St. Joseph farmers' market, Chris had to do the produce stand today, and the other chores could wait, so there was no real reason to get up. I'd barely slept last night, just stared at my ceiling for hours, thinking about what had happened on that blanket.

Marcus wanted me. It made it so much harder to fight myself.

I rolled over onto a cool spot on the sheets and tried to go back to sleep, but the temperature change woke me the rest of the way up. I squinted at the alarm. Eight-thirty.

Sighing, I slid out of bed. Sounds drifted back from the kitchen.

Marcus stood in the living room with his cell phone, wearing a tight black T-shirt and the baggy track pants he wore as pajamas. I had pants like that somewhere, leftovers from my one year of volleyball.

I paused with the fridge door open. Volleyball. Ellie. Playing without her wasn't the same, so I'd quit. I pulled out the juice and closed the door. No more news since the backpack. The field hadn't turned up any other evidence, but the backpack felt like only the first thing.

"Why are you up?" I asked. The drive home yesterday had been quiet, and he'd said he was sorry, and I'd told him not to be sorry. I still didn't know what else to say.

"I helped the parents load the truck. Sylvia texted me, but I get crappy reception in my room."

I poured myself orange juice. "Want some?"

He looked so worn out. I sometimes forgot he got up early on Saturdays to help load the produce. I'd be no help that early in the morning, and my parents knew it.

"Um—hot chocolate?" He set his phone on the window sill and walked to the kitchen.

I turned on the teapot. "Is mix okay?" It wouldn't be.

"The other way is better." He put a saucepan on the burner, poured in milk, then spooned in cocoa powder. Hershey's Special Dark.

I turned off the teapot. "But it's slow." We could do this. We could be normal around each other.

"But it's better." He added a third of the sugar I would have and whisked it.

"Is anyone else out of bed?" I asked.

He shrugged. "Don't think so. Hey." He paused. He wasn't looking at me, which meant something was up. "I didn't mean to be weird yesterday. Or make things harder."

I frowned at the bottom of my orange juice glass. I looked up to see him staring at me, a worried look in his eyes. I hadn't noticed before, but they were bloodshot. "It's fine," I said. "You didn't."

Except he had. He'd made it so, so much harder. He liked me. He wanted to be with me. And I so badly wanted to be a girl in high school with a huge crush on a guy who would kiss me slowly like that.

"You kept telling me we had to keep things low-key, and I didn't listen, and I've gone and made it worse." He gripped the whisk, his frown deepening.

"Shh!" I hissed. Chris could be up already. This conversation would undo a year's worth of secrets.

He sounded scared. "I can do it, okay? I can keep things low-key. I swear. We'll be more careful. We know we can't go that far, so we'll back off a bit."

Being more careful might help. Give us the chance to calm down and not give everything up right away. "It's fine," I said. "Don't be sorry. Let's try to take a step back and see how it goes."

He balled the dishtowel up in his hand. "It's not incest, you know," he whispered. "We can't—first cousins can't get married in Missouri, but it's not illegal for us—them—to be together."

Have sex. That's what he meant. It wasn't incest, but the fact that he'd had to check, had to see if us being together was illegal—that scared me. Maybe it wasn't wrong in a legal sense, but real couples, normal couples, never would have had to do that.

"I know," I whispered. I'd researched it, too. Once again, we fell quiet.

He sighed and hung up the dishtowel. "So, are we okay?"

"Yeah." We were not okay, but we were still here, still friends, still us. That mattered more than any limits we had to put on ourselves.

His face relaxed, but his eyes stayed serious. He shifted his weight to the other hip as he leaned against the cabinets. His fingers gripped the edge of the counter. "It's just, I've been thinking—"

I waited for him to finish, but he set his jaw and shook his head. He cleared this throat. "Never mind. Want to watch a movie?"

I blinked. "I was going to turn on *Casablanca*. But you can come if you want."

"Oh. Let's watch *Jurassic Park* instead." He turned around and poured the cooling hot chocolate into a mug. He rinsed the pan, wiped a drip off the counter, and rearranged the flour, sugar, and cocoa canisters so they descended in height.

"Sorry, but no way." I went back to my room and put in the DVD, Marcus tagging along. This felt normal. This was cousin stuff, friend stuff. I climbed back into bed and on top of the blanket. Limits. On top of the blanket, not under.

He closed the door then climbed in beside me and slouched against the headboard. The Warner Brothers logo appeared on the screen as I curled my arms around a pillow. Marcus drank his hot chocolate as the narrator marked a path on the map from Paris to Marseille; Marseille to Oran; Oran to Casablanca.

I exhaled and pulled the pillow closer. No one else here besides Marcus could stop moving long enough to enjoy a Saturday morning properly. Sometimes I felt like everyone else in this family was whirling in opposite directions and Marcus was the only one standing still, the only one looking right at me.

The magic about *Casablanca* was that it was just one story in all of World War II. It wasn't about a concentration camp or the Battle of Britain or D-Day or any landmark event. Ilsa and Rick's story was just one of love in the middle of war. About heroism in small things, and how much of a difference those small things made. Wars weren't made up of countries and allies and enemies. Wars were made up of people who loved and died and betrayed and left their loves behind. Ilsa and Rick's problems, in spite of what Rick said, did amount to more than a hill of beans.

When the Germans started rounding up the usual suspects, Marcus set his mug down and bumped my foot with his. I didn't move. I knew he was wondering how much was okay; if it would be weird to stay a foot away from me or weirder to be close.

He moved down a little and slid his arm around me. I hid my smile in the pillow and tried to focus on the movie. I could get over my crush on him or whatever this was. But for right now, this was good, and we could stick with our limits.

During the scene where Rick is drunk and Ilsa comes in to the bar, Marcus started playing with my hair. He twisted my hair around his finger, then straightened it out against the pillow. He looked serious, for the second time that morning.

Mom had taken a photo of us last year. We were sledding down the hill on the same sled, Chris behind us on his. My hair had been so red and his so dark against all the white of the snow. Marcus had put it in a flimsy, plain metal frame, and I liked that he'd kept it. "Your hair gets darker every year," I said. When we'd moved here, his hair had been light brown. Now it was the darkest of anyone's in the family. This year, he'd even passed his dad's height by a good two inches. Realizing we weren't kids anymore was strange, and maybe that was part of the stress. Everything was more serious now.

But we'd handle it. We always did.

He sighed, the serious look turning dramatic. "It's all the hot chocolate."

"You dyed your hair by drinking hot chocolate?"

"It's my secret. Women can't resist it."

I raised an eyebrow. "Clearly."

He propped himself up on his elbow. "I'll prove it. Look at me."

I did. His face was perfectly serious and very close to mine. Kissing was okay, when it was like this. Not smiling at his deadpan expression took all my concentration. But trying to keep a straight face made it even harder and I couldn't stop myself from grinning at him.

We were okay. We hadn't ruined anything. He slid an arm underneath me to pull me closer, but then instead of kissing me, dropped himself onto me and dug his fingers into my ribs. I shrieked and then kicked him, and he started laughing. I was trying so hard not to laugh and wake everyone up, so it kept coming out in squeals and gasps and I kept kicking. His fingers snuck around to my stomach and I could feel his chest vibrating with laughter. I grabbed his hair and yanked, and he finally lifted himself up off me, one hand braced on either side of my face and a knee between my legs.

"You fight dirty," he said.

"Look in the mirror," I panted.

He watched me breathing for a moment, looking pleased with himself. "Sounds like I took your breath away."

The door opened and something clattered to the floor. "What the hell is—Jackie!"

Marcus scrambled out of bed. Claire stood in the doorway, her backpack on the floor and a bag of dirty laundry over her shoulder.

I sat up slowly. "Don't you knock?" I looked at her calmly, but my hands trembled so I pushed them into the blankets.

She shouldn't even be here. She hadn't said she was coming. Marcus glanced at me, his eyes wide.

"I figured you'd still be asleep." She glared at both of us. "What's going on here? What the hell were you doing?"

She'd tell the parents. Aunt Shelly would literally go crazy and Mom and Dad would be so upset, they'd make us move out, move away. I wouldn't be here to see the twins grow up, to help Candace stand up to Angie, to help Marcus handle everything.

"Don't freak out. It's not a big deal." Marcus crossed his arms.

She turned on him. "What is wrong with you? If I find out you were—hurting her or something, I swear on all that's holy I'm going to—"

Fear stung me. "Claire, no, it wasn't him. Seriously. He didn't do anything wrong."

It had never occurred to me someone might think Marcus was forcing me.

He stared at her in shock. "Holy shit, Claire. I'd never—"

"Yeah, whatever. Take five, would you? I'd really love to talk to Jackie about this." She dropped her laundry on the floor and moved out of the doorway.

Marcus glanced at me before leaving. His shoulders were slumped, his hands shoved in his pockets. He didn't want to leave me here with her, but it was probably best.

Claire shut the door behind him. "Did I really just see that?"

I shrugged. "I don't know what you saw. Why are you even here?"

She put her hands on her hips and gave me a look. "I decided to come home. Now out with it. What's going on?" She sat down next to me, her eyes scanning my face. "You can tell me. I don't think Marcus would, but I want to make sure while he's not here—Jacks, he wasn't forcing you?"

I put my face in my hands because the idea was so awful. "Claire, no. It's both of us. I swear."

"Are you high? Drunk? Seriously ill? What kind of hicks-in-the-sticks business is going on here?" She looked a lot like Mom with her layered blonde hair, but her expression was all lawyer Dad.

I glared at her. "None of the above." This was classic Claire, barging in where she didn't belong and demanding to know why she hadn't been involved earlier.

I pulled the pillow onto my lap and leaned against the headboard. Claire and I weren't much alike, but we'd always gotten along. Right now wasn't the moment to make her my enemy, so I had to figure out some way to explain this. "Nothing's going on."

Just in case my irritation wasn't clear enough, I refused to make eye contact and yanked on the pillow tag.

"Give me something, Jackie."

"Fine. We have a thing. It's not a big deal."

"But *why*? He's. Our. Cousin."

"I know." It wasn't like I could have forgotten.

"How long has this been going on?" She had that concerned-big-sister tone in her voice.

"A year. You can't tell anyone. Ever. No one knows."

I knew she was going to flop back on the bed and say "Jackie!" before she did it. "Please tell me you're using, like, multiple kinds of birth control. Your kids would have six eyes."

"That's actually not true. The genetic issues are barely different than they would be if we weren't related." Research over popular myth was important here. I fiddled with the edge of the blanket. "And besides. We've never really . . . had sex." No way was I telling her about yesterday.

Claire sat up and crossed her legs. "You've had this friends-with-benefits thing going on for a year but never had sex?"

"Right."

"I can't wrap my head around this. I need a minute." She stood up. "Actually, let's go to town."

"Now?"

"We can talk in the car. Someone is going to overhear us here." She picked up her purse and dug out her keys.

I let go of the pillow. Since that might mean she didn't plan on telling, I slid out of bed. "Let me put on jeans."

Something like this was bound to happen sooner or later. I'd almost expected it, and now that it was here, my hands were clammy and I couldn't quite get my fingers to work correctly.

I'd gone on dates a few times before Marcus and I started this thing, and I didn't like them. Too much pressure. Too much talking with people I didn't know very well. Like the one time with Jared Sharp, and I didn't know what else to say so I talked the whole time about *Citizen Kane* even though it was a boring movie. Jared, it turned out, enjoyed hearing about it even less. Or my ill-fated date with Michael Findley, on which he got handsy before we even got our food, and I smacked him, and then he refused to pay. There had been a few more normal dates, but I was always thinking about what the guy was thinking, and worried

I'd done something stupid, and everything was awkward. Things with Marcus were good, and not awkward, and I liked it that way.

Marcus and Claire stood in the living room. His face was still flushed, which meant he was embarrassed or angry or both. He was texting one-handed with the other hand shoved into his pocket. Splendid. Texting Sylvia, probably. Why he had to do that right now, I had no idea.

Claire was glaring at Marcus, standing with one hand on the door knob. I followed her out the door and climbed into her car. As she backed out of the drive, my phone vibrated. Marcus. He'd been texting me.

Sorry. If telling her the whole story will help, I'm okay with it.

"So," Claire said. "I can't even really get this. How did this whole thing start?"

The secret was half his. I texted back.

No worries. We'll work it out.

The less of a deal we made this, the better. "When we were fifteen, and we played truth or dare that one time."

Claire braked too sharply at the stop sign. "When Candace dared Marcus to kiss you. I remember that. It was weird. And that was two years ago, not one."

Weird, yes. But it hadn't been bad. I'd thought Marcus was cute since he made me play his alien invasion video game with him when we first moved in, and he told me I was good even though I was terrible. That cuteness opened up a whole new range of possibilities spring of our freshman year when he kissed me, even though it was only a dare. When Candace dared him to, I'd figured he'd give me a that-barely-counts kiss and then never talk to me again. He actually kissed me, just briefly, but still a second longer than necessary. He'd turned red like he always did, and he didn't stop looking at me all evening. I'd looked back.

I shoved my phone back in my pocket. "We didn't talk about it for like three months, but then he brought it up." We'd been hanging out laundry. Naturally, the parents ran a dryer-free home in all but the dead of winter. The clothesline was behind the house, and since the house was built into a hill, it had no windows in the back. "He said something unconvincing about how weird that was, and I said it wasn't that weird."

I'd also said if he wanted, we could do it again sometime.

He'd looked so nervous when he'd brought it up. It had taken him until summer to work up the courage to mention it to me. Maybe if he hadn't seemed so nervous, I wouldn't have said we should do it again. But I had.

That was fifteen-year-old me. Brash. Brave. Fascinated by my cousin and his calm, unshakable nature. I'd felt certain I could rattle that responsibility, make him do something reckless.

I'd been right.

I'd never forget the stunned look on his face. His next words had been, "So—so like, right now?" and we spent the next half hour in the grass making out on a damp sheet from the laundry. But Claire didn't need to know that.

My prior experiences with kissing had so much buildup, and turned out so awkwardly, I was surprised when my first actual kiss with Marcus hadn't been anything like that. It wasn't awkward or clumsy and it didn't have that *oh crap what if I do it wrong?* factor.

"Ew. This is too weird."

"Stop saying that. You're not helping." After making out that first time, we'd let the issue drop again. I'd bounced between being excited and embarrassed over having made out with my cousin, and he'd acted awkwardly for the rest of the summer. We'd kept hanging out—we didn't have a choice, constantly paired up by the parents for chores and babysitting—but it was always there between us.

And then sophomore year started, we both turned sixteen, and we kept getting closer. One of my classmates asked me out, and I said no, because Marcus and Ellie and I did homework and watched my movies and went to the pool, and there just wasn't room for anyone else. And when the school year ended and Ellie moved, we found ourselves with a lot of time on our hands. In the vacuum of our trio turning into just the two of us, we finally acted on what we'd been pushing away.

We hadn't even talked about it. Most mornings I'd get too close to him on purpose during chores, touching his leg, brushing him with my hand. He'd watch me, his eyes missing nothing, until we were done and then we'd make out behind the toolshed. And he'd gotten really good at making up some reason he had to have help on a trip to town for errands; the parents would automatically send me. If I sat close to him on the way to town, he'd brush my leg with his fingers as he shifted gears. He'd park on some lonely road and the next half hour would be freeing, exciting—stabilizing, somehow.

After a few weeks of that, we'd finally talked about it. Asked the questions hammering in our minds. Admitted neither of us wanted to stop. We'd established our three rules and sworn no one would ever find out.

Except now someone had.

We fell quiet. Claire passed the city limits sign. Manson was only four miles away, and barely even a town. It was mostly a cluster of buildings around the school. A burger place, a convenience store, and a bar were pretty much the town's only businesses. A handful of houses flanked the four graveled streets.

We passed a small house with an unmowed yard on the outskirts of town. The Wallaces had moved to St. Joseph a year ago; selling their house had probably fallen by the wayside when Ellie disappeared.

Claire saw me look at the house as we drove past. "You haven't heard anything new about Ellie, have you?" she asked.

I shook my head. "Not since they found her backpack."

"She's been missing for what, four months?"

"Yeah." Maybe if our volleyball team had been better, she wouldn't have transferred. Maybe if I'd paid less attention to Marcus in those early weeks, I would have spent more time with her and she would have kept in touch.

Claire pulled into the burger place and parked. Todd's burgers were underwhelming, but they did perfect dipped cones. Claire and I had come here for them almost every Saturday since we'd moved until she went to college last fall.

"So, this is a no-strings thing?" she asked. "You're seriously just messing around?"

"Sure." Until yesterday, I'd thought that was true.

"You can't mess around with a friend. This whole thing is weird. You have to stop."

"It's worked so far." Marcus would call me on that, but Claire wouldn't.

We went inside and Claire ordered two dipped waffle cones with nuts. Since she ruined my morning, I let her pay. We took the cones outside and sat on the top of one of the picnic tables under the overhang. Potholes studded the crumbling asphalt and a big-eyed, bony hound wandered around by the curb.

My phone chimed, and I thought it would be a text from Marcus, but it was an e-mail. Claire was staring at me, waiting for me to say something, so I opened the e-mail instead. From Travis, the guy who followed my blog. He'd e-mailed me a few times once he found out I wanted to go to college for film studies of some kind; he went somewhere with a film program. I skimmed the e-mail. He wasn't saying much, so I shoved my phone in my pocket.

"I know it's weird," I said. "I don't know what to do about it."

Claire picked a nut off her chocolate. "Yes, you do. Stop making out."

"It's not that simple."

"It's exactly that simple. Listen to me, Jacks." She turned to face me. "I know you guys are close. But you're going to cause a big problem if you keep doing this."

I wouldn't. Whatever happened, we could work through it. "We've talked about that. We're not letting things get complicated." I could hardly believe what I was saying.

Claire tapped my hand so I'd look at her. "I know what I'm talking about," she said. "I have exes. Even the ones who were nice guys, even when we said we'd stay friends—we don't talk at all now. You know why?"

She didn't need to treat me like a child. "I know what breaking up is."

"Exes can't be friends. It doesn't work, because before you break up, things get bad. You hurt each other. You hate each other, even though you wish you didn't. I can't look at any of the guys I used to go out with without remembering it, even if I remember some of the good things, too. By the time I decided I was better off without those guys, we'd hurt each other often enough and badly enough that neither of us could fix it. And you know what eventually does fix it?"

Letting her talk now was my best chance for keeping her quiet later. "What?"

"Someone else." She licked a drip off her cone.

My napkin fluttered off the picnic table. Now I was listening.

"He's going to find someone, one day, and they're going to get married, and you're going to resent her because she's with your ex. You won't be friends with Marcus anymore, and you'll resent him for hurting you. Even worse, Marcus is going to tell her about you and him, and she will not like you. And you won't be able to get away from it, because he's part of your family."

Imagining myself married and seeing Marcus with his wife and kids at Christmas made my stomach turn. Even after we moved out and went to college and started our own lives, we'd see each other several times a year.

I said nothing. I'd thought maybe we'd quit when we went to college, mutually agree it was over and that would be fine. We'd be the cousins who were closest; we'd keep up with each other and stay friends. But with the way this summer was playing out—me resenting him already, him wanting a relationship, us crossing and recrossing our limits—it just wasn't going to happen that way. The thought of us hurting each other so much we couldn't get over it made my eyes sting.

"Oh. My. Word." Claire squinted. "Look at me." I did, not sure what she was talking about.

Her mouth fell open. "Jackie! You like him! Don't you!"

"What? No." I bit my chocolate even though I didn't feel like eating it anymore.

"Lies. I can see it. If it meant nothing, you wouldn't look like that. You need to end this, for real. It will be hard, but you need to make a clean break. This isn't healthy. Once it's done, you'll be glad you ended it, and you'll find someone else, and it will be fine."

She didn't get it. And I didn't need her to tell me it wasn't healthy. "But we'll still live in the same house. It won't be fine, because I'll see him every day."

"It will be weird for a while, but you'll get over it eventually."

That was where she was wrong. If Marcus ever started dating someone else for real, I wouldn't get over it.

Claire grinned, which was rude, because there was nothing funny about this. "See? You have a huge crush on him," she said. "I knew it. He's gotten kinda hot, I'll admit, but you seriously have to get over him. He's your *cousin*."

I whipped around to face her. Whatever I had for Marcus, it wasn't a passing, giggle-worthy attraction. "I know he's my cousin. Stop saying that. Being cousins is the whole problem. If we weren't—" I stopped.

What would happen if we weren't cousins? If he lived in town and our families only knew each other from school events? My ice cream dripped onto the picnic table.

His stability fascinated me. He was okay with how his family worked and he didn't worry about what other people thought of him. I wanted to be more like that. He was comfortable with who he was. Maybe that was why I could talk to him so easily, why I didn't feel the pressure I did with most other people. And he knew the family issues were hard for me, the same way I knew it was hard for him to shake off the responsibility of being a third parent in his family and act like the teenager he was. "I don't know," I said.

"That doesn't sound like a crush," Claire said, eyebrow raised. "Jackie. This isn't good."

I didn't need her to say it.

I wanted to cry or pound the picnic table or anything other than just sit there and pretend like it didn't matter.

I didn't only like him. I didn't just want our friends-with-benefits fling to be a real relationship. This was a mess. This wasn't the way it was supposed to be. I was supposed to find someone perfect for me. Someone my family would like and we'd make our lives good together.

But because it was Marcus, that couldn't happen and I had to fall out of love with him.

A crack in my warming chocolate let melting vanilla soft-serve seep out and sog my waffle cone. "Are you sure I'm not adopted?"

Claire's face softened. "Neither of you are adopted. Photos from the days you two were born are hanging right outside your room."

"Then where did I get my red hair?"

"Grandma had that red-brown color." Claire threw out the end of her cone and took mine from me. She broke off a piece of the chocolate then huffed. "This must be hard for you."

Just a bit, yes.

"So if you're so into him, why didn't you ever sleep with him?"

The thought made my hands sweat. "I figured, we can't undo that, you know?"

Claire shook her head. "You can't undo any of this. And I can't imagine how many times in the last year you must have given him blue balls."

Trust Claire to put it that way.

"You really have to end this. Seriously. Promise me you'll stop making out with him. If you end it, I won't tell anyone."

I didn't answer her.

"Jacks. Really. It's weird. And long-term, it's messy. You can't be permanently related to your ex. It'd be a nightmare. Plus, family is supposed to be a place where some things aren't an option. It's a safety thing."

It seemed so strange that out of all the people in the world Marcus could have been, he ended up being my cousin. Why couldn't he have been a guy from school?

Claire let me sit there. Maybe she knew I needed the space or maybe she didn't know what else to say. I couldn't handle any more questions, and I wanted to stop talking about it. Talking wouldn't fix it.

The hound wandered away. Sheriff Whitley drove past and waved. A rusty white pickup rolled up to a pump at the gas station across the street.

To keep Claire from grilling me further, I motioned to it. "Have you seen that truck before?"

She squinted. "Don't think so. Why?"

A man climbed out—the man who'd come to the produce stand and the pool.

He took off his sunglasses and went into the gas station. He was probably mid-thirties, fairly short, skinny. "I've seen him around a lot."

"Maybe he's visiting somebody."

"Do you need gas? I want to check out his truck." We were maybe thirty feet away and I could see something sticking up in his back seat. I didn't like the look of it.

"Right, because the natural response to seeing a strange man lurking around is to go snoop in his truck." We climbed in to the car and Claire drove across to the gas station. We pulled up to the other side of the pump where the truck idled. He was still inside the convenience store.

"We're in public. We'll be fine." I said the words like I knew what I was talking about.

Claire started filling her tank while I gathered up fast-food trash from the car floor to have an excuse for being next to his truck. Claire's car was almost as messy as Sylvia's. The garbage can stood right between our vehicles.

The windows weren't tinted. In the back seat of the cab was propped a compound bow, at least a dozen heavy aluminum-shafted arrows, a cooler, and a pair of expensive-looking binoculars.

"Well?" Claire hissed.

I scrambled back to the car. "Let's go."

She paid at the pump as he walked out of the convenience store, carrying a gallon of water and sliding on his sunglasses. We shut the car doors and he stared at us through the windshield as he walked past.

Claire pulled out of the gas station and turned right; the truck turned left.

"There's a nasty-looking compound bow and a pair of binoculars in his back seat."

"Maybe he's a hunter," Claire said.

"Nothing's in season right now. He doesn't have any camouflage stuff, no hunter's orange on anything, no boots."

"Who knows. People do strange things."

That was exactly my concern. Someone driving past my house with a compound bow doing strange things.

We hadn't gone a mile before I glanced into the rearview mirror and saw the white truck a half-mile back. "Claire. Look."

She glanced up. "Maybe he lives out this way."

"He turned the other way out of the gas station. He would have had to turn around immediately to be this close behind us."

Maybe he wasn't following us. Maybe he had some reason to be out here.

Claire pushed the automatic door lock and we drove in silence for the next three miles. The white truck hung back, still behind us. Claire turned off the blacktop and onto our gravel road. The parents should be home by now, so there wasn't much he could do on our own property. She parked but when I reached for the door handle, she said. "Don't get out. Wait a minute."

The truck crawled past our house but kept going.

"There's nothing down that road," I said. We sometimes got traffic past our house, but not often. The road connected to the blacktop highway a few miles down. Sometimes people used it as a shortcut, especially neighbors driving farm equipment and trying to stay off the main road. Unless he was after trees and cows, it would be a fruitless drive.

Thinking he was following us was silly. He was probably using the road for a shortcut.

I turned to Claire before getting out of the car. "Please don't tell anyone about me and Marcus. Let me figure out what to do."

She drummed her fingers on the steering wheel. "I won't tattle. Not if you're ending it."

I didn't have a choice. Just that morning I'd told him we could keep going, but I couldn't keep this up if I had to get over him.

We went inside to find all the cousins up and running around the house and the parents sitting around the kitchen table with their coffee. Green tea for Uncle Ward and Aunt Shelly.

"Claire, honey!" Mom stood up and everyone said hi to Claire and I just kind of stood there. I could hear Marcus in the living room, talking to someone. I recognized her voice, and it made me feel sick. Why now? Why before I'd had a chance to talk to him about Claire walking in on us? Why right after I'd discovered the one thing I didn't want to do was exactly what I had to do?

"Now, no teasing," Mom said. "Marcus has a friend over. Be nice."

I definitely wouldn't be teasing him.

Crossing the living room was necessary to get to my bedroom. Marcus and Sylvia sat on the couch, playing a card game on the coffee table with Chris, Candace, and Angie. He looked up as I walked past.

"Hey," he said. His eyes searched mine, glanced over to Claire, and then back to me. "Want to play?"

I did not. "That's okay. Have fun." She shouldn't even be here.

Sylvia sat next to him, smiling like she hadn't made my day exponentially worse simply by being there. One leg was crossed over the other, her small feet sporting a pair of cork-heeled platforms. She laughed at something, and, ever so casually, touched his knee.

Yesterday, that would have made me want to smack her. But today— no, today it still made me want to smack her.

I closed my door and sank down onto the bed. My phone beeped a moment later.

You ok? How'd it go?

Maybe this was good. He'd have a distraction for when I told him we had to be done.

I turned the TV on so I wouldn't have to hear Sylvia giggling in the living room and spent the rest of the afternoon hating how much I wished he was still in here watching *Casablanca* with me.

The TV flickered black-and-white. "Of all the gin joints in all the towns in all the world, she walks into mine," Rick said.

Chapter Eight

When someone tapped on my door an hour later, I thought it would be Claire, but instead Marcus stepped in. "Hey," he said.

"I take it you and Sylvia are getting along." I paused the movie. My eyes had to be red, and my head hurt.

"Oh. I guess. She was bored and asked if I wanted to hang out. Doesn't really know anyone in town yet."

"Are you sure that's why she came over?"

He sat on the edge of the bed and smiled halfheartedly. "You mean, she might have a secret mission? I guess she could be casing the house for a burglary."

I sat up. Screw him and his never saying what he meant. "She likes you."

His expression faltered. "Really. You think so?"

"Yes, really." I was being unpleasant, but I felt unpleasant. I pulled a pillow onto my lap.

He looked down at his hands and the smile left. I looked down at my own hands and played with my fingernails.

"She just came over to hang out," he said. "Don't worry about it."

Don't worry about it. That pretty much summed up Marcus. Sometimes that was great, but sometimes it meant he'd landed himself in a mess. And he had, even though he didn't know it yet. Sorting this out wasn't going to be fun for anyone.

He looked down again. "How'd it go with Claire?"

I played with the hem of the pillowcase. I didn't want to talk to him about it right then, not with Sylvia hanging over my head. "She says it's a bad idea and wants us to quit, but she's not going to tell. For now, anyway."

His shoulders relaxed a little. "That's good."

"Yeah." Neither of us wanted to say anything else. One wrong phrase, and we'd be asking each other if we should call it off now. As much as I needed to tell him we were done, I couldn't right yet. I wasn't ready.

Even if we could have done something, there was no problem here to handle. Just the simple, awful truth. I wasn't fifteen, this wasn't a crazy dare, and it couldn't be fixed.

A dozen things could have happened. I could have asked him what was wrong, why he was looking at me that way. He could have moved closer and told me what he was thinking. I could have told him I loved him. But instead he stood up, hesitated in the middle of the room, and then walked out.

I thought I'd felt sick before, but this ache in my stomach felt like an actual wound.

Less than a minute after Marcus left, Claire came in. Knowing her, she'd been listening in the hall. "Are you okay?" she said.

"So you admit you were listening in." I didn't appreciate her invading my privacy, but it was an invasion I was used to.

"My sister's in love with our cousin. Of course I was listening."

"Claire. You can't do that. It's rude." Sometimes I felt like the more mature one, but it wasn't really true. Claire just didn't care much for social conventions like knocking before opening doors or, in general, respecting anyone's privacy.

She glanced at the TV. "I never understood why you like these old movies so much."

"They're interesting. Complex." Especially Hitchcock. I needed to watch *Psycho* again. I hadn't seen it in a while because Marcus didn't like it.

"Slow, you mean."

"Not all of them." Going from my life to the world of, say, *My Fair Lady* could be a bit of a culture shock, but I enjoyed it. I liked their traditional, Old-World charm. Plus, they were mine and no one else in the family watched them.

Claire wanted to talk more about Marcus, but I didn't. Having her here made me pull myself together. I yanked the blanket around me and turned the volume up a little. She narrowed her eyes, but then lay down on the bed beside me. "So what's this one about, anyway?"

"A lot of things. Rick, mostly."

A strange thought occurred to me, so I reached for my computer. Maybe I could find out if Sylvia had actually gone to Ellie's school before moving out here.

But Google wasn't cooperating. Sylvia had no Facebook page I could find, no Twitter, and not even an old Myspace profile. She didn't come up connected with a search for St. Joseph, Missouri, or any other local search terms I could think of. A Sylvia Young theater school in London, a Sylvia Young from Georgia, and information on Sylvia Plath were all I could find. The Internet hadn't heard of her.

I closed my laptop harder than necessary.

Marcus stayed in his room the rest of the evening and did chores without me the next morning. I tried to not be upset about him ignoring me, because neither of us knew what to do and it wasn't his fault.

I pulled my hair into a ponytail and slid on my running shoes. I whistled for Heidi, clipped a leash on her collar, and hit the road.

Running on gravel was a unique experience. Not only was the road uneven because of potholes and washed-out edges, but since the center was graded higher than the edges, one foot always hit slightly higher ground than the other. Larger rocks were always an ankle-turning peril, as were potholes hiding under the fine bits of rock and dust. But running still seemed like the best way to get over being in love with my cousin, so I ran.

Heidi trotted along beside me, glancing at me every once in a while as if she were wondering why we weren't going any faster. Chris ran with her more than I did, but today I wanted the company. Her heavy tail swished side-to-side as we ran.

I'd never had to get over a guy before. Introverted as I was, I rarely put myself out there to be noticed. I wasn't shy, exactly, I just didn't find the same thrill in social events that Claire did. Guys had asked me to school dances, and I'd gone to a few, but before the evening was over, Marcus and I usually ended up sitting on a picnic table outside, sometimes with Ellie, laughing about someone being high or drunk or both. No matter who else was around, we'd always gravitated toward each other.

Kelsey and Hannah made me jealous. They were so normal, with their part-time summer jobs and single-family homes. They had nothing to hide. No major topics to avoid when they talked to their friends. No reason they couldn't giggle about their crushes to each other.

About two miles past our house, I nearly tripped on the leash when Heidi stopped running and woofed. The creek cutting through our ten acres meandered down here through a stand of pines and knee-high chicory. New tire tracks ran the ten yards from the road out to the trees, and faded green fabric flapped in the breeze not far into the pines.

"Come on." I twitched the leash and Heidi trotted beside me into the pasture. A tent. Whatever vehicle made those tracks wasn't here, so hopefully no one was inside the tent. Beer cans littered the grass, and a protein bar wrapper fluttered silver, caught on a rock in the water.

The tent wasn't huge—a standard canvas, single-person thing. The area around it hadn't been mashed flat, so whoever it was hadn't been staying there for very long. The tent flap was closed but unzipped. Any smart camper would have zipped it to keep raccoons out. I pulled the flap aside. A backpack and a sleeping bag lay inside. Two one-gallon water jugs sat on the sleeping bag. The overflowing backpack was stuffed with T-shirts, jeans, and protein bars. Men's jeans. No women's clothing.

Maybe he was hunting out of season. He could be homeless, but the jeans were an expensive brand and looked almost new.

Across the creek, the tall grasses rustled. I stood straight up. A rabbit burst from the grass and dashed along the bank.

No axe-murderer, thank God.

Glancing behind me every few steps, I walked back to the road, tufts of grass catching my sneakers and weeds stabbing me in the ankles. Heidi whined and tried to pull back to the rabbit trail, but I could just imagine someone pulling up as I was about to leave.

The run back seemed to take twice the time it had taken to get down there. I usually didn't run four miles and I had been sweating and desperately sucking in air for far too long by the time I was halfway home. A cramp in my side demanded I slow down and walk the rest of the way.

A crowd of people stood in the driveway. The parents stood in a circle looking worried, while Claire, Chris, and Marcus crouched by his truck. "What's going on?" I asked. If all four of the parents were there, something had to be wrong.

Marcus looked up. "Someone slashed my tires."

His rear tires rested on their rims, stab marks in the tire walls.

"That's illegal, right?" Claire asked.

"Of course it is," Dad said. "Intentional destruction of property."

Uncle Ward ran his hand through his hair. "Do you have any idea who would do this, son? Some kid from school?"

Marcus stood up. He frowned, but his eyes were more worried than angry. His dark hair was damp and stood up all over; he'd probably just gotten out of the shower, which meant he'd slept until noon. Not unusual for Marcus on a Sunday. "Maybe the Harris basketball team, if school weren't out for the summer. But I quit playing last year, so they don't care about me anymore."

The Manson-Harris school rivalry was nothing new.

"We'd better call the cops," Aunt Shelly said. By "cops" she meant octogenarian Sheriff Whitley. He'd bend down, say, "Yep, them tires is cut alright," we'd get a police report for the insurance claim, and that would be about it.

Aunt Shelly was one of those people who, if there was nothing in her life to freak out about, felt she must be overlooking something. Cancer-causing foods, non-SPF Chapstick, high-fructose corn syrup, margarine, first-person shooter video games, and treated tap water dared not be in the presence of her children, or else suffer the wrath of a vegan-raised ex–New Yorker.

Uncle Ward pulled out his cell phone and stepped away from the driveway to call the sheriff.

"If it was the Harris basketball team, Will would know," Chris said. "I can ask him if he heard anything."

"That must have been a big knife," Mom said.

Marcus looked a little pale, but Claire was watching me suspiciously, so I just stood close to him. She was on "get Jackie over Marcus" patrol now, and I'd get away with nothing while she was here.

"Nothing else is damaged?" I asked.

"Nope. But tires are expensive." He exhaled.

"You should wait out here with me and your parents," Dad said. "The sheriff will have questions. But everyone else can go inside. We don't need a crowd."

I followed Mom and Claire and Chris inside. Of all the stupid things to do to someone. This made no sense. Marcus didn't have enemies. None of us did. The local farmers thought we were a bit strange and a little too "city," but they had no real problems with us that I'd ever heard. Occasionally Dad even did free legal consulting for them to be neighborly.

The sheriff pulled up half an hour later. He stood in the driveway talking to Marcus, and then while he talked to the parents, Marcus pulled out his phone and texted someone. I sat at the kitchen table watching my phone, waiting for it to vibrate, but it stayed silent. Marcus kept texting.

Mom sat across from me, telling Angie, Chris, and Candace not to worry. Chris didn't look particularly worried, but he rarely looked like he felt any emotion beyond skepticism. So unlike Marcus.

I walked over to the coffee pot, chose the largest mug from the cupboard, and filled it two-thirds full. I added a packet of hot chocolate mix to my coffee—intentionally using the mix—and poured in several tablespoons of Kahlua. My mom raised her eyebrows but didn't say anything when I pulled the container of whipped cream out of the fridge and heaped the mug.

Another reason my parents were unusual: She raised her eyebrows at the whipped cream, not the Kahlua.

A bowl of homemade whipped cream usually waited in the fridge, ready to pile on strawberries, peaches, or whole-wheat waffles. Aunt Shelly declared at least once a week that laziness outweighed the desire for junk food in adolescents, so having an easily accessible, cancer-free dessert option around was improving household health. To Aunt Shelly, all preservatives equaled cancer. All it meant to me was I could put both cocoa mix and whipped cream in my coffee.

Mom smiled at me licking whipped cream from my fingers. "Why the heart attack in a mug?"

"No reason." Because, unlike my life, I could make it exactly how I wanted.

I stole my mom's straw out of her coffee and put it in mine because I was getting whipped cream on my face. She pulled the mug over to herself and took a drink, then wrinkled her nose. "Oh, hon, that's too sweet."

I reclaimed my mug and drank half before admitting she was right. Claire took it from me and I let her keep it.

Marcus and the rest of the parents came in as Sheriff Whitley pulled out of the driveway. "He thinks it wasn't targeted at Marcus in particular," Uncle Ward said. "His truck was closest to the road. Probably some bored kid on a dare."

"Unless it's one of the neighbor kids, which I doubt, someone drove a long way for a prank," Mom said. "And cutting tires isn't like toilet-papering a house. That's aggressive."

"Could be revenge for something," Dad said. "Maybe someone didn't like my legal advice. Maybe something I advised on turned out badly."

Aunt Shelly shook her head. "Let's hope that's all it is and this is the last we hear of it. Kids—Chris, look at me—no one goes outside after dark for a few days. We'll keep the outside lights on. We'll lock the windows and the door at night, so don't unlock them once the house is shut up. And tell us if you see anything strange, okay?"

At least she wasn't handing out Tasers, rape whistles, and pepper spray. She must be mellowing out in her middle years. She and Mom had gone head-to-head a few times, and it was a good thing, because living by Aunt Shelly's rules would kill me. Particularly the one that required her children to track their television time on the kitchen wall chart.

"Speaking of strange," I said. "I found a tent when I went running this morning."

"An abandoned one?" Mom frowned.

"Someone's living in it. Down by the creek. There were clothes and stuff."

"Could be a poacher. Across the road?" Dad asked.

I nodded. "Yeah. I don't think he's been there very long."

Dad ran a hand through his hair. He didn't handle stress well—half the reason he quit working for the firm and we moved. "Okay. I'll go check it out."

"Oh, Cliff, have lunch first," Mom interrupted. "I think everyone needs to sit down and eat."

Dad sighed. "True. Okay."

"Do you want coffee?" Mom stood up. "I'll get you some."

"Oh, I'll get it. How long til lunch?" Dad asked.

Aunt Shelly opened the oven. "Ten minutes. Chris, get the salad from the fridge? Angie and Candace, the table needs setting. Texting every minute isn't necessary, Marcus. We need the water pitcher and the wheat rolls." Aunt Shelly's meals might sound normal, but the lasagna was eggplant lasagna, the salad would have tofu and bean sprouts, and the rolls probably had flaxseed or something in them.

If Aunt Shelly ran this house, my soul would shrivel up and die.

I glanced at my dad. He looked more rested now than he ever had in California, but he still had deep lines around his eyes. The coffee pot was right next to me, so I poured him a mug and stirred in two spoons of sugar. He liked it black.

"Oh, thank you, sweetheart." He took the mug from me. "Good thing coffee is a natural beverage, right?"

"No kidding." I glanced at Marcus as we sat down at the table. He'd shoved his phone in his pocket to help set the table, but he pulled it out and started texting again.

"No phones at the table," Candace said in a sing-song voice. Aunt Shelly raised an eyebrow, looking around for the offender.

Marcus put his phone away and poked her in the ribs. "Snitch. Not cool. I thought I was your favorite."

Candace passed him the salad. "You are. But I have to be fair. I told on Claire, too."

There were times when I enjoyed the tattle-tale stage that followed Candace turning nine.

"So, we need to get those tires replaced, I guess," Uncle Ward said. "What do you have for spares?"

"Well," Marcus set down his fork. "I have one. It's just a donut, though. It won't work for long."

"You'd better call Riley's, then. You can use my truck to pick them up Monday. We can cover it so you don't have to wait on the insurance check. This wasn't your fault."

Judging by the crabby looks on the twins' faces, they weren't too happy about the eggplant, either. Nate wailed and shoveled his off his plate onto the table. "Hey, hey—don't do that." Marcus took away his fork and scooped the mess back onto his plate. Nate grabbed a handful and dropped it onto the table again. Gage watched him, then deliberately picked up a handful of his own lasagna and dropped it on the floor. "Mom," Marcus said, "this may be too much of an acquired taste for the twins."

She sighed. "Can you get them some peanut butter bread?"

"Sure." He stood up and walked over to the pantry.

I'd heard Marcus complain about the twins maybe a handful of times since they were born. I loved them, of course, but I didn't have the patience he did. Maybe because they weren't my siblings.

He never seemed to mind watching them, washing their hands, cleaning up their mess, or answering their million toddler questions. But he did mind, sometimes. I knew he did. He just knew if he didn't do it, it probably wouldn't get done.

Dessert was only a Sunday thing, and of course Aunt Shelly served whipped cream over berries. Thankfully, blackberries and whipped cream were in a much superior food category than tofu and eggplant.

"We have Chris and Angie to thank for the blackberries," Aunt Shelly said. "They picked them yesterday."

"Thank you, Chris and Angie," Marcus and I chanted.

"Yeah, whatever," Chris said. "I ate half of them already."

"Well." Dad pushed back his chair. "Shall we go see that tent, Jackie?" He stood up and put a hand on Mom's shoulder. "Be back in a bit."

I carried my plate to the sink and followed Dad out the door. "So this is down the road, by the creek?" he asked.

"Yeah." I didn't see my dad a whole lot, since he spent most of the day in his office, but on weekends he tried not to work. That was one rule Mom insisted on making, and Dad had been pretty good about it since we moved.

He started the truck and backed out of the driveway. "Dad," I said, "did you date girls besides Mom?"

"Of course I did. Why?"

"I asked her why she married you, and she was vague."

He grinned. "You did, huh? What'd she say?" When my dad smiled like that, it took ten years off his face.

"She said, 'lots of reasons.'"

He laughed and I raised an eyebrow.

"Sorry," he said. "Inside joke. I had a few girlfriends before her, but she hadn't dated anyone seriously before me. She was a choosy woman. Still is."

"Why did you marry her, and not one of the others?" Everything was so mixed up with Marcus. There was a sliver of a chance that I could talk myself out of believing I was in love with him. I didn't have much to compare it to, so maybe this horrible sick feeling was something else.

"Oh, the usual things, I suppose. She challenged me. And we weren't just dating—we were good friends too. I knew whatever I did with my life, I wanted it to be with her."

Damn it.

He glanced at me sideways. "So. Your aunt thinks you're seeing some guy."

I froze. It took a minute for me to get words out of my mouth. "What?"

"She says you weren't at the pool the other day when you said you were. I guess she checked. She says she overheard you arguing with Claire this morning about some guy, too."

I adjusted the shoulder strap on my seatbelt. Thank God Claire had insisted we leave before talking about the rest of it. "I'm not dating anyone." Breaking up was the opposite of dating.

He rested his hand on the gear shift. "If you ever are, we want you to feel like you can bring him to the house. If he's important to you, we'd want to meet him."

No. No, they would not. "I know."

"Well, don't hide him just because he's some pierced, tattooed punk skater or whatever they are now. After your sister's boyfriends, I'm all prepared to handle that." He winked at me.

I almost grinned. "I'd tell you if I was dating someone." And normally, I would have. I wanted my parents to like the guy, and think he was good for me, and ask me nosy questions I could roll my eyes at. All the normal things other girls got to have.

He smiled. "I figured you would. And I don't care whether or not you were at the pool, as long as you're being safe." He pulled the truck to the side of the road.

Aunt Shelly must have only heard scattered words of what Claire said to me, or she'd know exactly what was going on. The fact that she'd nearly discovered us made my skin prickle. If she was being that nosy, we definitely had to end it.

We climbed down from the truck. "It's in the trees, over by the creek." I walked in the tire tracks of crushed grass over to the trees, but halfway there, I stopped. "It was right there."

The grass was mashed down where the tent had been, and the protein bar wrapper still fluttered in the creek, but the tent was gone.

Dad stepped on a rock partway into the water and fished out the wrapper. "Well, I guess that solves our problem. Probably just some kids having a camp-out."

So there had been a tent in the field. That was no reason to be worried or suspicious. I shouldn't have made a big deal out of it.

Between Ellie's backpack, Claire's ultimatum, and my discovery of how screwed up my brain was, I wasn't seeing things straight. I had to do something. Get out of the house more. Anything to distract myself and take a step back.

Dad headed to the truck. "So Shelly's just being overly concerned? There's no guy?"

I climbed into the truck and closed the door. "Nope. There's no guy."

Chapter Nine

The house was quiet when we got back. The twins were down for a nap and the rest of the cousins were doing the dishes, Marcus supervising. When parents cooked, kids did the dishes—another household rule. I preferred the days kids cooked. Mom, Aunt Shelly, and Uncle Ward were watching the news in the living room. Since Uncle Ward and Aunt Shelly approved of being informed, news was an appropriate use of the television.

I glared at the back of her head when I walked into the living room. Aunt or not, Shelly Reed had better stop following me around.

"Hey." Dad sat on the couch beside Mom. "The tent's gone. So, I guess problem solved."

Something wasn't right. Everyone was too quiet.

Mom glanced up and took his hand. Aunt Shelly and Uncle Ward looked grim.

I frowned. A girl's photo was being broadcast on the news. Ellie. "Mom! That's Ellie." *Sixteen-year-old St. Joseph girl's body recovered* scrolled across the bottom of the screen.

"I know, honey," Mom said. "How awful."

Body.

Recovered.

Sixteen. She should have been seventeen by now. But she wasn't, because she was dead.

I sat down on the arm of the couch. Ellie. Dead. Her body turned up now? My vision swam. Drugs, an accident, an aneurism or blood clot, some kind of illness she hadn't told anyone about? Maybe someone had kidnapped her.

No, no, no. There was no reason for her to be dead.

She'd always been so cheerful, even when we lost games. She'd been a competitive player. I had a particular memory of her jumping during practice, her whole body primed and under control. The slap of her hand on the ball still rang in my ears. I was nowhere near that good.

Found in the woods, west of St. Joseph. After this long, her body must have been barely identifiable.

Marcus walked up behind me. His hand brushed my shoulder and I looked up at him. Looking in his eyes hurt.

Mom glanced up at us from the couch, and Marcus dropped his hand from my shoulder. He walked back into the kitchen, and Mom turned back to the news.

My cell phone buzzed.

Outside?

I caught his attention and nodded. I pulled my shoes back on and went out the kitchen door, and a minute later he followed me. He caught the screen door and kept it from banging. We walked around the back of the house. The sky was overcast, gray but thin, like an old wool blanket. He reached over and took my hand.

I let him, because she was gone.

We sat down on the hill our house was built into. "I should have tried harder," I said.

Marcus shook his head. "You can't do that." He shifted around so he could see me. "You're always so hard on yourself."

Ellie was dead. This shouldn't be about me. "Someone—someone must have killed her."

Marcus touched his hand to my face and brushed my cheekbone with his thumb. "I'm sorry," he said.

I leaned my head on his shoulder, but my insides were too numb for me to cry.

By the next morning, the gray blanket of clouds had turned into an oppressive layer that mirrored the heaviness in my lungs.

Muggy and warm, the day was already too hot by the time we left to get the tires for Marcus's truck.

Somewhere, someone was doing an autopsy on Ellie's body, and here we were buying tires. The unfairness of the world and my own insensitivity stunned me. I shouldn't be buying tires, I shouldn't be sleeping and eating the day after my friend's body had been found.

The mechanic's was a twenty-minute drive away, in Harris, and for most of the way there, Gorillaz pumped from the speakers and Marcus told me about this new online game he was playing with three guys in Idaho and somebody in England. Something about spaceships and mining ore on moons.

Talking about normal things hurt.

We pulled into the parking lot by a steel building marked "Riley's Auto Shop." An old Coke sign hung on the building, and buckets and various hunks of metal lay scattered around the lot. Tires were lined up against the exterior and stacked inside.

"I'll be two minutes." Marcus left the truck running for the air conditioning and went inside. My phone buzzed a second later with a text from Claire.

How're you? Doing okay?

She'd left late last night to get back in time for work this morning. I was surprised she'd stayed as long as she had, but then most of her friends weren't on campus for the summer. I texted her back.

I'm glad they found her, I guess.

My phone vibrated again almost immediately.

Yeah. Horrible. They'd better find the bastard. Keep me updated on Marcus.

Having someone know about me and Marcus was an inexpressible relief. So many times I'd wanted to talk to someone, but I'd never been able to. She'd been right that I had to end it, but at least she hadn't called me a freak.

The tailgate clanged down. Marcus and Riley heaved a set of tires into the truck bed. "Thanks again," Marcus called, then climbed back into the cab. "Okay, let's go."

I loved driving on this highway. The blacktop rolled over hills, wound around S-curves, and stretched over half a dozen creeks. It wasn't a safe road, especially during the winter. Deer were constant casualties out here, as were coons and the occasional cow.

Marcus was a good driver. Watching his arms and shoulders move as he shifted, I settled back in the seat. I could drive a stick, but not very well. I needed more practice, and the parents' cars were both automatic.

"Admiring my mad shifting skills?" Marcus asked, grinning. He was trying to take my mind off Ellie. "You know how good I am with my hands."

"I can't believe you just said that." I adjusted the vents to blow on my face. He acted like he'd forgotten all about yesterday.

Marcus squinted into the rearview mirror, his smile disappearing. "Is that the white truck you've been seeing?"

I sat up straight. A truck crested the hill right behind us, going way over the speed limit. "Yeah."

Marcus frowned. "Is your seatbelt on?"

"Yeah, why?"

"He's way too close."

The truck was close enough now I could see the bald man in sunglasses. He was less than three feet behind us. Marcus drifted to the side of the lane, a clear invitation to pass. The white truck only accelerated.

"Don't stare at him. I don't like this." Marcus shifted and sped up a little. "I'm already going ten over. Faster isn't good on this road."

I looked in the side mirror. He was right on our tailgate, and inching closer. I dug an old receipt out of my purse. I could see his license plate if I looked in the rearview. I jotted it down. At least now we could turn in the plate number and figure out who this guy was.

The truck jerked forward and something banged. I slammed forward into my seatbelt. Marcus gripped the steering wheel. "What the hell is his problem?"

He'd just rammed our tailgate. The white truck's engine roared above our own and fear settled in my gut. If we pulled off the road, this guy would stop too. I'd rather keep moving. We were still at least ten miles from home.

The highway rolled over another hill and around a curve. Marcus had a good grip on the wheel, but we were driving too fast. The road swung back into an S-curve and a tire slipped off the blacktop, grinding on the gravel shoulder.

The white truck pulled into the opposite lane. Marcus's jaw tightened. "He'd better be passing. Oh, shit, Jackie—call your dad. Right now." Calling 911 would do nothing. They took nearly half an hour to respond out here.

I already had my phone out. The truck pulled up beside us and drifted closer as we sped downhill. He was half in the oncoming lane and half in our lane.

The phone kept on ringing. Marcus braked hard a second before the man in sunglasses jerked the wheel. Our truck dropped back half a length and his bed slammed into Marcus's door. The side-view mirror crumpled and fell and my shoulder cracked into my window. We spun sideways, tires screaming on the asphalt. The tires hit the gravel shoulder and the truck rocked as we plunged off the road. Pain split through my head. I gripped the door handle as we careened down the slope. The truck jerked and bounced at the bottom of the incline and we plowed straight into a cornfield.

Stalks crunched beneath us, but the field swept uphill and we ground to a halt. The white truck roared over the next hill and kept going.

Marcus leaned his forehead on the steering wheel for barely a second before asking if I was okay.

"I'm fine. You aren't hurt, are you?" Pain radiated through my head and neck.

"I don't think so."

I sank back onto my seat. We sat there for a minute before I touched the bruise on my shoulder. No blood, and it was throbbing less now. The window wasn't cracked. My head was sore, too, from smacking into the window. "He could turn around and come back. What do we do if he comes back?"

Marcus forced the door open, cracking cornstalks. "I can't hear his engine anymore. He's gone." He looked around and exhaled. "If there had been any kind of ditch here, we would have rolled the truck."

It was a miracle we hadn't. "Why would he do that?"

"I don't know," he said. "I'm gonna see how bad the damage is." He forced the door open farther and jumped out.

My hands shook as I brushed the hair out of my face. I didn't think I'd ever been so scared in all my life. If the truck had rolled, who knows what would have happened. He could have killed us.

Marcus crashed around in the corn and banged on the tailgate. He came back after a minute. "The tailgate is dented and I can't get it open. The side mirror is broken, obviously, the whole side of the cab is scraped, and my door is dented. But otherwise, I think we're okay. We'll have to get the suspension checked out and we plowed a darn good trail through this corn." He leaned back in his seat and finally looked at me. "Are you sure you're okay?"

"Just a bruise on my shoulder. And my head hit the window."

"What?" He leaned over and gently turned my head so he could see. "Oh, Jackie, that's swelling."

"Not much." It didn't hurt that badly. I held still while he touched my face.

"Can you see okay? Are you dizzy?" He peered critically into my eyes. "Do you think you have a concussion?"

"No, I'm okay. I can see fine. I can count backward. It's just a bruise."

If we could do over our fight in the garden, I'd tell him I didn't want him to find a girlfriend. If I could go back to that moment on the blanket, I'd tell him I'd wanted to stop not because we should but because he meant too much to me.

His thumb slid over my cheek. "Okay. Let's go home. But you tell me if you start to feel dizzy or nauseated or get a bad headache."

"Deal." I'd had a concussion before, from a four-wheeling accident shortly after we moved, and this didn't feel like that. My head hurt, but it was just a bruise.

We drove the rest of the way home in silence. My whole body felt like a wet rag from the adrenaline crash. I called Dad again, and this time he answered.

The parents were all standing in the driveway when we pulled up. "Good lord, son," Uncle Ward said. "What did you do to my truck?"

"Well," I said, because Marcus was having trouble with his door, "someone ran us off the road."

"Oh honey, are you okay? Are either of you hurt?" Mom hugged me, a little too tight. My shoulder had to be all sorts of colors by now.

"Jackie has a wicked bruise, but I'm fine," Marcus answered. "The truck's banged up, though."

Chris let the door bang behind him as he walked down the steps. "Geez, Marcus. Who'd you piss off?"

Marcus slammed his door, and it finally latched. He told the story and the gunmetal sky hung over us, no longer thin and woolly but heavy with rain.

Chris frowned. "I asked Will, but he hadn't heard of anything going on in Harris. He said to put your truck in the garage next time."

Will. Chris's hero, to hear him talk. What brilliant advice.

Marcus shook his head. "Well, a garage wouldn't have helped me with this."

"Oh. I forgot. I got his plate number." I pulled the white paper out of my pocket.

"You did?" Marcus asked, surprised.

Uncle Ward reached for the receipt with the number. "I'm calling Sheriff Whitley. This is ridiculous. That man needs to be locked up."

"Thank goodness you're okay," Aunt Shelly said. "These roads. I swear." She hugged Marcus. "I'm so glad you aren't hurt."

Dad frowned, heavy lines on his forehead. "First the tires, now Ward's truck."

Uncle Ward was still on the phone, gesturing wildly as he paced around the yard. We went inside, Aunt Shelly fussing over Marcus and even me as if we were desperately ill. "Do you want some hot chocolate, honey?"

Marcus sank into a chair at the table. "Sure. But can you make—"

"I'll make it from scratch," she said, hurrying over to the stove.

"Okay." He grinned. "You want some, Jackie?"

I shook my head. Sugar didn't sound good right then. I wanted a nap.

"So, this guy doesn't go to our school, right?" Chris asked. "You saw him?"

"He's definitely not in high school," I said. "He's probably thirty. I don't know."

Uncle Ward came in. "Sheriff Whitley said the truck is registered to someone in Kansas City. That's all he'd tell me."

"Kansas City? He's a ways from home," Marcus said. That was a good four hours away.

Aunt Shelly poured hot chocolate into six mugs and I took it as a sign of acute distress that she made one for herself. I let my mug steam in front of me while Mom got me ibuprofen and looked at my bruise.

"Until we get this figured out, no one goes anywhere without one of us," Dad said. "We know you won't do anything stupid, but you could have been seriously injured or even killed."

Clearly. Of all the ways I'd expected my drive with Marcus to go, this wasn't it. "I'm going to go to my room." I'd wanted to talk to him on the way home about what Claire had said and his mom's suspicions. And he needed to know that we were done.

"No sleeping after a head injury. Watch a movie or something. I'll come check on you in a bit," Mom said.

I carried my hot chocolate with me. I probably wouldn't drink it, but leaving it on the table would hurt Aunt Shelly's feelings.

I crawled up onto my bed and crossed my legs. My drink had cooled off a little, and I took a sip.

As much as I wanted to sleep, I put in a movie, then drank half the hot chocolate before pulling a pillow onto my lap and reaching for the television remote. I'd been wanting to watch *Psycho*, but that movie wouldn't sit well right then.

The floor creaked and I looked up. Marcus stood in the doorway. I'd left the door open, hoping he'd follow me. Angie and Candace tagged along behind him, carrying throw pillows. "Marcus said you were going to watch a movie," Candace said.

"That was a good guess. Climb up." I made room on the bed. Aunt Shelly wouldn't make them stop watching a movie if I turned it on. They lay down on their stomachs at the foot of the bed and Marcus sat next to me.

"Any chance you put in *Jurassic Park*?" Marcus asked.

I smiled. "Nope." We leaned back onto the headboard and I hit play.

As rain poured down on the wealthy leaving the opera and Henry Higgins shouted about Eliza being an incarnate insult to the English language, I leaned my head on Marcus's shoulder. "I need to talk to you," I whispered.

My tone told him what about and he turned to meet my eyes. His breathing paused. "Um. Can it be tomorrow?"

After this afternoon, it could wait until tomorrow. I nodded.

He moved his shoulder lower for me. The girls shifted in front of us, working their feet under the throw blanket. Marcus started playing with his phone, eyes on the screen, but moved his other hand to the bed between us. Without looking, he moved his hand until his little finger, rough and warm, brushed the side of my hand.

Chapter Ten

A sprinkle of rain fell during the night, but the air was muggier and the sky hung even lower by morning. Ceiling fans beat the air quietly, moving a slight breeze through the house. Since our house was dug into the ground, it didn't absorb much heat, especially away from the kitchen windows, but it was still muggy and uncomfortable. We almost never used the air conditioning, but this was insane.

My phone beeped with a text from Claire.

Did you tell him you were done yet?

I turned my phone off and set it on the desk where I couldn't see it from the bed.

All afternoon I'd been on my computer trying to write a blog post, but I kept getting distracted and clicking random links. I couldn't write, couldn't pull my thoughts together, couldn't care about movies with this hanging over my head. Today was the day, and he might hate me for it. He'd resent me for hurting him.

I'd given up on blogging and was reading when I heard her voice. Sylvia Young was in my kitchen. Marcus laughed at something she said. Last I'd seen, he had been mining ore in the Andromeda Galaxy. Clearly plans had changed.

I closed the browser and snapped my laptop shut. My neck and shoulder were stiff and painful from skidding around in the truck, and I really wanted to stay in bed, but I straightened my tank top, ran a brush through my hair, and went out to the kitchen.

Aunt Shelly was making lemonade in a sunny yellow glass jar. She'd love to be June Cleaver.

And that would be fine with me, because June Cleaver wouldn't spy on her niece.

Marcus leaned on the counter and Sylvia stood by the table, twisting her blonde hair around her finger. Again. Powder-blue backless heels, this time. They made her legs look tanner and her shorts look shorter. Naturally.

"Oh, hi, Jackie," she said. "How are you?"

"I'm fantastic," I said. "Reading *Where the Red Fern Grows*, and it's just as heartbreaking as everyone says. How are you?"

"Oh." Sylvia smiled awkwardly. "Well—I'm good, thanks."

Marcus raised an eyebrow. "We're going to play a game. You want in?"

I looked into his brown eyes for a second too long and I knew why he was letting Sylvia Young play cards in my kitchen. It wasn't a bad idea, but I still didn't like it.

"Sure." I poured myself a glass of lemonade and, after hesitating, poured some for Marcus and Sylvia. I then resolved to think of them as "Marcus and Sylvia" never again.

"Ace high." Marcus shuffled and then dealt. War usually only had two players, but in this house we had learned ways around the rule. We each turned our first card face-up. Sylvia's card took the other two. Then Marcus and I both turned up jacks, I won the war, and Sylvia took the next two cards.

After watching her for a minute, I said, "So, you said you moved from St. Joseph, right?" I smelled her lilac perfume as she leaned forward to lay down a card. I liked the scent, actually, but I really wanted to hate it.

"Right."

I might as well ask. "Where'd you go to school?" I took the third set of cards.

"Edison." She sighed when Marcus took her jack with an ace. He looked at me.

I stopped, holding my card in the air. That was Ellie's school. She had to be the same Sylvia Ellie's e-mail had mentioned. "Did you know Ellie Wallace? She transferred from Manson last year."

Sylvia took a long drink of her lemonade. Too long. Her hand gripped the glass. "I saw her around. I barely knew her. Really sad, though."

"Yeah," I said. "Have you heard anything new about it?"

"No. I knew she was from this area, but I didn't know she went to your school. Your turn, Jackie."

I laid down my card. "Saw her around" was not the same thing as playing on her volleyball team. Maybe Sylvia had quit the team. Or maybe she and Ellie hadn't gotten along well.

We'd been playing for twenty minutes when Mom came in and asked me to help her make dinner.

Twenty minutes of war was enough. Marcus headed outside to help Chris and Angie close up the henhouse and feed the calves, and Sylvia followed him. Of course she did.

"You don't like Sylvia, do you?" Mom turned on some rock violinist's newest album and then poured a cup of dry oatmeal into a bowl.

"She seems fine." I started to mince an onion. She hadn't wanted to talk about Ellie, but it was horrible, so that might be why. "What are we making?"

She added two pounds of ground beef, one of ground turkey, and one of venison to the bowl. "Meatball subs. Why is Sylvia only 'fine'?"

I poured a puddle of olive oil into the heating frying pan. "I don't know her very well. She definitely seems to like Marcus, though." The onion hit the pan and sizzled. Sautéing was a good excuse to not make eye contact.

"I noticed that. Do you think he's going to ask her out?" She kneaded the oatmeal and spices into the meat.

"I guess we'll see." I watched the onions searing in the pan.

"He hasn't dated anyone since that Amy girl, right?" She turned to look at me, and I whirled around to dig in the fridge. Anything to hide my face.

Last year, Marcus's parents had pushed him to date someone. For some reason, they were obsessed with it. He needed normal teenage socializing, they said. Personally, I thought it was a ploy to get him to stop playing video games.

We'd talked about it and he said he didn't really want to date any of the girls he knew. But his parents kept at him, so he asked out one of the girls who played basketball. She said yes, and wanted to get all serious after one date, so he quit seeing her. Our solution to the problem was Amy.

Amy was me. He'd tell his parents he was going to go see Amy and drive off, and then I'd head out to "do chores" or something vague, and he'd pick me up down by the creek. Marcus and Amy did a lot of swimming in their day. They'd broken up shortly after his parents relaxed about his social life.

"Yeah. Amy." I shut the fridge and crushed two garlic cloves with the flat side of the chef's knife.

"Did you hear what they found out about that white truck?" she asked.

I minced the garlic, relieved she was done talking about Marcus. "No, what?"

"Apparently the owner doesn't fit the description of the man you saw."

Weird. "Do they have any idea who the guy is?"

"The sheriff said to keep an eye out for the truck again. He's going to try to get someone from Kansas City to talk to the owner and see if he loaned the truck to anyone, but I doubt it's actually going to happen."

Sheriff Whitley wasn't known for following up on details. Uncle Ward could holler into his cell phone all he wanted, and as soon as he hung up, Whitley would forget about it. Even if he did remember and was industrious enough to get hold of the Kansas City police about the issue, a dented truck in the Missouri sticks wouldn't be high on their priority list.

I mixed the sautéed onions into the meat and made the mistake of looking out the window. Marcus and Sylvia stood talking in the middle of the yard. The bright evening sunlight lit up her skin. He made a face at something, and she laughed and shoved his arm. If standing there grinning like an idiot was any indication, he didn't mind.

Mom chatted on about the library and how she had to go in and talk to the librarians this week about the summer schedule, but I barely listened.

I couldn't really blame Sylvia for liking Marcus. The most fair thing of me would be to let it happen. Claire was right—the best thing for getting over someone was finding someone else. I just had to get over the fact that when I watched her with him, my lungs needed to be reminded to pull in air.

The night was almost as oppressively airless as the day. I couldn't sleep, so I watched *Rear Window*. Jimmy Stewart made the humidity almost bearable, but I'd forgotten how creepy the movie was. Or maybe it was just the dark and the accident making me jumpy.

After the credits rolled, it was still too hot to sleep. I laid there dozing and waking for an hour, but my fan made little difference so I gathered up my blanket and went out to the living room.

I still hadn't talked to Marcus.

The living room was always a bit cooler because it was the room farthest back in the hill. I curled up on the couch, mostly hugging the blanket because it was too hot to cover up with it. My phone buzzed.

Still up?

My phone glowed blue in the dark. He knew me too well.

In the living room. Hot as Hades.

The stairs creaked a moment later as he tiptoed down. He wasn't wearing a shirt, just basketball shorts. Way to make this harder, Marcus.

He flopped down onto the couch.

"I don't know how everyone else is sleeping," I said.

"Maybe they all passed out."

Marcus's hair was damp and his face was sweaty. "Eww," I mumbled, pulling my feet closer to me. "You're gross."

"Yeah, well, heat rises. Upstairs is a freaking sauna."

We lapsed into cranky silence.

Finally Marcus turned toward me and said, "I can't believe Claire didn't tell the parents."

I sat up a little. "I know. I thought she would."

"She was kinda freaked out." He shifted on the couch. His voice fell to a whisper. "I'm surprised no one else has caught us."

"She's serious. She says she's going to tell if we don't quit."

He said nothing. I couldn't see his eyes in the darkness, which made it easier.

"Your mom found out I wasn't at the pool. She told Dad I was sneaking around with some guy."

He straightened up. "What? Does she know?"

"I don't think so. But between her and Claire, we have to do something." Not the main reason, but still a convincing one.

Silence, still. Finally he said, "Sylvia's been texting me a lot."

"Yeah." Believe me, I'd noticed.

"I can't believe she went to Ellie's school." He turned to look at me again. "You want to go swimming?" Apparently he was done talking about Sylvia. Fine with me.

Swimming. Cool water and the night breeze. "More than anything." I rolled off the couch and went back to my room to dig through my drawer. After hesitating, I pulled on my skimpiest swimsuit, a green string bikini with tiny white dots, and then my T-shirt.

I grabbed two beach towels from the bathroom and met him in the living room. We left the house as quietly as possible, and Marcus turned on a flashlight a hundred yards from the house. The creek cut across the back of our ten acres. It wasn't a very wide creek, but it had deep spots.

Running through the grass with Marcus felt so familiar I could hardly bring myself to remember that there wouldn't be a good way to explain this if anyone woke up and found both of us gone in the middle of the night. The adrenaline and expectation made me forget Claire and Aunt Shelly and anything but the good parts of us.

We were even sweatier by the time we got to the creek, but the water was right there. I pulled off my T-shirt and jumped into the creek, the shock of cold water an instant relief from the miserable heat.

Marcus dove in beside me and came up grinning. He'd jumped in wearing his basketball shorts. "A bikini? Not skinny dipping? No fair."

"Yeah, well, take what you can get." I splashed him, coming close enough he could almost touch me.

"Oh really. Take what I can get?" He lunged and grabbed my legs, pulling me under. I came up gasping. I yelled and sputtered while I pulled my dripping hair out of my face, but he pushed me up against the bank, muddy and root-covered as it was, and kissed me.

I was going to tell him it was over. I wasn't even going to tell him I'd found out I loved him, because him knowing that might make it worse.

His skin burned warm against mine in the dark water. I could hardly see through the water streaming from my hair but I kissed him back, wrapping my arms around his neck and pulling him closer.

His mouth was tight and demanding. This was not the slow, patient kiss from our picnic. Every muscle in his body tensed and his hands trembled where they touched my skin. He knew.

He shuddered and pulled away, just an inch. He leaned his forehead on mine. "You know, you're not as different as you think you are."

I leaned my forehead on his chest, feeling his harsh breathing and hearing his trip-hammer heartbeat. Claire said I would move on, but I couldn't move on from this. Marcus wrapped his arms around me and in all the heat and cold water I barely noticed my own hands shaking.

He pulled away to look at me, but I shook my head and his body came back, his lips back to mine. We stood together in the creek while the black water whirled downstream away from us.

I couldn't do it. I'd tell Claire we'd broken it off and we'd be more careful than ever. Both of us wanted this, and that was what mattered.

I pulled away. "Claire was talking about exes."

He looked at me and then downstream, his jaw set.

I could hear my own breathing and the words spilled out of me before I could sort through them. "I kind of panicked, because I—I don't want you—" I started over and slowed down. If I could just get this out, if I could just tell him, then we'd be fine. "I don't want you to be an ex. I think I love you."

His arms fell away from my shoulders and he stepped back. Water rushed between us. "Love me?" His voice was tight, strained. Echoing off the water and against the dark. "Love me how?"

My words came out a whisper. "You said you wanted me. I want you."

"But you don't. You think it's wrong."

"Not wrong. I think it's—" My voice cracked. "I think it's hard. But it's you, and I don't care." I stepped toward him so he was against me again. I found his hands, put his arms around me. Looked into his face.

Watching me, he took my hands and pulled them away from him. "You're shivering," he said. One hand still holding mine, he walked toward the bank and we climbed out of the creek.

I shook out our towels and he sat down next to me. Not a single star shone through the leaden sky and the air lay like a heavy blanket over us.

He said nothing, so I moved to his lap, one knee on each side of his legs. Both of us were dripping wet. "Did you hear me?" I gripped his bare shoulders. "I said I love you."

The vein in his neck thumped against my hand. Drops of water collected on his skin and slid downward. His breathing turned harsh.

I was fifteen again, and nothing mattered except getting him to react to me. My hands slid down to his chest. I pushed him backward, and he let me. I stretched out my body on top of his and touched my lips to the cool, wet skin of his collarbone. His chest rose and fell beneath me. I brushed my mouth over the vein that beat in his neck.

His arms gripped my rib cage and hauled me upward. My mouth connected with his and the air left my body. Arms wrapped around me, he rolled us over so he was on top of me and his shoulders blocked out the sky. His hair brushed my forehead. He linked his fingers behind my neck, his thumbs pressing into my jawline, asking me to open further to him.

I did, and I couldn't stop, because I didn't want to.

His lips, the heat of his tongue with mine. My hands were all over him, every part of him familiar but so different from me. His weight was safe and thrilling and mine.

Limits were for people who were afraid.

He was sucking in air, still kissing me, his stomach pressing into mine and a hand tracing up my thigh. I tipped my head back, letting him kiss down my neck, one hand over his heart, fascinated by how hard it beat. My own made me dizzy. He slipped his hand under the side string of my bikini bottoms, over my hip. The fabric pulled tight.

"It's okay," I said. People couldn't stop us. Not if they didn't know.

He made a sound low in his throat when I slipped my hand under the band of his wet shorts. His stomach muscles contracted. He nodded.

I raised my arms over my head and untied the string around my neck. His lips paused on my skin. His hands skated up my body, over my bikini, to the strings that lay loose on my shoulders. Without moving the fabric, his fingers traced all the way across me from my right shoulder to my left, his eyes burning a trail I could feel.

And then he moved on top of me again, over me, and something about his chest and stomach right there against mine was perfect, and I knew I could never be like this with anyone else, because he belonged to me. He moved up, pressing against me, his hands in my hair, and my mouth went to his neck. Smooth, warm, the edge of sweat and his blood in a slow beat right there. My lips and tongue moved against his skin, but also my teeth, harder than I meant to.

He held still, and then his breath left him in a rush and a half-laugh. "You're going to kill me," he whispered. "I love you."

For a moment I thought he'd lower his head to my neck and his lips and teeth would be on my skin. But then his eyes met mine, and went wide, and then he closed them for a second. "I don't have—"

No, no, no. Shit. I knew exactly what he didn't have. It didn't matter. Yes, it did. It had to. We stared at each other.

He grunted and rolled off me, staring at the sky that was too dark to see. He sounded hoarse. "Can you fix—tie your—"

Somehow this had ended, and now he was over there away from me, and the space that had been so safe just a moment before was gone.

I retied my bikini and rolled toward him, trying to close the distance, but he stopped me with a hand on my shoulder. "Gimme a second."

We lay on our backs on the towels and I watched a sky I couldn't see and hoped the cloud cover meant it couldn't see me, either. When his breathing evened out, I rolled over on my side toward him. I could barely make out his face in the pale wash of the moon. His mouth was drawn tight, and his face was set when he opened his eyes.

"I can't do this," he said.

My stomach sank. "We don't have to. We can wait."

"I mean, I can't do this to you." He spoke to the sky, not to me. "I'm screwing up your life. I'm the reason you have to sneak around and most of why you think you don't fit in. I'm tying up all of high school for you in a dead-end pseudo-relationship."

I said nothing because anything I said wouldn't be the right thing.

"People are going to find out, and you're going to get hurt, and it will follow you around for the rest of your life, and it will be my fault."

I closed my eyes. Loving me was not a reason to leave me.

"You're going to move on to some other guy, eventually, and he'll be the real thing. And when you have that awkward exes talk, you'll have to tell him your first relationship was with your cousin. Your first kiss. Your first everything, if we hadn't stopped."

"Yours, too, though," I said.

"I don't care about that."

"Then why would I?"

He rolled toward me and touched my hair. "But you do. Maybe if it was just us, we could. But someone at school would find out. Senior year would be horrible for both of us. Chris and my sisters would get bullied over it. Teachers would find out, and since—it's not normal, so they'd call social services."

He was probably right. A caseworker would come to the house and talk to all of us, make sure our home was a healthy environment for children. The official stamp we were abnormal. Who knew what social services would decide.

And everyone at school would hear about it.

My parents would be so ashamed of me, and they'd blame Marcus even though it was almost entirely my fault. My family would leave. I'd have split up our home.

But he was wrong about me finding the real thing with some other guy.

"I wanted to hear you say that, you know," he said. "I've wanted to hear it for a long time."

I hadn't known that. I hadn't known any of it and I wished I had. I touched his face and did what he always did to me: I brushed my thumb over his cheekbone. The hardness in his eyes faded a little, and when he sighed, it was so heavy.

We hadn't broken any of our rules, but somehow we'd leaped right over them and off the edge of something much worse.

Every bit of pain on his face was something I'd put there. We never should have started this. I'd been so wrong to push him.

We lay there on the towels by the creek under the heavy night sky, and his hand touched my face and slipped through my hair, and at that moment I wouldn't have noticed if the world had fallen in on us. It wouldn't have made much difference.

Chapter Eleven

Morning was a little cooler than the night. I slept in until Mom woke me, asking me if I was sick. I told her sort of.

Marcus and I had stayed out all night and snuck back in before dawn. I'd fallen asleep for a bit wrapped in my towel, my head on Marcus's chest, but every time I moved, I'd felt him lying there awake.

After Mom left my room, I rolled over and my gritty hair scraped my skin. Creek water. I heaved myself out of bed, hoping a shower would wash away both the grit from the creek and the awful feeling in my stomach.

We had new rules. We'd talked them over for hours last night. No more making out, no movies just us, no walks or trips alone. As much as possible, we'd only see each other when other people were around. I'd treat him like he was Chris. He'd treat me like I was Claire.

I let the pounding water beat on my skin for longer than usual.

I dried off, pulled on my jean shorts and a yellow tank top, then headed out to the kitchen. Mom handed me coffee. "We aren't going to work outside today," she said. "There's a heat advisory. You could get sick. We'll make sure the animals have water and then stay inside."

"We have to turn on the air conditioning. At least knock the house down to eighty degrees." She nodded and I shoved my feet into my sneakers and went outside. I turned on the water to the garden, filled the chickens' waterer, and pushed them aside to get the eggs, even the old hen who refused to leave her nest. Chickens weren't going to be my undoing today. The duck's pool was getting silty, so I tipped it over and refilled it while she stalked around, quacking her worry at the muddy water draining into the ground.

Chris and Angie stood by the calf fence feeding the bottle calves, giant strands of slobber stringing down from the bottles as the calves noisily sucked down a half gallon of milk each. Marcus showed up while I was rinsing Heidi's water bowl. He poured dog food into her bucket and opened the garage door to make sure she had shade. The parents would probably let her inside for the afternoon.

"How'd you sleep?" he asked.

"Fine," I said. He hadn't done anything wrong, but we had to push each other away. I stood at the row of three washing tubs, industrial sinks on PVC legs, near the garage and washed radishes and carrots for an hour while he finished watering the garden. Even though Mom had said we didn't have to do all the chores today, having my hands in the cold water made the temperature bearable, and I couldn't follow Marcus around right then.

What I'd almost done last night tied my stomach in knots. Heat crept up my neck. So I was in love with him. And so what if he loved me, too?

If I had a wish, I'd undo all of that.

I picked a few ripe tomatoes before I went inside, then curled up on my bed. After a minute, I pulled out my phone and texted Claire.

Marcus and I are pretty much done now.

A moment later my phone buzzed.

Yeah? Good. Sorry though.

I pulled my laptop off my desk and took it back to my bed. Acting normal around everyone wasn't going to happen.

Just to prove to myself that getting over Marcus really was the best thing to do, I Googled "first cousins marrying." The hits showed up purple and blue—most of these links I'd already clicked. The first was a list of states in which it was illegal. But it was legal in half the states, including California. Maybe I'd go back to California for college.

I closed my computer, annoyed with proof that being in love with my cousin was a bad idea, and picked up *Where the Red Fern Grows* again. I knew the dogs were going to die, but I hoped they wouldn't.

The dogs did die. One died of wounds and the other died of heartbreak. I cried on my bed and ignored whoever knocked on my door at lunchtime. I heard Sylvia giggling mid-afternoon, which meant I wasn't coming out of my room, so I turned up the BBC/Colin Firth version of *Pride and Prejudice* because it was six hours long. Twenty minutes into the movie, I realized that in *Mansfield Park*, Fanny and Edmund are first cousins who get married, and that did not improve my mood or the likelihood of me emerging from my room.

I was getting hungry, however, so I dug around in my desk and found a candy bar. Under the junk in the drawer lay a photo of me and Ellie at the pool. I picked it up. We both were making silly faces, sucking on straws buried in a giant plastic cup of lemonade slush.

The photo was from before she moved, before my deal with Marcus started, before I had any idea what my seventeenth year was going to be like. I tucked the edge of the photo between my mirror and the frame so it lay pinned against the glass.

Sylvia was not going to be the reason I skipped lunch, so I paused the movie and went to get actual food. From the racket going on upstairs, I guessed the twins were playing in their room and Angie and Candace were banging around up there with them. Dad was in his office and Mom was probably at the library. Relative peace, for once.

Chris sat in the living room reading a graphic novel on the couch opposite Marcus and Sylvia, probably trying to annoy his brother with his presence, but Marcus didn't seem to care. He was telling Sylvia about the truck that ran us off the road, and she was frowning dramatically and sitting too close to him. Little red boots, this time.

"You didn't find out who he was?" she asked.

"Nope. Some guy from Kansas City owns the truck, but he's not the guy who was driving it." He stiffened when I walked through the room, so he knew I was there, but he didn't look my way.

Sylvia, of all people, was the one who looked up. "Hey. Want to play a game?"

"I'm watching the BBC *Pride and Prejudice*. Sorry."

"Isn't that thing like ten hours long?" Chris lowered his graphic novel. If he was around on a weekend, it meant Will and his other friends weren't.

"Six hours of witty social commentary," I said. "If you plan on dating someday, you should watch it." Chris made a face and went back to his reading.

Sylvia laughed. "I've never seen it. We should all watch it sometime."

Nice try, Blondie. "We could play basketball at the park once it cools down."

Marcus finally made eye contact, but his face gave nothing away. Sylvia smiled. "Hey, that would be fun."

I decided to ask. "Did you play anything at Edison? Did you play basketball?"

"Um, yeah. But not basketball."

I knew it. She didn't want to tell me. I shoved my hands in my back pockets. "Marcus played for two years, but I was never any good. What did you play?"

She glanced at Marcus then fiddled with her phone. "Oh, just volleyball."

Okay, she'd admitted it, but she was reluctant to tell me. She picked at her fingernails. "Are you going to play this year?" I asked.

She pulled her legs up onto the couch and tucked her feet to the side. "No. I think I'm done."

She didn't say anything else, and Marcus was still giving me a weird look, so I quit trying to make conversation and walked into the kitchen.

I loaded a bag with a jar of nuts, a banana, string cheese, and peanut butter. After grabbing a glass of grapefruit juice from the fridge, I sealed myself in my room.

Playing on the Edison volleyball team was the main reason Ellie had wanted to move. I opened up my laptop and waited for it to wake up. Sylvia said she barely knew Ellie. But she had to have known her pretty well if they were on the same team. All those hours at practice. Competing together. Trips to games. The sleepovers Ellie mentioned in her e-mail. Sylvia couldn't have barely known her.

I logged into Facebook. Sylvia might not be on social media, but Ellie had been.

Her profile hadn't been taken down. She smiled back at me, holding her cat and looking super excited about something. It took me a minute to remember that she was no longer smiling, no longer fluffing her cat's fur. Her hands and her face and her whole body were buried in the ground.

Or maybe she hadn't been buried. I had no idea how the investigation was going; maybe she hadn't even been put in a coffin and lowered into the ground yet.

I scrolled down her wall; it had turned into some kind of strange memorial.

I'll always remember those sleepovers in 7ᵗʰ grade. Nail polish everywhere! Miss you. ☹

We miss your smile down here—Mrs. Shepherd

We love you, sweetheart. I just wanted to tell you that one more time. —Aunt Kathy

Awful. The one from her aunt was dated two days after they found her body. Most of the other posts were cheesy sentiments that sounded like they'd been taken straight from a badly written greeting card, like most of the posters barely knew her.

The blank box stared back at me. *Write something!* it demanded.

What would I even write? *I'm sorry the world is screwed up. I'm sorry someone killed you. I'm sorry we didn't stay close.*

Ultimately, me writing something on her wall wouldn't help anyone. She'd never know.

I clicked on her photos and scrolled through the most recent ones. She'd been tagged at someone's party, in her mom's photos of the new house in St. Joseph, and driving the second-hand car that was her sixteenth birthday present. Her last birthday present.

There. Fuzzy photos from some mother's cell phone of a game. Several girls I didn't know were tagged. Teammates. Ellie was jumping in the air, and right behind her stood a blonde girl. The photo was taken from a long enough distance, I couldn't tell for sure who it was.

I flipped to the next photo. Fuzzier. Why did people bother posting ones like that?

I stopped on the third. A clear, in-focus picture of Ellie high-fiving Sylvia. Unmistakably Sylvia. The date on the photo was in the middle of the fall semester. Sylvia hadn't quit the team, so she must have gone to the sleepovers and team activities.

I leaned back against the headboard and stared at the photo. Sylvia had lied. Maybe it didn't mean anything. People lied for lots of reasons.

An e-mail popped into my inbox, so I switched tabs. Another one from Travis—I'd forgotten to reply to his last one. I clicked it open and replied.

Hey,

No, sorry, I'm fine. My life just kind of exploded this week and I can barely remember what day it is. Glad you enjoyed the last post—have you studied anything about adaptations or spinoffs in your classes? I'm thinking my next post will be discussing Bates Motel, *that modern prequel to* Psycho, *or else maybe the BBC's* Sherlock, *and compare it to some of the earlier adaptations.*

~J

I wanted to make some comment about Benedict Cumberbatch being the ideal man, but that was the kind of joke I'd make to Ellie, not to some Internet guy. Besides, it was a toss-up between him and Johnny Depp.

Adaptations usually fascinated me. Just a few twists, and the story would turn out so differently. Minor changes meant Henry Higgins and Eliza either stayed together or couldn't overcome their pride.

Right then I wasn't fascinated so much as seeing depressing parallels.

Sylvia giggled in the living room until dinner, at which point she went home and I emerged from my room.

During dinner Aunt Shelly and Uncle Ward pretended they weren't overly interested in why Sylvia had been coming around and tried to come up with casual-sounding questions. Marcus deflected most of them, staring at his plate and not reacting to their baiting.

Chris waved his fork. "You know, maybe this is late notice, but Sylvia's actually been hanging out here for me. We're getting married this weekend. You guys should totally come." Candace and Angie giggled and Aunt Shelly told him not to be mouthy.

Halfway through dinner, Marcus tried to get my attention by bumping my foot, and I ignored him the first two times, but when he huffed and mashed his peas with his fork, I looked up. He simply watched me, his brown eyes worried, and I shrugged. What could I say, "Don't worry, leaving me after two years probably won't hurt that much"?

Secret messages and covert whispering simply weren't part of the twelve-step program to getting over one's cousin. If I didn't treat him like Chris, I was never going to get over him, and I didn't want to feel like this for one minute longer than I had to.

I passed the butter to Angie and asked Mom about the library. Her eyes brightened. "The summer reading program's in full swing. I'm doing a lot of planning for the carnival. The soap slides are always a hit, and we're doing face painting and water balloons again. We're going to try to rent a bouncy castle for the big attraction."

The reading carnival was usually pretty fun. Kids earned points for each book they read over the summer, and they spent them at the end of the summer at a mini-carnival put on by the library. All of us cousins usually got roped into helping. If Claire came home for it, I could attach myself to her and not get paired up with Marcus for all the games.

After dinner Mom and Dad made decaf coffee and Aunt Shelly and Uncle Ward brewed green tea in their tiny pot. I was heading back to my room when Mom stopped me. "Come talk with us, hon. You've been in your room since I got home."

Marcus had gone upstairs to play his computer game, so I came back.

Mom was a big fan of conversation. I didn't mind, but I didn't really have anything to say, and the one thing I could have used some help with was the one thing I couldn't talk about.

"So, senior year," Aunt Shelly said. "ACTs, senior prom, all that. Are you excited?"

"I took the ACT and the SAT last year, but yeah, it should be cool." I read once that *prom* was short for *promenade*, which was a ridiculous word, and when paired with "senior" it just sounded like a geriatric parade.

Around here, proms were pretty lame, since the junior and senior class combined would be about forty students max, and everyone would leave about nine at night for a field party and some idiot would have a gun and everyone would use beer cans for target practice. Bonfires, kegs, tequila, and much making of prom babies would go on until four A.M., and everyone would be violently ill for the rest of the day.

Maybe I'd enjoy it more if I had people I wanted to share it with.

"What are you thinking about college?" Uncle Ward asked. "You want to study English, right?"

"Maybe film, actually. Film criticism or cinematography or something." I wasn't entirely sure yet.

"Really?" Mom said. "You'd be great at that."

Aunt Shelly pursed her lips. "I'm not sure I'd encourage one of my children to spend so much time with television, though," she said.

This conversation wasn't one for in front of Aunt Shelly. Mom set down her mug. "Well, that's your decision, but we don't have a problem with it, and even if we did, it's Jackie's choice."

"But medical reports show the long-term damage to the brain is—"

Uncle Ward broke in. "So then you might go back to California? L.A. and all that?" He refilled his green tea.

Maybe if Aunt Shelly had smoked pot in college, she'd be more like Uncle Ward. "If I wasn't going to teach film at a college or something." I'd barely thought about what career I wanted, beyond something in film. Being in love with my cousin was taking priority at the moment.

"That sounds great, honey. We'll have to look at some of the good programs." Mom was making a point to be supportive, and I appreciated that, but if I stayed here much longer, the conversation would turn into an argument about the effect of screen time on the adolescent brain, so I excused myself, saying I was tired.

"Be up early, please," Dad called after me. "That garden needs a serious day's work."

I didn't see Marcus for the rest of the evening. He stayed upstairs and I stayed in my room. Day one: successful.

Success felt an awful lot like loss.

The engine of the Gator rumbled through the morning. Dad drove it past the house as I closed the storm door and walked through the dew-damp grass.

The day would get hot fast, so I wore my raggiest pair of jean shorts and a sports bra under a T-shirt. I'd cut the sleeves off and slit the sides last summer. My arms might get scratched up, but there was a humidity point where personal injury ceased to matter.

Marcus held the hose, filling five-gallon buckets every few rows down the length of the garden for plunging our arms into to cool down. Aunt Shelly had turned on the soaker hoses, and they steadily dripped water onto the bases of the plants.

Mom stood up from over by the tomatoes. "Jackie, would you and Marcus start on the green beans?"

Beans couldn't be watered until we were done handling the plants. If the plants were damp, our hands could spread bean blight bacteria from the leaves to the rest of the plant, so they had to be weeded first.

I grabbed a bucket and we went over to the six rows of beans, two each of pole beans, snap beans, and yellow beans. Beans were my least favorite garden chore. Not only were there a million of the things to pick every time I came out here, but it was like they deliberately hid from me behind the leaves.

Marcus knelt in the dirt and clipped a bean from the plant. "Hey," he said.

"Hey." It had only been a day, and already I missed talking to him. I picked up the garden scissors and snipped off a handful of ripe beans. The scissors meant we didn't have to pull on the bean and damage the plant.

"You okay?"

"I hate picking beans."

"I know that's not all you're thinking." He tossed a bean past its prime to the edge of the garden.

"It's not, but normal cousins don't tell each other everything they're thinking." I walked back to the bucket pile and picked up another; several of the beans I'd seen so far were either withered or overripe. We'd need a bucket for the bad ones. Between only doing basics on the weekend and then Monday and Tuesday being too hot to work, the beans, and probably the rest of the produce, were not happy.

We worked in silence for almost twenty minutes. Candace came over to help, working in the pole beans row and talking about how Angie was being annoying and could do the tomatoes herself.

Dad drove by in the Gator, the bed loaded with flats of Roma tomatoes and buckets of spinach. Chris and Uncle Ward were on wash duty over by the garage. Dad waved, and I was glad he was out of the office for at least a little while.

Mom stretched an extension cord from the garage. She up-ended a bucket and plugged in an old radio, then turned the dial to the local classic hits station. Mom and her music.

When Candace left to drop off her bucket, Marcus said quietly, "There's no reason we can't talk anymore. Why are you ignoring me?"

"We can still hang out. I just need some space for a while." I searched through one of the bushy plants and snipped off a bean. Across the rows, Aunt Shelly was staring at me, her eyes narrowed. I kept my eyes on the plants.

His shoulders were hunched as he worked. "Okay." He wouldn't look at me, which meant I'd hurt his feelings, which made me crabby. I didn't want to hurt him, but we couldn't jump from more than friends to only friends and expect that to work without changing how we treated each other.

The cloud cover broke up into patches, letting the sun through for a few minutes at a time. As the morning wore on and the temperature rose, Candace and Angie argued about who had to weed the tomatoes and spent half the time playing in the water buckets to cool off, Chris turned on his iPod and ignored us, and Mom and Aunt Shelly discussed how much of what to bring to the farmers' market this weekend.

Marcus and I spent nearly the entire morning picking beans and then washing the produce in the industrial sinks, which turned out to be a very solitary job for having him right beside me.

Near lunch time, Aunt Shelly called it quits, and we all went inside. It was partially the heat making me so irritated, so I tried not to talk to anyone and made a beeline for the shower.

Marcus said Sylvia wanted him to come see her place, so he got dibs on the second bathroom and was done showering and gone before I got out. He was being too deliberately casual about going to Sylvia's, which meant he was excited about it, and I hated knowing she'd put that look on his face.

If he was gone having fun, I wasn't going to sit around, either. I texted Kelsey, she came to get me, and for the next two hours, I thanked God for the theater's air conditioning. Kelsey laughed through the movie, mocking everything from the superhero's clothing to the laws of his abilities.

"I can't help it," she said. "*Avengers* was so much better."

"Never seen it."

She smacked my arm. "Yes, you have. Say you have."

"Nope."

"I'm going to make you watch it. Sleepover, ASAP."

I grinned and shrugged. "Okay."

When we were heading home, Travis replied to my e-mail with some interesting links on the principles of adaptations and the success rate of spinoffs. Kelsey wanted to know why I was asking him for that, so after taking a deep breath, I told her about my blog. To her credit, she seemed vaguely interested. "Can I read it?" she asked.

My face grew warm. "Uh—if you want. You'll probably think it's boring."

"I'll show you all my horrible photography if you let me read your blog."

I laughed. "Deal."

My high was ruined when Marcus came home that evening and told me he met Sylvia's dad, and then he had the nerve to say he thought Sylvia and I would like each other.

I said nothing and waited for him to notice. We were crouched on the living room floor, helping the twins put their blocks away before bed.

"She's nice," he said. "And I have to do something."

I understood. But oh, how I wanted to be angry at him for it. I sat back on my heels and stared at the carpet.

He snapped the lid on the bucket for the blocks. "We said—"

"I know what we said." I could do this. I could let him go and be fine with him hanging out with other girls. He was doing it for us, and me getting hurt would only make it worse for both of us.

When I went to bed, I had another e-mail, but not from Travis. Kelsey had followed my blog.

Chapter Twelve

Dinner Friday night was mostly Aunt Shelly questioning Marcus about Sylvia, Marcus having what amounted to a staring contest with his plate, and me failing spectacularly at pretending nothing was wrong.

My introverted silence and Marcus's plate-staring were spared the limelight when Mom mentioned she'd seen the white truck at the library.

"It was sitting outside after the library closed, just idling," she said.

Uncle Ward set his water down. "Was someone in the truck?"

She nodded. "It was getting dark so I couldn't see who, but someone was in it."

"You should have called the police," Aunt Shelly said.

Mom gave Dad a look, then shrugged. "I called Cliff. Telling Whitley a truck was sitting in a parking lot wouldn't have done any good."

Conjectures and speculations floated nervously around the table, and I excused myself without anyone noticing and started doing the dishes. My parents would come find me if I hid in my room any more than I already had, and then it would become an "issue."

Mom got up to help me load the dishwasher. "Shelly and I can get these. Do you and Marcus want to go shut up the henhouse and check on the calves for the night?"

Marcus looked up.

I rinsed a plate. "Oh, that's okay. I haven't done dishes in a while. I can help."

Marcus shoved back his chair and the legs scraped on the floor. I expected him to bang out of the house, but he just put on his shoes and walked outside. Guilt crowded out some of my determination, but I wasn't trying to be mean. The parents had gotten used to pairing us up for chores and errands and everything under the sun, and it had to stop. This was exactly why most people didn't continue to live with their ex after a breakup.

Mom put soap in the dishwasher. "Are you two okay?" she asked quietly. The twins were still goofing around with their food, and Uncle Ward was chatting with Dad about expanding the garden to include a potato field next year.

"Oh, yeah, we're fine," I said.

"You've been pretty quiet lately, so something has to be wrong." She dried her hands on a dish towel, frowning. "Is it Sylvia? I know it can be hard when a friend starts dating. Friends take second place to girlfriends sometimes."

"He's not dating her." She was partly right, though. "But it is kinda weird."

"Oh honey, I'm sorry." She hugged me. "Just remember—if she makes him happy, then you want him to be happy, right?"

"Yeah." Except it was a whole lot more complex than that, because he'd said he loved me, and he was what made me happy.

"We've been so glad to see what good friends you two are. It'll work out, honey. Don't worry about it."

Everyone kept saying that.

Mid-morning Sunday Chris stumbled down the stairs in his pajama pants, shirtless with his blond hair standing on end.

"Hey," I said. "You look fantastic."

"No sarcasm before noon." He shuffled over to the couch and collapsed. "Did Marcus go off on another hot date?"

I followed him into the living room. "No idea." I knew exactly where he was. He was hanging out with Sylvia, and sitting here by myself was not helping.

Chris was shorter than Marcus, but more muscular, even though he was almost three years younger. He'd probably be one of those guys girls giggled over—he sort of was already.

Chris sighed. "Why are you moping?"

"I'm not moping."

"You're moping because Marcus has a girlfriend and now you're bored because he's not your pet anymore."

That entire sentence was wrong. "I'm not moping, and he was never my pet. And she's not his girlfriend."

He rolled his eyes. "Give it a week. The stars have aligned."

I didn't reply.

"Okay, fine, I'll take pity on you." Chris rolled off the couch and stood up. "I'm gonna take a shower then go out with the guys. Want to come?"

I raised my eyebrows. An invitation from Chris. "Um—okay."

"Wear something different. I have a reputation, you know." I couldn't tell from his smirk if he was serious or not. I was perfectly comfortable in my tank top and jean shorts.

All the same, I didn't want to screw up the one time Chris deemed me cool enough to hang out with his friends. I went back to my room and changed into dark jeans and a black sleeveless shirt with a drapey neck. I debated whether it was worth putting on makeup, but settled for mascara, light lip gloss, and long silver bars for earrings. Whatever I was doing with Chris, it couldn't be necessary to go all-out. I brushed my hair up into a ponytail, then because Chris still wasn't out of the shower, I tried on three pairs of shoes before sticking with my black flip-flops.

Chris pounded down the stairs. "Jackie! They're here. Come on."

I'd never met his friends because they never came inside. Chris nodded his approval in the living room. "That's better. Thanks." I gave him a weird look and we headed out, waving to Aunt Shelly as we went.

A green Neon idled in the driveway. Chris motioned to the passenger door. "You can sit up front, I guess."

Generous of him. I opened the car door and almost did a double take as I climbed in. Chris's friend was hot. Really hot.

I buckled my seatbelt to hide my face while Chris said, "Guys, this is Jackie. Jackie, Will is driving and Mara and Kyle are back here." A girl and a guy sat in the back, and Chris was sitting closer to Mara than strictly necessary, but I didn't waste time thinking about it, because this was Will?

The black wife-beater he wore—whose name I objected to but whose cut I did not—stretched over muscles that bulged in his shoulders and upper arms and stretched down to cord and flex in his forearm when he adjusted the rearview mirror.

He dangled a lit cigarette out his window over the driveway. No way was he Chris's age. "Geez, Chris." He put the car in reverse. "You didn't say you were bringing your girlfriend."

"She's my cousin, moron."

"Well, now. That's marvelous news. You're his older cousin, I take it." His grin lit up his face. Messy black hair and a fringe of dark eyelashes over pastel blue eyes. Two inches of his boxers rose above the narrow waist of his jeans.

I tried not to look at him, because my face would be a dead giveaway. Talk to the windshield, not him. "I'm seventeen."

"Perfect. I'm nineteen."

Leave it to Chris hang out with someone older than me. "You're from Harris?"

"Yep. You go to Manson? Right." He glanced at Chris in the rearview mirror. "You should have told me years ago you had a hot cousin."

I flushed. So he was an unapologetic flirt, too.

Chris ignored him, talking instead to Mara and Kyle.

Will grinned. "So. Jackie. You have a boyfriend somewhere, right?"

"It's irrelevant, but no, I don't." He was smoking, and I didn't like smokers.

"It should be relevant. I'd love to make it relevant."

I fought back a grin, in spite of myself. "Me being single will never be relevant to anyone who smokes."

He dropped his cigarette out the window.

Will parked the car in front of a creaky old house in Harris. Beer bottles littered the yard and the grass hadn't been cut in weeks. The garbage can looked like someone had missed trash day. Several times.

"It's a bachelor pad." He grinned, but his smile was a little less natural than before. "I rent with two other guys. They do construction work, so I hardly see them. Pretty sweet deal, right?"

We got out of the car and Chris and the others followed us up to the house. "Yeah," I said. "You rent your own place?"

"Well, there're the other two guys. But hey, it's awesome. Girls love it." He unjammed the door by ramming it with his shoulder and I stepped into a mud room off the kitchen. The interior of the house was about what I expected, given the outside. A mineral-stained cast-iron sink, peeling linoleum, and shaggy rust-colored carpet in the living room. The house smelled like stale smoke, but it was clean. Surprisingly.

Chris opened the fridge and grabbed a six-pack like it was his—which it probably was. Will glanced at me while the others tramped into the living room. In spite of his confidence that girls loved the place, he seemed like he might not be convinced himself.

He hung back with me in the kitchen. "I can see the charm," I said. No reason to crush the guy. "This place is a real chick magnet."

He grinned. "Can I get you a drink?"

I hesitated. "What do you have?" Beer wasn't my thing.

He opened the fridge. "I can offer one of Chris's beers, a screwdriver . . . hmm. Coke and whiskey?"

Coke and whiskey on Sunday morning. Why not. "The last one sounds great."

He pulled a frosted glass from the freezer and poured in about two fingers of whiskey. He kept the Coke from fizzing too much, and bubbles snapped to the surface and burst when he handed me the glass.

"So you'll be a senior this year?" He leaned on the counter, his arms braced on the edge, which raised his shirt enough I could see a strip of skin between his shirt hem and the band of his boxers.

The rim of the glass was incredibly cold on my lips. I didn't know what to do with this much attention from a guy who wasn't Marcus. "Yeah." I sipped the drink, avoiding looking at his arms. And that strip of skin. "You?"

"Nah. I quit my junior year."

Chris stuck his head into the kitchen. "Stop flirting and get out here."

"Cocky little shit, isn't he?" Will poured himself a drink and followed me into the living room.

Everyone was sitting on the floor. Chris sat close to Mara, a cute brunette with a pixie cut, and Kyle, who looked about my age, sprawled on his stomach by the armchair. Will waited until I picked a spot on the floor with my back against the couch and then sat next to me. The six-pack rested on the carpet.

"Okay, 'Never Have I Ever.' Everybody show your hand." Will pointed to Chris. "You start."

"What? I want to play Xbox," Chris said.

"We can't play *Halo* with this many people. 'Never Have I Ever.' You start."

"Umm—" Chris leaned back on his arm. "Never have I ever . . . gotten a speeding ticket."

"Really? I've had two." Will put down a finger and so did Kyle. I'd never gotten a ticket, but I'd talked my way out of two.

Games like these with people I didn't know made my brain stall. I tried to think of something as the game progressed around the circle, and then it was my turn. "Um—never have I ever . . ." Thinking of something I'd never done was a lot harder than it sounded.

"Gone out with a guy who had his own place? Dated a guy just for his body?" Will suggested.

I gave him an almost-serious glare. "Never have I ever played 'Never Have I Ever.'"

"Cheater. And seriously?" Kyle asked. "It's a good drinking game, but we're all broke. So you only get to see the mostly sober version."

The mostly sober version sounded fine. I wasn't sure what I'd do if I got really drunk, but I was certain I didn't want to do whatever it was around Will. He stretched out his arm—tanned skin, defined muscle—to reach his drink on the coffee table and I vaguely wondered if that muscle was as hard as it looked. Just briefly.

His other arm brushed mine, and I had my answer. Goose bumps trickled down my skin.

The game went for half an hour, during which time I managed to blurt out something lame on four or five turns, while Will casually suggested everything from romantic to dirty things I might not have done, and all of it only reminded me of Marcus.

I'd done several of them, but I wasn't going to tell him.

"Okay—'Truth or Dare,'" Kyle said.

Chris moaned. "That's so middle school."

"No, I love that game," Will said, looking at me. "Let's play it."

I groaned and leaned back against the couch. Candace's infamous dare had started things between me and Marcus, and I was not kissing anyone this time, dare or no dare.

"Okay, Mara, you're up," Kyle said. "Truth or dare?"

"Dare," she said.

"I dare you to chug the rest of that beer."

"Ugh. Lame." She squinted through the amber glass to check how much was left, then tipped the bottle up and chugged the last half. "Also nasty. Chris, your turn."

"Dare."

"I dare you to . . . give me the rest of your beer since I had to chug mine."

Chris sighed and handed it over. "Will. Truth or dare?"

"Truth." He rested his arm on the couch behind me. I swirled the ice in my glass and pretended I hadn't noticed.

"Why are you flirting with Jackie? It's weird."

For the second time that afternoon, heat rushed to my face. Chris had never been one to hold back. Will was being pretty obvious, but still.

"Flirting is one of life's finer pleasures, and I strongly recommend you do more of it," Will said. "Now Jackie, truth or dare?"

Of course he'd pick me. No way was I doing a dare. "Truth."

"Hmm." He watched my face, his blue eyes studying me. I met his eyes because if I didn't, I'd turn even redder. He grinned. "Yes or no—do you think I'm hot?"

My eyes widened. The raging confidence of this guy. That cocky grin qualified, but he didn't need help with his ego. "You're okay."

His grin widened. "I knew it. She thinks I'm hot, guys. Outrageously hot."

"This is so dumb," Kyle complained. He turned on the TV and flipped channels. Chris and Mara moved onto the couch so they could see, repositioning themselves much closer to each other than they were on the floor.

Kyle stopped flipping when he came across *The Fast and the Furious.* "Here we go. This is how Will got his speeding tickets."

"It's true. Just like that," Will said. "But those rides don't hold a candle to mine."

"Really," I said. "The Neon?"

"Hey, don't say it like that. I'm telling you, that lady will do zero to sixty in under five minutes."

I almost choked on my drink. "Sounds like a winner."

"She is. Not for sale." He pulled a lighter out of his pocket and lit a cigarette.

This guy could hardly be more different from Marcus. I turned back to the TV, but glanced back and caught him staring at me. Smoke swirled toward the ceiling.

We didn't say anything for a moment. He blew smoke at the ceiling again.

"So." He nudged my arm. "Can I get your number?"

His grin was the same self-assured one I'd been seeing all afternoon, but his eyes weren't quite so confident. I hesitated, and his grin fell just a bit. For that reason alone, I caved. "If you put out your cigarette, I'll even let you text me."

He ground it out in the ashtray on the end table. "Deal."

Maybe I had a distraction now, too.

Chapter Thirteen

The weekend had come and gone without Marcus doing more than passing through the house. Everywhere I went, he'd already been there and left. His keys on the counter, or his folded stack of laundry the missing one in the row on the living room couch, already taken up to his room, or his chores done and his truck gone already. I couldn't seem to find a room with him in it.

The few times I saw him, his glance burned into me for the briefest second on his way out the door or up to his room. I'd texted him on Saturday, but no matter how long I stared at the bubble that held my words, no reply ever popped up.

When I'd backed off, I'd at least told him I needed some space. I hadn't given him the cold shoulder. I hadn't ignored his texts. This wasn't him treating me like Claire, this was him pretending I didn't exist.

I let the dog into my room Monday, a rare privilege for her. She leaped up onto the foot of the bed and beat her tail against the blanket before letting out a deep sigh. Researching college film programs would keep me busy for the afternoon, and Heidi would be good company.

Spreading out index cards and my top-bound college-ruled notebook on the bed made me feel better. Legs crossed, I opened my laptop and clicked my bookmarks. Each program I was considering had an index card—pros on one side, cons on another. General questions and new universities to check out I scribbled onto the notebook, organized into sections by state.

A big stack of the index cards had a note printed neatly on the "cons" side from the beginning of summer—*no degrees Marcus would want.*

Mostly film or arts-only schools. I'd requested information on all the programs except the ones in that stack.

College would change so much. Those four years would pretty much be nothing but change, and if Marcus wasn't part of it in some way, if he missed it all, that kind of gap would keep us apart for good. He'd go his way, I'd go mine, and what we'd been would be left behind in high school.

I huffed and Heidi pricked her ears. I scratched her head and opened a new tab on my browser. A new message from Travis in my inbox. E-mailing with a college guy was kind of fun, and talking about films with someone who really got it made me feel like I wasn't completely on my own with this. My hand stilled on Heidi's fur.

> *Jackie,*
> *I keep seeing coverage of that story about Ellie Wallace. Is that your area of Missouri at all? Such a sad story.*
> *Hope your life is calming down some. Sometimes getting out of the house can help; can you go out with friends or something?*
> *~Travis*

Ellie kept cropping up everywhere I went. Somewhere in the woods, trees had hidden her body, and every time I saw a stand of pines and oaks, I wondered what they were hiding, if a girl's life had ended there with no one to see or hear. The empty-window eyes of her old house watched me on the way past to the pool. Even Sylvia reminded me of Ellie, because somehow they'd been friends.

I hadn't kept up our friendship, but at least I hadn't lied about knowing her.

I replied to Travis's e-mail right then so I wouldn't forget.

> *No, life isn't really calming down much, but whatever. Yeah, Ellie was a friend of mine. I'm still in shock, I think. It's true*

*what they say about not realizing what you had until you can't
have it back. Hope classes are going well.*

~Jackie

I searched the university websites for information about their film
programs until that evening, which did not keep me from thinking
about Marcus.

His footsteps would beat down the stairs, and I'd look up from my
computer, expecting him to come to my door. His voice would answer
someone in the living room, a low, even sound I'd conditioned myself
to listen for, but no part of it would be for me.

It was only because I knew him so well, it wasn't true, but a small
part of me felt like it had been a part of him for so long that it just hadn't
come back to me yet, and that was why I could tell where he was, know
where he'd been.

I left the cards for universities Marcus wouldn't go to on my dresser
in a neat white stack.

I could watch *Psycho* now. Marcus had never liked it, but I knew
how Marion Crane felt, having to meet Sam in secret. I wasn't planning
on staying in any cheap motels, though, so hopefully I'd avoid being
stabbed to death in a shower. Plus, my secret relationship was over.

As the discordant orchestra played in the credits, my phone buzzed
with a text. An unknown number.

Will. I smiled, then frowned and re-read the text.

Marion and Sam argued onscreen.

*Dude, you should have seen this girl I met. Total babe. Can't stop
thinking about her.*

For half a second, I thought he'd accidentally texted me something
meant for someone else. I rolled my eyes and texted back.

Yeah, I've seen her. She's okay.

My phone buzzed immediately.

Oh no—this is Jackie, isn't it? I thought this was Eric!

What a giant dork.

Right. Sure you did. Flattery will get you nowhere, BTW.

Will probably did this to every girl he met. If he wasn't serious, he couldn't expect me to be.

It usually works for me. Watch this.

After a minute, a second text popped up.

Hey there, gorgeous. Go out to dinner with me tomorrow?

I blinked. I hadn't thought he'd follow through.

Hmm. Nope, doesn't work. Try asking Eric.

A minute lapsed before another text arrived.

What would work?

I was light-years away from being ready to focus on someone else, especially someone who flirted so much winning a medal in the sport must be his life's ambition. But if Marcus was hanging out with Sylvia, maybe hanging out with Will would help.

Try not flirting at all.

My phone buzzed almost immediately.

That might be hard. I'll try, though, just for you.

I'd texted my way through the stabbing scene, which I'd never been able to watch without looking away. When I leaned back to watch Norman cleaning up the mess, something occurred to me.

Flirting with Will was something I could tell Claire about. And Kelsey and Hannah. They'd laugh and demand details, and I'd say, "I'm sure it doesn't mean anything," but then tell them everything. It would be very normal.

The heat finally broke with a sprinkle of rain during the night. When I came in from chores, I stopped in the driveway, staring at Marcus's truck. Ugly scratches ran the length of the body, fresh scars in the gray paint.

The tires, his dad's truck, and now this.

The parents and Marcus sat in a ring around the table. Shadows lined his eyes and he was leaning back in the chair, his arms crossed.

"What happened?" I asked. Dread curdled in my stomach. Maybe all this was because of us; maybe someone knew about Marcus and me.

Marcus leaned forward braced his arms on the table, and his eyes met mine for a second. He looked away. "Someone keyed my truck last night. I was at Sylvia's, and when I came out . . . it was like that." He lined up the salt and pepper shakers.

Wait. If it happened last night, and he was telling the parents just now, he must have been out until late. Very late.

"The good news is we think we know what's going on," Mom said.

I glanced out the big kitchen windows. Between being run off the road and having the tires cut, and now this, I suddenly felt exposed. Like I shouldn't be standing in the middle of a room with one wall almost completely glass.

"Sheriff Whitley says there's been vandalism over in Harris, too. Someone had their gas siphoned, someone else had prank gifts on their doorstep—disgusting ones, I might add. It's just school rivalry stuff again, he thinks."

Our basketball team had a long-standing rivalry with Harris, and it had gotten aggressive before, but keying a truck was extreme. And school rivalry didn't explain an adult wrecking Uncle Ward's truck, unless it was some student's irate parent. "That's dumb. I mean, I'm glad it's not a crazy stalker, but still."

Mom frowned. "It's an expensive prank."

"It's not a prank," Dad said. "It's a crime, and kids should know the difference."

"Well, now, I remember us doing some pretty risky stuff in college," Uncle Ward said with a grin. "Illegal, even."

Mom's eyes narrowed. "You don't need to imply things, Ward. Everyone knows we smoked marijuana. But pot doesn't cost some young man who never hurt me several hundred dollars."

Dad put his arm on the back of Mom's chair and massaged her shoulder. "That's debatable, and you never know the ripple effects." Mom gave him a sideways glance. He cleared his throat. "Not the time for that, probably. It's just good to know it's a school thing. But be smart and don't provoke anyone, Marcus. Lock your doors, keep your phone with you, and when you go see friends, maybe stay in instead of going out."

"Yeah." He stood up and walked out of the kitchen, right past me. He didn't so much as glance in my direction.

My eyes burned. I crossed the living room, fully intending on slamming my bedroom door, but I stopped in the hall and stared at the stair-step arrangement of baby photos. Mine hung right beside Marcus's in matching frames. Mom held me, Dad standing by the bed, in one frame. The other showed Aunt Shelly and Uncle Ward in a similar position, Marcus only three weeks younger than me.

Our new rules said no seeing each other when other people weren't around, but screw that. Marcus was worried more than he would say about the tires and the damage to his truck. He had to be. Our parents hadn't been in the truck when we were run off the road. It wasn't some random, unexplainable road rage.

I turned around and marched up the stairs. He was halfway to his room already. "Hey."

He glanced back. "I'm fine."

Right. "The parents weren't there when that guy ran us off the road. I don't think this is school rivalry."

He stood with his body turned away from me, still pointedly intending on going to his room. "It could be."

"But you don't think so."

"The sheriff is handling it. I can only do so many things at once."

This new edge to his voice cut me. "Marcus. Come on." I took a step toward him. "This is hard on me, too. I'm just trying to make sure you're okay. Giving each other space doesn't mean we can't talk anymore."

He ran both hands through his hair, making it stand on end. "Yes, it does, damn it." He walked toward me, his attention finally on me, and his voice dropped lower. "Eventually, maybe we can, but not now. I can't handle it. Hang out with Kelsey. You've been doing that more. Maybe finding friends other than me would help. I can't be around you right now, or this is never going to work. I can't—when you—I just can't."

He turned around and walked away, leaving me in the hall. I sat down in one of the computer chairs and put my face in my hands. "Breaking up" was such an accurate phrase. Him, me, everything.

If Will ever asked me out again, I'd say no.

Aunt Shelly sat at the kitchen table, sorting through a stack of bills and newspapers. Cutting coupons out of the paper was taking up most of her attention. Ellie's school photo peeked out from the stack of newspapers beside her; she hadn't even seen it yet.

The local media loved that story. Some real news, for once. I picked it up and folded the paper so I could read the article but not see her face smiling back at me.

No arrest had been made. The article called her a normal teenage girl—a volleyball player from St. Joseph. The police had found her body in the woods fifteen miles from the city. She'd been strangled.

I gripped the paper and read the line again. Not drugs. Not alcohol poisoning. Not a horrible accident. I sat down at the table and stared into my coffee until it turned cold.

I took the paper with me out to the truck for my turn at the produce stand again. Chris was going with me this time; Marcus was helping his dad with something.

In other words, he didn't want to go with me.

I couldn't talk to him about Ellie, so at the park I opened up my inbox on my phone and replied to Travis's latest e-mail.

Hi Travis,

You remember the girl you asked me about last time? Someone killed her, and I found out this morning by reading the newspaper, of all things.

I don't even know what to do. She was upset at me when she died, I'm pretty sure. I can't get away from feeling like I hurt her, made her think I didn't care enough. I had so many chances to fix things with her, and I didn't take any of them.

Sorry to dump this on you. There just isn't anyone here I could tell.

~J

I could have talked to my mom or dad, but they'd tell me it wasn't my fault and that a lot of people don't stay close friends when one of them moves away. But that wasn't my version of the story. What everyone else saw as normal didn't affect what I knew I should have done.

Chapter Fourteen

No one said anything about the number of nights Marcus came home after everyone else was in bed. I'd hear him coming in, since my room was closest to the door, and each time the door creaked open and closed quietly, I'd roll over and try to go back to sleep, but I never could.

We hadn't so much as had a conversation in a week. He'd still helped with the twins and been in charge of dinner on the kids' nights to cook and harassed Chris into helping with the dishes on the other nights. He just acted like I wasn't there. When we were in the same room, he looked over me, around me, through me. Anything but at me.

He drove up to the house shortly after lunch. The sleeves of his black-and-gray button-up shirt were rolled up neatly on his forearms. His nice jeans were wrinkle-free. He was grinning, and for a moment I forgot the last few weeks. "Hey," I said.

I stopped on the steps, holding a basket of laundry. I did my own, because otherwise Angie ended up with my underwear and Aunt Shelly took all my socks.

He climbed down from the truck, spinning his keys. The grin faded a little when he saw me. "Hey."

I shifted the basket on my hip and glanced around. No one else was in the yard, but Uncle Ward was down by the chickens.

Marcus shoved his keys in his pocket. "Can we talk for a minute?" He was back to the grim, pale Marcus I'd known from the last few weeks.

I raised my eyebrows. "I thought we weren't going to do that."

"Well, I need to for this."

I headed back to the clothesline behind the house. He stared at his shoes as we walked, then stopped by the clothesline and met my eyes. "So, last night I asked Sylvia to go out with me."

"You did?" My chest suddenly hurt, so I set down the basket.

"Yeah."

I shook out a T-shirt and pinned it to the line to give myself a moment. It didn't help. "So, like on a date?"

"I mean, I asked her to be my girlfriend, so it would involve dates."

Socks needed careful pinning so the cuffs would dry. "And she was all for this?"

"She said yeah, so I guess."

I turned away from the clothesline. "Why?"

He crossed his arms. "You know why. Asking me repeatedly doesn't help."

If he could be this walled-off and act like he didn't care, then so could I. "Us backing off doesn't mean you have to immediately go find a girlfriend."

He shrugged. That's it. After nearly two years, I got a shrug.

"That's not fair," I said. "It's not fair to me to bring her around all the time. Not this soon."

He leaned against the clothesline pole, not meeting my eyes. "What wasn't fair was starting something with you in the first place. If I could go back and stop my fifteen-year-old self, I would."

Him wishing we'd never started being us shouldn't have hurt so badly, because I wished it, too. "Do you even like her?"

He re-pinned the crooked hem of a T-shirt so it hung straight. "She's nice, and she's fun. And she really likes me. She says she does, anyway."

"So you just like her because she likes you." I gave up pretending to hang up laundry and just stood there. "That's kind of low, Marcus."

"You know what?" His voice grew sharp. "I like being able to talk to my girlfriend's dad like a man, and not constantly feel guilty that if he knew what I was doing to his daughter, he'd have me thrown out of the house. I like being able to tell her what I think about her without being told to back off. And I like being in a relationship. A real one."

I stood there by the laundry basket, in love with him and trying to unlove him and hating every minute of it, and he thought we hadn't been real. This was not the Marcus I knew. I went back to hanging up my T-shirts.

His voice fell to a whisper. "We knew this was coming. Now we're paying for what we did, and we have to deal with it. I'm trying, I really am."

I barely heard him because I felt sick. "You're trying? Being gone with her til midnight every night is trying?"

"How do you know when I come in?" He stood close enough I could smell the scent of laundry soap on his shirt, and it only made me feel further away from him than ever.

"I hear you. The door wakes me."

"I guess I'll be quieter."

That last night at the creek, he'd kissed me like it meant something. I turned on him. "I know you're trying. So am I. But you can't bring her around here and ask her out and all this so fast. I can't stand seeing her in my living room all the time. It's not fair."

His eyes grew hard and his jaw tightened. "See, that's what I don't get. You were the one always telling me we meant nothing. For more than a year, you told me that over and over again and said we were just burning time and it was all going to end. Every time I tried to show you I cared about you, you shut me down and pushed me away. That was hell, Jackie. You put me through that for over a year. I kept up with it because I thought you didn't really mean it, but you're so ashamed of us it doesn't matter if you meant it. Can't I be happy? Can't you handle that?"

I threw down the wet jean shorts. "We agreed to those things together. All I'm asking for is for you to be more careful about bringing her around." And to not run off immediately to some other girl like I meant nothing.

His voice turned bitter. "I can't be careful about everything all the time. I just can't. I'm done." He turned around and walked away.

I dropped the clothespin I'd been holding. The wind teased my hair and picked up the leaves on the ground, swirling around in the space between us.

I didn't know it was possible to feel so hollow. Like my chest was my own personal void. I'd had no idea I'd hurt Marcus so much during the past year, and he was right; I wasn't brave enough to pay the cost of being with him. But I wasn't sure it was bravery if it hurt the people around me. Anna did not give herself to the King of Siam. The fox and the hound didn't stay friends. Rick and Ilsa went their separate ways.

Travis's reply to my e-mail about Ellie didn't help.

I'm so sorry you're having to deal with that. And that must be tough, knowing you didn't get the chance to patch things up with her. Life is so short. I can feel it slipping away from me, too, sometimes.

I hope you have at least someone you can talk to. I'm sure you have other friends who can help you deal with this, though I shouldn't assume that. When I was a teenager, my girlfriend left me, and all her friends were my friends, so I pretty much had no one my final years of high school, either. You can always talk to me, if you need someone. The death of a friend is a lot to handle on your own.

~Travis

At least he didn't freak out about me dumping my emotions all over him in my last e-mail.

I have a friend, I suppose, we're just not superclose. My cousin and I used to be great friends, but he's been a jerk this last month, and we're not really getting along. So, I guess this is my chance to get out and make new friends. Senior year, here I come.

I did not feel nearly as excited as I sounded.

Sylvia, oblivious to the fact that I never wanted to see her again, came over that afternoon. Oblivious really was a good word for her. She kept trying to be friendly to me even when I barely responded, and she was clingy with Marcus. Everywhere he went, she followed. Everywhere he sat, she scooted closer.

All the parents but Aunt Shelly were gone. Again. Which meant even though I was trying to put the twins down for their nap, I was the one who had to go see what happened when something crashed to the floor upstairs and one of the girls started crying. Marcus made no move to get off the couch. He glanced toward the stairs, but that was it.

They were sitting much too close to each other, watching a movie. TV rules didn't apply to dating couples, apparently. She was whispering, and Marcus was laughing.

By the time I came back, she'd moved—her back was against the arm of the couch and her legs lay across his lap. Marcus paused the movie. "What happened?"

"Candace bumped her head on the bedframe when they were jumping around." I watched him, surprised he'd even talked to me, and Sylvia looked from me to him and back again. It didn't take me long to figure out him asking was only about Candace and had nothing to do with me.

"You should come watch the movie with us," Sylvia said. "It's really bad." Her purse was tossed on the end table, keys and lip gloss spilling out of it. One of her purple heels was under the table, and one of them was on the couch next to Marcus.

Just to annoy Marcus, I sat down in the armchair. "What's it about?"

"Oh, I haven't been paying much attention. These kids go up to a cabin in the mountains and there's this crazy mountain man. It's supposed to be scary but it's really bad."

Marcus glared at me. He knew exactly what I was doing.

He could glare all he wanted. "What do you normally like to watch?"

"Oh, I love reality TV shows." She grabbed her lip gloss, reapplied it, and tossed it back on the table.

Reality TV. It figured.

"But," she said, "I also really love *The Truman Show*, and my favorite movie, hands down, is *Breakfast at Tiffany's*."

My mouth fell open. "Seriously?"

She waved her hand. "Oh, yeah. I get the mean reds all the time."

Now I felt bad. "I love that movie. I mean, she's self-destructive, but I can see why."

Sylvia leaned forward. "And you know what? I love that she wouldn't name the cat. It says so much about her. And everything hinges on the final moment, and whether or not she can change."

Marcus glanced at me and then her and a crease formed between his eyebrows. He tapped her bare foot with his finger. "Hey, you want to go get dinner?"

She tilted her head. "This early?"

"Yeah. We can go somewhere nice."

A huge smile split her face. "Okay. Let's go." She swung her legs off his lap and grabbed her shoes. Marcus stood up and she haphazardly stuffed her things back into her purse.

Sylvia waved to me. "See you later."

Marcus spoke over his shoulder as they walked out of the house. "Tell Mom I won't be back til really late, will you?"

I glared at him and didn't answer. He didn't want me to tell his mother anything. He just wanted me to know he'd be out with Sylvia until late into the evening, because he knew I'd hate it. And he was right.

I was still sitting in the living room when a text popped up. Will.

Hey. I'm texting you but not flirting.

I moved to the couch and flopped down on the cushions.

Wise choice.

The reply came immediately.

Which—texting you or not flirting?

I almost smiled.

I'll never tell.

A pause, during which I grabbed the throw pillow and played with the fringe.

Jackie Lawrence. I think you're flirting with me.

I wasn't sure if I was or not. I lay there on the couch for a while longer, texting Will, and opened Facebook while waiting for him to reply. I commented on Kelsey's status and tagged Hannah in it, then scrolled through my feed. But I stopped cold when I saw a stupid little heart next to Marcus's name. *In a relationship.* Awesome. It might as well say *I've got a real girlfriend now, one I can put labels on and bring around in public.*

Labels must make things real.

That evening, I went back to the stack of white notecards on my dresser. I filled out the forms for the colleges with film-only programs and requested their information.

Chapter Fifteen

I didn't see Will again until Wednesday evening. Chris wanted me to go hang out with his friends again, saying something about how Mara liked having another girl in the group.

Will picked Chris and me up in the green Neon. Plastic bags from the store were heaped on one side of the back seat.

"Look at that," I said. "This guy doesn't even know to use reusable bags. Or paper bags, at the very least."

"Ouch. And to think I didn't smoke just for you." Will backed down the driveway.

Chris peered into the grocery bags. "What the heck did you buy?"

"Just stuff. It's for a game." Will braked at the stop sign and turned toward Harris.

"Disgusting. I don't want to play that game."

I was a bit worried about what was in the bags, but decided not to ask. "So, are you working somewhere this summer?" If he actually was going to ask me out—which he might not, since I'd turned him down already—I wanted to know more about him.

"Oh, yeah, I work at Walmart. Pays rent but not much else. Hence the beer shortage."

"Well, beer is gross, so that's fine with me." I found myself scanning the streets of Manson as we drove past, looking for the white truck, but I didn't see it. The parents had relaxed a little now that it had been a while without anything else happening. We still had no explanation why that guy had run us off the road, and no word from Sheriff Whitley on who he might be. School rivalry, he said. Right.

When Will parked in front of his house, Chris helped Will carry in the bags. Kyle and Mara were already inside. Will and Chris set the bags on the end table in the living room and unloaded them. I gathered up the plastic bags as they set out a bottle of cheap butterscotch schnapps and club soda. Will opened the fridge and pulled out Tabasco sauce, mustard, soy sauce, and lime juice, and carried them out to the living room.

"You don't cook much, do you?" Mara crossed her arms.

"I can cook well enough," Will said. "But this is our new favorite drinking game."

"Hell, no," Kyle said. "I don't even know what the game is, and I can already tell it's a bad idea."

"Just listen." Will went back to the kitchen and came back with five shot glasses. "Turn on some music, Chris."

Chris flipped through Will's iPod and hooked it up to the stereo.

"Here's how it works." Will lined up the condiments.

He wasn't standing too close to me, wasn't finding ways to "accidentally" touch my arm, and he was talking to everyone instead of directly to me. Hardly even any eye contact. He must be taking my no flirting comment seriously. "These are numbered one through five. Soy sauce is one, schnapps is five. Now, everyone pick one of the dice." He shook six-sided dice out of a small cloth bag. "The number you roll corresponds to one of the condiments. Put that condiment and club soda into your shot glass. We'll shoot them together."

"Wait. What if we roll a six?" I asked.

He looked over at me, and never had I felt eye contact make such a difference. He grinned. "Well, that would be a suicide. Put everything in your shot."

"What's the point of this?" Kyle demanded.

Will shrugged. "No one wanted to pay last time, so the first person to drop out has to buy. Because this is going to be disgusting. Everybody ready?" He sat across the circle from me instead of next to me.

This was ridiculous, but I grabbed a die and pleaded with fate for the schnapps.

"Roll!"

I rolled a two. Lime juice. I grabbed the lime and filled my shot glass a third full then added the club soda. Kyle swore—he got a three. Tabasco sauce. Will and Mara had mustard. Chris got the schnapps.

"Okay, go!" We tossed back the shots. Mine wasn't bad, but Kyle gagged and Will and Mara nearly choked. Kyle stood it for five seconds before running to the kitchen. He came back swigging out of the milk jug.

"Hey!" Will yelled. "Use a glass!"

"No time." Kyle wiped his mouth on his sleeve and sat back down. "My whole mouth is burning. That was disgusting."

"No spitting it out, or you lose," Will warned. "Again. Roll!"

I rolled four. Mustard. Chris got a six—the suicide shot. Mara looked sympathetic, but Kyle laughed and pounded the table.

We all watched as Chris mixed Tabasco sauce, lime juice, soy sauce, schnapps, and mustard in the shot glass. The glass was brimming with a fizzy, murky red-brown liquid that looked like some kind of disease-causing potion, and I could only imagine what Aunt Shelly would say if she knew what her son was about to ingest.

"You can back out if you buy us all beer," Will said. "You don't have to do it."

"I can take it," Chris said. "You guys ready?"

We raised our shots. Mine was a lumpy, foaming yellow. "Go!" Will yelled.

Chris gagged and I nearly did. Fizzy mustard tasted about like I expected. Chris looked like he'd just eaten garden fertilizer. "That tastes like sin. Sin in a glass."

I couldn't believe he'd done it. Apparently Chris and his friends did whatever Will told them to.

"Okay, booze round!" Will poured us all a straight shot of schnapps and I tossed it back. The butterscotch still tasted faintly of mustard, but the sticky sweet was blessed relief.

Three more rounds, interrupted by a second round of schnapps shots, went down before Mara caved when she rolled a six. "Nothing's worth drinking that. I'll buy next time," she said.

No one really wanted more schnapps—it was a little like drinking pie—so the boys pulled out the Wii, but that only lasted about half an hour before they felt sick. "Jumping up and down with fizzy Tabasco in my stomach is like the second worst idea I've ever had," Chris said, collapsing on the couch beside me.

"Yeah, well, you drank it," I said. My own stomach was a little queasy, too.

"And that one was the worst." Nevertheless, when it was his turn again, Chris got up to play, changing out with Will.

"Sure you don't want to play?" Will asked. He sat half a cushion away from me.

"I'm not good at sports, real or virtual." Chris and Mara were now completely absorbed in some kind of kickball game. My aim and coordination were decent, but I couldn't jump or throw to save my life.

"So, tell me something about yourself." He leaned back on the couch and stretched his shoulders.

I watched, in spite of myself. "Like what kind of something?"

"Anything. Like, what's your favorite thing to do with an afternoon?"

I turned sideways a little and crossed my legs. His glance darted down to my legs but then right back up to my face. "Either go to the pool and bake in the sun," I said, "or watch an old movie in my room." With Marcus.

He frowned. "Darn it. I was hoping you were cool. How old of a movie are we talking here? Please don't say silent films."

I laughed. "Not silent films. A few black-and-whites. Really, it's not just old ones. It's the great films. Classics. Like *The Godfather* and *Schindler's List*." I pulled one of the grungy throw pillows onto my lap. Kyle cheered Chris on, but Chris wasn't playing nearly as well as I knew he could. He was letting Mara win.

Will leaned toward me a little. "So what's your guilty pleasure movie?"

I rolled my eyes. There was no question, but not very many people knew. "*Raiders of the Lost Ark.* What about you? Do you have a favorite movie?"

"I like pretty much all sitcoms. *The Office* is sheer genius. *Arrested Development. Parks and Rec.* I don't catch much TV, but when I can, that's what I go for."

I hadn't gotten into television shows much. Chris yelled when he scored and Mara sat down looking glum. Even Chris going easy on her wasn't enough to help, apparently. I knew how she felt.

Will laid his arm along the back of the couch and leaned toward me. "So," he said. "You said to try asking without flirting, and that means all my usual cards are out. But I really would like to take you out on a date sometime."

I didn't really get why. "How come?"

He looked me straight in the eyes and grinned like I'd just said the silliest thing in the world. "Because I like you."

Ballsy. I looked down, playing with my nails and trying to hide my smile. "I'm not a huge fan of dates." A date wasn't a relationship, and dates could be fun, right?

"You can't say that until you've been on one with me."

Screw it. Marcus was off meeting Sylvia's dad and making her official on Facebook and taking her to dinner in the city. I'd tried everything else, so I might as well try this. "I guess one date couldn't hurt."

"Awesome." He grinned. "How's tomorrow sound? I promise I won't make you do Tabasco shots."

Tomorrow was too soon. I hadn't entirely made up my mind I would say yes until that moment. "How about Saturday?"

We got home barely in time for dinner. Chris grabbed my arm as Will pulled out of the driveway. "Hold on." When the Neon turned at the stop sign, Chris said, "I heard him ask you out."

My face warmed. Blushing gave me away, every time. "I think everyone did."

"Well." Chris cleared his throat. "He's a decent guy. But he's kind of a player."

His awkward expression made me smile. "Are you trying to warn me or something?"

He shrugged. "He's always kinda been that way. Nothing sticks. He gets all serious about some new girl, and then two months later, he loses interest. Maybe he wouldn't be that way with you, but I thought you should know."

I nodded. "It's just a date. I don't want it to be serious or anything." We turned toward the house. "Why does he live on his own? Do you know why he dropped out?"

Chris shrugged again and walked ahead of me up the driveway. "His dad got remarried. I think they kicked him out or something, and then he had to work to pay rent."

I knew the story behind it wasn't going to be a happy one, but what shitty parents. Maybe I'd seen my parents making out one too many times, but at least they hadn't cost me my diploma.

Marcus was home without Sylvia, for once, helping the girls with their summer reading hours in the living room and doing that thing where he stared at me but kept his face so blank I couldn't tell what he was thinking. I hated it and he knew it.

I missed him. I missed his voice and his laugh and the way he used to look at me. But I was angry at him, too. People, it turned out, seemed perfect until you needed them, or they moved away and you wanted them to try harder too, but they couldn't or wouldn't. And here I was left dealing with all his little barbs and flaws that he'd left out for me to trip over.

To avoid seeing Sylvia in case she came over, I went with Kelsey to Todd's for ice cream, but because the world is a cruel and heartless place, my break from my ex's new girlfriend was short-lived. Marcus and Sylvia showed up not fifteen minutes later.

I waved to Sylvia and she came over to our picnic table. "Hey, I just realized I don't have your number," I said. The evening was warm but not stifling, and there was a line in front of the walk-by pickup window.

"Oh." Her eyes widened a little, and she smiled. "Here, I'll text you mine and you can reply with yours." Her long nails clicked on her phone.

Marcus shoved his hands into his pockets and stared at me, but I didn't look at him. "Thanks," I said when her text came in. "We should hang out more."

"We should." She smiled again. Glossy coral lips, professionally whitened teeth. Guaranteed, those lips had touched Marcus. I turned away from her, but then turned back.

"Are you sure you didn't know Ellie very well? Because she mentioned you in an e-mail. It sounded like you two were pretty good friends." Her lie about it was still bothering me, and if there was something

Sylvia knew, I had to know. I'd already let Ellie down too many times. I wouldn't be giving up any more chances to make that right.

Sylvia paled. "She did? What did she say?"

"Not much."

She moved closer to me and bent down. "What did she say?"

I moved back so she wasn't in my face. "She mentioned a sleepover."

She straightened up. "That's it?"

"So you were friends, then?"

She walked back toward Marcus. "No. Not really."

Marcus put a hand on her arm. "Let's go to the store for ice cream instead. We can get toppings and do sundaes." The reference wasn't lost on me.

And for some reason, Sylvia had been awfully concerned about that e-mail.

She let Marcus pull her away, and Kelsey turned to me. "I always thought your cousin was gay."

I choked on my spoon of mint chip. "Gay?" I could swear in front of a judge and jury that Marcus was not gay.

She shrugged. "I flirted with him all through freshman year. Asked him to the Sadie Hawkins dance. He said no. I've never seen him interested in any girl ever, so I figured he was into guys."

Freshman year. Right after I'd moved in with his family.

Kelsey wound a springy blonde curl around her finger. "Now I'm insulted that he wouldn't go out with me. I hope it's not weird that I'm talking about your cousin, but those hands? His shoulders? Yes, please."

"It's a little weird." Just not for the reason she thought.

"Maybe I'll have to keep trying." She licked her chocolate cone. "He's got the cutest smile."

He did. An unselfconscious, whole-face kind of grin. I hadn't seen it in a while.

So I didn't have to talk to keep talking to Kelsey about how cute my cousin was, I checked my e-mail.

Something new from Travis, finally. As strange as it was to be talking about Ellie to someone who hadn't known her, it was also a relief.

That's too bad about your cousin being a jerk. At the risk of sounding old, I'm going to tell you that we men do eventually grow out of that. Did you guys have some kind of falling out? I've noticed the blog has been quiet for a while. If you ever need an idea for a post, a comparison of the different Wuthering Heights *adaptations would be interesting to see. Heathcliff comes off so differently in each one.* Wuthering Heights *and* Tess of the d'Urbervilles *were two of my favorites in high school. Have you read either of them? Usually when someone recommends Gothic tragedy, they point to Poe's work, but it's so much bigger than that.*

I raised my eyebrows and skimmed the rest of the message while stirring my melting ice cream. He argued that *Tess* should be called a Gothic tragedy too, and that Heathcliff was misunderstood. Maybe he should just write the blog post for me.

Of course, the whole story is riddled with passion and emotion that were scandalous for the time. It seems like hiding those things damages people. Sorry, I'm rambling now. I had a professor my freshman year who loved the book, and I guess her enthusiasm was contagious.

Misunderstood. Not the primary word I'd use for Heathcliff, but whatever. Treading the line between romantic hero and anti-hero, and then plunging catastrophically over the edge to anti-hero wasn't something I had much sympathy for.

I shook my head. I wasn't going to debate Heathcliff with this guy. Plus, the two novels he pointed out were ones in which people were perpetually miserable. Thanks, but no thanks.

Anyway, I hope you're handling things okay. I lost a friend to suicide in high school, and you just have to adjust and move on, and try to not let it make you too upset. They made their own choices, tragic as it is.

Hold on. How in the world could I not be upset about Ellie? Someone had killed her. Her life had been brutally cut short. She hadn't killed herself; suicide was not the same as murder. Annoyed and not sure how to reply, I switched to Facebook, only to see six people had commented on Marcus's relationship status. Woo-hoo, indeed.

Chapter Sixteen

Saturday morning, I woke up much earlier than I wanted to because Claire slammed my bedroom door.

"Oh, sorry, did that wake you?" She stood there grinning at me, like this kind of behavior in the morning wasn't borderline criminal.

"You did that on purpose," I groaned.

"That's what sisters are for. Now get up. I was sent with a message." She dropped her laundry bags. Claire was the only person in our entire family who actually liked mornings. Her ability to function this early was almost inappropriate.

I sat up partway and looked at the alarm. Eight fifteen. Too early for the weekend. Much too early. "What message?"

"The second hottest guy I've ever seen is sitting in the driveway. He says he's waiting for you. He's got flowers."

"What?" I sat upright. "Why?"

"He says you have a date. We had a good talk about you. And wow, Jackie, I'm jealous. He looks so good I want to eat him."

I slid out of bed. Will couldn't be here now. Our date was tonight, so I couldn't imagine why he'd be sitting in the driveway. Some horrible mix-up—this was why I hated dating. My face was already red with embarrassment over being asleep while he waited in the driveway, and I hadn't even seen him yet.

I washed my face and then reached for my toothbrush. We hadn't actually said our date would be for dinner, though. Had he said he'd pick me up this morning, and I'd missed that somehow? Claire watched me, one eyebrow raised, as I raced around the room brushing my teeth and searching for something decent to wear.

She shook her head. "Take it easy, Jacks. I'll go entertain your gentleman caller. I'm a pro, remember."

Claire was a pro. Dating for her was as easy as it was horrible and awkward for me. Mortified. That was a good word to describe my feelings at that moment. I dragged a brush through my hair, pulled on jeans and an oversized gray hoodie, and ran outside. I could tell him to come back tonight and then I'd have time to shower and get cute before he came back.

Claire sat in the passenger seat of Will's car, the door hanging open. She laughed at something, and she kept laughing as I walked up. When she got out of the car, she whispered, "If you don't take him, I will."

I glared.

"I'm going, I'm going. Have fun." She ran up the driveway.

I put a hand on the car roof and leaned inside. "Hey. I guess I thought you were coming tonight. How long have you been—"

"I know, don't worry," he interrupted. "We never said when. But you did say you didn't like normal dates. So, I figured I'd just take you out for breakfast."

What kind of plan was that? He so didn't know me. Still, it was hard to criticize a guy who handed me daisies. "Oh. Thank you." They were pretty; tiny and white with bright yellow centers. His hand brushed mine, and my skin warmed where he'd touched me.

"Come on. Let's go." He winked. "I've been waiting."

Boys. "You could have texted me to say you were here." I got in and closed the door.

"I didn't want to wake you. I figured you'd be up soon enough and I'd wait."

Creeper. "What a lovely thought."

"I mean, I was just watching for lights or something. You guys sleep late."

"It's not late. How could you think eight fifteen was late?"

He shrugged. "Well, I work nights, so I got off work not too long ago."

"Oh. Walmart, right?" I buckled my seatbelt and desperately wished I'd had time to dress up a little more. I was wearing a hoodie on a date.

"It's my dream job. I'm the king of stocking shelves." He grinned. "But since I figured I'd be waking you up, I brought you coffee. It tastes like crap, but it's hot."

The cup holder held one of the sixteen-ounce cups from the Manson gas station. I reached for it. He was right, their coffee was crap, but it was better than nothing. Something inside me relented. "Okay, you're partially forgiven for waking me."

His eyes widened. "Only partially? Geez. What else do I have to do?"

"Not sure yet. I try not to waste owed favors." I was trying to tease him, but it wasn't coming out right. Stupid mornings.

"Well, let me know when you think of your wishes," he said. "I figure I owe you at least three more for waking you up."

"Three?" I sipped the coffee. It was almost too hot, and much too sweet.

"Breakfast will be your first wish, the pleasure of my company can be your second, and then that leaves one more for whatever you want. Is the coffee okay?"

"Did you put in like six sugar packets?" I wouldn't have said anything, but he asked, and it did taste like syrup.

"Four of those hazelnut creamer things. Girls like coffee sweet, right?"

I assumed he was joking, but he looked a little concerned. "Well, it depends on the girl, I suppose," I said. "It's a little sweet, but it's still good. Thank you." The blue in his eyes was even brighter because of his dark eyelashes. He had such a pretty face—not feminine, really, but gorgeous all the same.

The drive to Harris was over the same meandering, hilly blacktop where the truck had forced us off the road. We passed the trail Marcus and I had plowed into the corn. Black skid marks still scarred the asphalt and a shudder trickled down my spine.

When we pulled into the parking lot for the diner in Harris, Will leaped out of the car and ran around to open my door before I could do it.

The bell on the diner door tinkled. Tiny tables with red vinyl chairs lined the room, mostly empty except for a group of farmers with their coffee. The smell of hot griddles and brewing coffee permeated the air. We seated ourselves.

Breakfast for me was normally just coffee, but nothing in the world smelled as good as this diner, and suddenly I was hungry.

Our waitress walked up and handed us menus, smiling. She must like mornings. "What can I get y'all?" Without hesitating, I ordered coffee, eggs, and pancakes. Will glanced at the menu and asked for an omelet. She disappeared and came back with my coffee.

I stirred in a packet of sugar while Will watched how I fixed it. "Is this particularly interesting?" I asked.

"I want to know for next time."

Next time. I set down my spoon. "Do you pay such careful attention to every girl you go out with?"

He cocked his head to the side. "Generally. I mean, why not?"

"It doesn't seem like a first-date thing." I liked him, and I didn't want him to get the wrong idea. Honestly, I might be tempted by a second date if it didn't involve mornings, but not only did I think he wasn't as serious about me as he seemed, I knew I wasn't serious about him. But if he was serious, using him to get over Marcus wasn't fair. I sipped my coffee and waited.

He leaned back in the red diner chair. "People are worth noticing. If I'm taking the time to go out with you, I'm wasting it if I don't notice those things. You think it's weird?"

I finished half my coffee and relaxed into my seat. "Not weird. It's nice, actually." So far, he was a good date. Since I hadn't ever been on a legitimate one with Marcus, this was the least worst date I'd ever had. "I wish I'd had more time to get ready, though. I wasn't planning on wearing this."

"You were going to dress up for me?" He leaned forward, his smile splitting his face.

"Of course I was." Our food arrived. The waitress refilled my coffee and I poured syrup on my pancakes. Once she left, I said, "I didn't know it was going to be for breakfast. I guess a dress would have been weird."

"Well, I think you look great how you are." He cut into his omelet.

I rolled my eyes. "I'm sure you tell all your dates that."

He shrugged. "I try to. Most girls are beautiful, and you're no exception."

I didn't have a comeback, so I poured more syrup on my pancakes.

I didn't think I was ugly, but beautiful girls had a certain polish that I'd never been able to achieve. That straightened hair, luminous skin look. Sylvia, basically. Like everything else, I was just a step to the right or left of fitting in.

Will pointed his knife at my plate. "So, coffee with barely any sugar, but pancakes as an island in a sea of sugar. Got it."

I ignored the observation and cut into my pancake island. "So you work nights? That sounds like it sucks."

"Well, it sucks less than being evicted, so I deal."

True. And practical, which I appreciated. I wanted to ask him about why he didn't live with his family anymore, but that didn't seem like a first-date question. "You hadn't met Claire before, had you?"

He shook his head. "I mean, I'd seen her around. What's she like?"

"We get along. She's louder than I am."

He grinned. "I could tell."

I'd never have Claire's outgoing nature, but I didn't want to. If everyone was outgoing, the world would be a really annoying place. He leaned back in the chair and stretched his legs out. His leg touched mine, and I instantly thought of Marcus. I poked my eggs with my fork and yellow spilled over the white. "Do you read much?" I asked.

"Nah, not really. I watch movies of books, sometimes."

"But not other movies?" I wasn't getting the feeling he'd want to watch *Casablanca* with me.

"I guess I like the newer Bond films."

I'd seen some of them. "You really have to see the Indiana Jones movies, then. You'd like them."

"Maybe we can do a marathon." He stabbed a sixth of his omelet and swallowed it in one bite. "So, what was California like?"

"Different." I didn't miss it so much anymore, but I had for a long time. "The air smells different. The trees and grass and colors are different. Things are bigger and louder than out here."

"I've always wanted to travel," he said. "I don't see myself getting to, but maybe someday."

He shouldn't give up like that. "Of course you can travel. Make it happen," I said. "You can totally do that."

His smile made me glad I'd said it. I looked down at my coffee. "Where would you want to go?"

He was quiet for a moment. "I have no idea."

I refilled my mug from the carafe.

"So," he said. "I thought after breakfast, we could go to the park."

"The park?" I looked up and his eyes were focused on me. Intently. For a moment, I forgot what he'd said.

"Just to walk or something. I thought an elaborate date might weird you out, so I didn't plan anything superfancy. Should I have?"

I shook my head. If dating could be like this most of the time, I might not mind it so much.

Will paid, and we walked out to the car, where he opened the door for me again. It felt strange with him standing there waiting on me as I got in. No one had ever done that for me before. I'd never let Marcus.

Harris wasn't a big town, but it took pride in its park. A bandstand with an acoustic shell presided over one end of the square, while a new fountain and koi pond stood at the other. The library reading carnival was always held on the green space behind the bandstand.

Will parked and I got out before he could open the door. "I bet those fish don't last long," I said.

"Yeah. I'm seeing a gruesome end for them. Firecrackers. Beer in the fountain. Something like that."

More likely, children would climb in the water and give them heart attacks. We walked over to the fountain and Will put a quarter into the little stand that vended food pellets. He tossed them into the water one at a time while the fish surged around the kernels.

He handed me a few pieces. The food smelled funny, but it was fun. One of the fish swam up to the edge near me and poked its mouth out of the water, making an odd gulping motion. I dropped the pellet and he seized it as it hit the water. I tossed in the rest and brushed my hands off on my jeans while the swarming bodies fought over their plunder.

We walked toward the playground equipment. Sparrows hopped and chirped along the picnic shelter roof on the shingles already warm from the sun. "So, do you know what you want your third wish to be?" Will asked.

"My what?"

"Your third wish. So I can be forgiven for waking you up." His shoulder brushed mine as we walked. Even through the sleeve of my sweatshirt, I felt his warmth.

"I'm not sure. I'll have to think about it." I'd thought he'd been teasing about a third wish, but maybe he really did want me to pick something. He headed for the bandstand, and I almost said something, but then I followed him up the steps.

I'd never been up here with a guy before. I sat on the stage, leaned up against the curving band shell, and stretched my legs out in front of me. He sat down close enough that our legs touched.

The band shell faced the middle of the park. Because the giant trees blocked it from the view of the road, it was a popular place for making out. I wasn't quite sure I wanted to be here with him.

He couldn't like me as much as he seemed like he did. Will was just a flirt. Next month he'd take another girl out to breakfast and sit on the bandstand with her. I didn't really care.

He was so different from Marcus, but somehow it only made me miss him more.

When I didn't shift away from him, Will took my hand and threaded his fingers between mine. I should have let Marcus hold my hand more. At the beginning, he'd wanted to.

"Hello in there." Will turned toward me a little, leaning his shoulder against the band shell. "What are you thinking about?"

"Nothing." I looked down at our hands. This guy, this superhot guy, was into me for whatever reason, and I was daydreaming about my cousin. Claire would tell me I was an idiot. She'd be right.

The blue in his eyes darkened. "Well, do you know what I'm thinking about?"

I did. Every time I looked at him, a shock went through me at how light his eyes were. He hesitated, and I moved toward him, just an inch.

He leaned down. My stomach tightened and my brain turned to fizz. I hadn't kissed anyone but Marcus for years.

His lips touched mine and he held still for a moment, asking. I touched his ribs, slid my hand around to his back, and pulled him closer. He kissed me, eyes closed and eyelashes dark on his skin. I pulled in a deep breath, closed my eyes, and kissed him back.

My fingertips traced his chest, feeling the strength of his muscles and the heat of his skin. Will might not be in love with me, but at least he knew what he wanted and went after it. That, more than anything else, made me want him.

His chest pressed against mine, and he slid an arm around my waist. He pulled out my ponytail and ran his hand through the layers of my hair the way Marcus used to.

Marcus had to get out of my head. I leaned back on an elbow and pulled Will down beside me, a little surprised at myself but not really caring. We lay on the bandstand floor, him kissing me, his hand on my side and mine curled in his shirt. Not hiding was a relief.

I broke away. I looked into his eyes for a moment, catching my breath. He lifted my chin with a finger and kissed me again, but I pulled back. This was too much for a first date. He was going to get the wrong idea. "Just so you know, I don't—I mean, I'm not . . ."

He grinned. "Oh, don't even start." He came back, his shoulders looming over me. I ran my hand up his back, feeling the warmth of his skin and muscle through his shirt. I relaxed and let him kiss my cheekbone and my lips again.

Forget Marcus. My world didn't hang on him. Guaranteed he'd been doing this with Sylvia. I pushed toward Will and he leaned back so I was above him. He kept on grinning.

"What?" I demanded. He didn't answer. I'd never wanted to kiss anyone besides Marcus, but right now, I wanted Will. Kissing him was easy. Surprisingly easy.

His face turned serious. He reached to tuck my hair behind my ear and brushed his thumb along my cheekbone.

I froze. His thumb traced my eyebrow, his lips touched my neck, and I couldn't move. If I closed my eyes, this was the basement and he was Marcus. The tightness in my gut turned to the stab of a half-healed wound splitting open.

Will paused. He sat up a little. "What's wrong?"

I shook my head. If I could just breathe for a minute, I'd get over it. Marcus wasn't an option. He never really had been. I bit my lip but it didn't help, and hot tears spilled down my face.

He sat up all the way. "Did I do something? I swear, I wasn't—you seemed—only whatever you wanted, nothing else."

"No. I'm just being dumb. Never mind." He hadn't done anything except exactly what Marcus had always done. I'd remember the callus on Marcus's thumb brushing my skin for the rest of my life.

"Shit. I'm so sorry. I didn't mean to make you upset." His eyebrows drew together.

"No, I'm sorry. It's not you. I just . . ." Breaking down crying was high on the list of things not to do while making out, but that didn't stop me.

"Tell me," he said.

I shook my head. "It's just that I broke up with someone, sort of, not too long ago." He didn't have to know who.

"You did," he said. "Okay. Well, I was dating this other girl a few months ago. It's not a big deal. I don't care."

I almost laughed but cried instead. Having dated other people wouldn't make me cry while making out. "That's not it."

"Oh." He got it. "So it's too soon."

I nodded and wiped my face. I had a feeling it would be too soon for a long time.

"Come here." He leaned against the band shell again. I scooted back. Crying like this was so embarrassing.

"So, if you're crying, it's not just that making out is a little weird. You're not over him yet?"

"Not really." I hadn't talked to anyone except Claire about this, but as long as Will didn't know who, it helped to say it out loud.

"But you said you broke up with him, right?" He was still confused, but I could hardly blame him.

"Yeah. I mean, it wouldn't have worked."

"Were you together a long time?"

"A year." The words sounded strange, even to me. I'd never said them to anyone but Claire.

"Wow. Well, this is awkward. You didn't love him, or what?" He picked up a stick from the bandstand floor. The trees around the band shell had littered leaves and twigs across the stage.

I wasn't expecting him to ask that. He sounded like he didn't really want to know the answer. "I did, actually."

"Then why wouldn't it have worked?"

I hesitated. "We had a lot of problems."

"Chris never mentioned you dating anyone. He said you were single." He said it too casually, turning the stick over in his hands.

"Chris didn't know. We didn't really tell anyone."

"Why, was he married?" he teased, but his voice had an edge. "Was he a teacher or something?"

"No." I almost smiled. "Mostly the problem was my parents. They weren't okay with it." All true things. I wasn't lying. I shoved my hands in the pockets of my hoodie. The day was already too warm for wearing it.

He stilled. "Was it Marcus?"

I looked up, too stunned to think of a convincing denial.

"A few nights ago he came over to my place with Chris, and he said something," he said. "Once he got drunk, he kept talking about Sylvia, wouldn't shut up about her, but then out of nowhere he said, 'I thought Jackie loved me.' He just kept saying 'I thought she loved me, I really thought she loved me.' I figured he said the wrong name or was talking about a different Jackie. But he wasn't, was he?"

My face flamed. I couldn't look at him. By now, he'd be regretting that he ever asked me out.

And why had Marcus said that? I'd told him I loved him. He should know it.

Will was waiting for my answer. I shook my head.

He was quiet for a moment, staring at the bandstand floor. After a minute, he sighed. "Well, I guess that makes sense. But it's a bummer. I like you."

What did that mean? "Please don't tell anyone. I can't believe he told you."

He squeezed my shoulder. "Well, he told a whole room of guys, but they weren't paying any attention. Unless they heard him say your name, it just sounded like he was mooning around about Sylvia. Seriously. I've never been that broken up about a girl." He paused. "So, why'd you break up with him for real?"

My face was still hot. I couldn't believe he'd figured out my secret so fast. "We weren't ever really dating. I mean, we're cousins. It had to end sometime." He was judging me for messing around with my cousin. He had to be.

He didn't say anything for a minute. When he did, his words were careful. "Do you still want to be with him?"

I shook my head. "Our parents would throw a fit. We'd have to move out. School would be miserable and they might call a social worker. It's not worth it."

I shouldn't tell Will all this. It was my secret. Guilt had hung over me for years because of it, and I'd stopped trying to get to know people because I'd been afraid they'd find out. But it had been almost a month now, and I wasn't getting over Marcus, and I didn't think I ever would.

"You do want to be with him, but you don't, because he's your cousin." He broke the stick in half. The broken ends splintered.

The truth might be embarrassing, but at least it was the truth. I did love Marcus. I did want to be with him. "Right."

"Well, that's a problem, but it's not so bad."

He couldn't know how much of a problem it was or wasn't. "It seems bad enough to me."

"I mean, him being your cousin might be weird, but it's not like it's wrong or anything."

I just sat there. I'd never felt like it was wrong, exactly, but it certainly wasn't good. "You don't think it's weird?"

"Well, it's strange. My dad married a twenty-five-year-old two years ago. They swear it's true love and all that, so whatever. Stuff happens."

"Is that why you moved out?" I asked.

"They wanted their space." He played with his cell phone instead of looking at me.

Clearly not the whole story. "That sucks. I'm sorry."

"Thanks." He shoved his cell phone back in his pocket. "So, you're telling me you went out with me, and made out with me, but it's not going to go anywhere because you want Marcus instead."

For the millionth time this summer, I hesitated. "Not necessarily."

He shrugged. "I mean, it's okay. I get it. It's just not exactly how I'd planned on the date going."

I played with the broken stick he'd tossed aside. "No, I mean, I really want to get over him. I just don't know how. He's always bringing Sylvia around, and no one at home even knows, so we can't even fight like normal exes. And everything he says—" Shit. I was still crying. "It just sucks."

He picked up one of the broken pieces. "It sounds like you want him back."

"No. I don't." Sunlight crept across the bandstand stage. Getting over him was the plan, not getting him back. Plus, I'd literally offered myself to him, and he'd said no.

"If it worked out, you could just move to another state."

"We can't do that."

"If you love him enough that you'd fall apart while kissing a hunk like me, it's clearly a big deal. I mean, I've never had a girl break down and cry while making out with me before. It's a pretty big shock to my pride." He gave me half a smile.

I raised an eyebrow. "I think your pride will be okay." I didn't know how to handle his reaction to the whole thing. "Why don't you think it's weird?"

He huffed. "You were together for an entire year, which is normally a lot, but between cousins, that's a heck of a lot. I mean, you're obviously still hung up on him, and he is too, or he wouldn't have blabbed about it to a whole room of guys. I just think—" He pulled away a little and turned to face me. "I just think there are enough hard things in life you can't do anything about. Parents get divorced. Dads kick their kids out of the house. Don't let something make you miserable if you can do something about it. If that's what makes you happy, go for it."

I stared at him. "You really think that?"

He threw the sticks off the stage. "So what if it causes some family disruption; it's causing that already. And honestly I don't see how the relationship can be wrong if you really care about him. If you've got a chance at something good, I think you'd be crazy to not go for it. Besides, it's not like it's never happened before."

My world was tilting too fast for me to keep up. Not wrong. He didn't think it was that big of a deal. I ducked my head. "Even if we could, he's dating Sylvia."

He gave me that cocky grin. "If being cousins isn't a problem, Sylvia had better not be what stops you."

It was so tempting to decide what we had was worth it, to try to dissolve the last month and take him away from that lip-glossed messy blonde. But we wouldn't last, and we'd damage too much. "I can't do it."

Frown lines creased around his eyes. "Then what do you want?"

I wiped my face and sat up straight. "I'm trying to change what I want. And I really like you."

The frown disappeared and a corner of his mouth tipped up. He looked down at the bandstand floor, then over at me again, for all the world looking like I'd just embarrassed him. "Yeah?"

"Yeah."

"Then—would you go out with me again?" His confidence returned. "Say you will. Come on. A second date."

I'd laughed more in the last week than I had all summer. "You can't mean that. I just told you I'm in love with someone else."

"I'll take my chances. Besides, I've been told I'm pretty charming."

I'd told him pretty much everything. If he wanted a second date that badly, then okay. "Alright. That sounds fun. But nothing fancy."

"And no more early mornings." His grin was back in place.

"You got that right."

He stood up and offered me his hand. "Come on. I'll take you home, and sometime in the next week, you can count on me taking you out again."

For the first time in a long while, I was looking forward to something.

Chapter Seventeen

It was nearly eleven by the time I got home. "Mom?" I walked into the living room. She and Dad were on the couch. Dad had his arm around her shoulders, and she was leaning on him. No making out, thank God. "Do you care if I start lunch?" I asked. It would be a good way to make up for missing chores this morning.

"That would be great," she said. "Thank you."

"Sure." They were kind of cute, actually. I liked seeing my parents like that. Dad had been tense in California and they'd argued too much. They were happier out here.

If our families split up, my dad would have to go back to a full-time practice with a firm again, my mom would have to get a job that paid more than the library, and they wouldn't be able to help Claire out with her college finances anymore. That couldn't happen.

We'd decided to quit to keep our friendship and our families together, but I couldn't stand Marcus thinking I didn't love him.

Will had to have misheard him somehow. And no matter what Marcus had said to me recently, a few weeks of hurting each other couldn't make me forget all of high school.

I pulled potatoes out of the crate in the pantry along with an onion and a few carrots.

"Hey, I thought I heard you." Claire came in. "How was the date?"

"Really good." Just not in the way it sounded.

She shook her head at me, short layers of blonde hair flicking over her shoulders. "How did you get a guy like that to ask you out?"

I shrugged. I probably should have been annoyed by the way she'd said it, but I didn't have the energy. "He's friends with Chris and Marcus. From Harris."

"So he told me. Want help?"

I handed her the potatoes to scrub. I poured olive oil in a pan on the stove to heat and then started dicing an onion.

I wet my fingers under the faucet and spritzed the pan to see if it was hot enough. The water snapped in the oil, so I scraped the diced onion off the cutting board into the pan.

Claire had the potatoes cubed shortly after I was done with the carrots, and she put ground sausage in another pan to brown while I seasoned the potatoes.

Marcus came in while we were still working; I'd thought he'd been out with Sylvia, but he must have been working on one of the cars, because his hands were blackened with grease and his jeans were dirty.

"Hot out there?" Claire asked.

"Yeah." He gave me a look. "Last night. What did you want Sylvia's number for?"

I stood by the stove turning the hash in the skillet. I hadn't planned on doing much with her number, but now maybe I would. "I figured since you two seem to be getting along so well, maybe she and I should become best friends."

Something flickered through his eyes before the look turned into a glare. He walked straight through the kitchen to the shower.

I let the hash fry while I wiped the counter. Claire shut the dishwasher. "Way to piss him off, Jacks."

"He's been an ass lately."

She leaned against the counter. "Well, a broken heart will do that to a person."

"I really doubt his heart is broken." And even if it was hard on him, it was just as hard on me.

"It's pretty obvious he's miserable."

"That makes two of us."

She shook her head. "I thought you guys would be doing better by now." She gave me a soft smile, but I didn't say anything. "So do you think you'll go out with Will again?"

Finally. A topic change. "Yeah, I think so. He's fun." And charming. And funny.

And not the one being a jerk.

"Just fun?" She opened the cabinet and lifted out a stack of plates.

"Well, he's smart. He works hard. He got kicked out of his dad's house two years ago, so he's had it pretty rough."

Claire grabbed silverware from the drawer. "Are you serious? That's crazy."

"Yeah. He was upbeat about it, but he seems that way about everything. I'm pretty sure that's why he dropped out." The potatoes were browning, so I turned the hash.

Claire shook her head. "That's stupid."

The television went quiet in the living room and Mom came in. "Oh, thank you, girls. This looks great. Your dad went to call the kids. We can just do a buffet line—I have to get to working on some things for the library carnival, and Ward is still out cleaning the henhouse."

I moved the skillet to a hot pad on the counter. The library carnival was next weekend, which meant we'd hardly see Mom for the days leading up to it.

Marcus came in, texting again. His hair was still damp and he frowned.

Trying to act on what I knew instead of what I felt, I tried to keep that tone out of my voice. "What's wrong?"

He looked a little surprised that I asked, but he frowned again. "Sylvia thanked me for sending her flowers. But I didn't send her flowers."

Claire raised her eyebrows. "Sounds like you have competition."

"Who are they from?" I asked.

He shook his head. "She says there's no card or anything. Last week a movie showed up in her mailbox she told me she'd been wanting to see. She thought I'd done that, too."

"Sounds like you'd better step up your game," Claire said. "Or, you could say they're from you. If the guy's going to crowd your girlfriend but not sign his name, you might as well take credit."

Marcus looked skeptical. "That would never work." He shoved his phone in his pocket, scooped hash onto his plate, and walked into the living room.

The morning had been draining. I'd gotten up too early, gone on a date, made out, and cried, all before lunch time. I carried my plate out of the kitchen intending to shut myself in my room and watch *Roman Holiday*, but stopped at the foot of the stairs. I could hear the sounds of Chris's computer game. Hanging out with him for the last week had been fun.

I started up the stairs but stopped when Marcus's voice drifted down, telling Chris about the flowers Sylvia had gotten. So much for escaping Marcus.

"Well, send her flowers yourself. Nicer ones." The stutter of video game artillery fire followed Chris's words.

"Good idea. I don't know what kind she likes. Roses are cliché, right?"

"Have Jackie help you. I think she's mad at you for hanging out with Sylvia so much."

Marcus snorted. "Jackie's mad because she's crazy."

I leaned against the wall and slowly let the breath out of my body.

"Are you guys having a big fight or something?" Chris asked.

"I guess. Sometimes I think she does stupid things just to make me angry. I don't even care anymore. She can do whatever she wants."

I almost dropped my plate. My hash was getting cold, but I just stood there.

"Well, she can be crabby. But normally she's fine."

That was Chris's attempt at defending me. Awesome.

Marcus didn't reply.

"Maybe she won't be so mad now that she's dating Will," Chris said.

Something clinked, like silverware on a plate. "I thought he just took her to breakfast. Are they dating for real now?"

"I dunno. But Will really likes her, I guess. He's been texting me asking what kind of stuff she likes."

"Well, good luck to him."

I walked down the three stairs I'd climbed and took my cold lunch to my bedroom.

Will was looking better and better. And that was a good thing, because I could bring him home and tell Claire about him and ask him to take me to senior prom.

I lay there in bed and stared at the photo on the mirror of me and Ellie at the pool. A year ago I never would have believed what was going to happen to us.

Her killer was still out there. And the more I thought about it, the more I needed to know why Sylvia had lied.

Sylvia came over again Sunday evening and sat too close to Marcus on the couch. They'd been hanging out at our place more because even though Sylvia didn't have a curfew, the parents had started enforcing his. He'd been mad, but having them here meant I could work on Sylvia more, and if that annoyed Marcus, then he'd have to be an adult and deal with it.

Chris had his graphic novels spread all over the living room floor, and I was pretending to read *Where the Red Fern Grows* in the armchair.

I'd finished the book already, but re-reading the first half, when things were good, took some of the sting out of the ending.

"So, Jackie, Marcus says you want to study film," Sylvia said.

She was a nice enough girl, and she had no idea she'd caused a problem between me and my cousin. But if she was lying about something, I needed to know the reason. "Yeah, I think so. What about you? Are you going to college?"

She shrugged. "Maybe. I'm not sure yet." This time she wore platform heels splashed blue and white. The blue matched her halter-neck top exactly, which showed off her neck and the subtle hollows around her collarbone. Marcus put his arm around her shoulders and I tried to look like I didn't notice, or even better, like I didn't care.

"Would you go back to St. Joseph?" I asked.

"No," she said casually. "I don't think so."

I set my book on the end table. "Do you know where you want to go?"

"Um, no. I don't know." She fidgeted with the throw pillow, then leaned over and whispered something to Marcus, and he nodded.

They stood up, and Marcus said they were going out for a walk. I went back to my book.

Sylvia had left an empty Coke bottle and a gum wrapper on the end table. The twins could choke on the wrapper, and leaving trash laying around was just rude. I grabbed them and tossed them in the trash can in my room.

Too annoyed to drown my sorrows in television, I opened my laptop. Travis was right. I hadn't blogged enough lately. I clicked "new post" and stared into the white void for a few minutes before giving up. Nothing I wrote would sound coherent, so I went to my e-mail instead.

One new message.

Okay, so no more talk about books. I get preachy about things I like, I guess, and I'm sure it's boring. I'm assuming you're blowing me off, since it's been a while and you haven't replied. It's my fault, of course—sorry for all that weird stuff about Heathcliff. I guess talking about creeps makes me sound like a creep myself. ☺ Hope you're having a good weekend.
~T

I hadn't been blowing him off at all. Had he missed one of my e-mails? It had only been a day since he e-mailed me.

Sorry, I've been superbusy. Mom's got this big library carnival coming up soon and my cousins and I are all helping.
Yeah, my cousin and I did have a falling out, I guess. He's dating some girl who just moved to town now, and therefore he has no time for anyone else. But hey, that's how it works, I suppose. Hope you're having a good weekend too.

Sick of sitting around the house, I slid on flip-flops and went outside. Sylvia's little blue Buick sat in the driveway. After glancing around, I peered through the windows. Fast-food trash littered the floor; water bottles, a jacket, and two pairs of heels were thrown on the back seat; headphones and sunglasses with a lens popped out lay on the back dash. Scattered bits of trash were in the front, and the cord to something that looked like a phone charger lay in the console. Nothing suspicious. I huffed.

Done feeling sorry for myself, I walked around back of the house to make sure the animals had water. The chickens were scattered over the back half of the yard, pecking at the bugs hovering over the grass.

I leaned against the giant oak tree and watched the hens for a minute. The whirring song of the cicadas rose and fell around me in a numbing cadence.

The evening hadn't cooled down much. The late-summer heat was back in full force, the air muggy again, hot and breathless. I pushed off the tree.

I filled the chickens' waterer and lifted the lid off the tub of feed. The clatter of their feed on metal always brought them running, so I took out a scoop and poured the grain slowly into their feeder. When they were all inside, I counted the hens twice and latched the door. Coyotes were always looking for stray chickens.

I turned to head back to the house, but stopped. Around back, sitting against the hill our house was built into, were Marcus and Sylvia. He had his arm around her waist, and she was giggling. Her heels were tossed aside in the grass. That I shouldn't be watching had barely occurred to me when he kissed her. He took his time, and it clearly wasn't their first kiss. Sylvia climbed onto his lap, one knee on either side of his legs. His hand worked up her back, making those lazy circles. Even from this far away, I could feel them on my own skin. Something hot burned in my stomach.

Knowing she was a relatively nice girl—except for what she was doing to my ex—couldn't keep me from wishing she'd burst into flames.

The calves saw me and mooed for their dinner. Marcus looked up just as I turned away. I heard scrambling, but I didn't stop. Instead of going inside, I kept going down the road. My eyes stung. My hands shook, so I stuffed them in the pockets of my jean shorts.

Marcus certainly didn't miss me very much. I'd barely been able to go out with Will, and when I'd kissed him, I'd broken down crying.

I wasn't going to beg Marcus. If he wanted Sylvia to giggle and climb all over him like he was playground equipment, then she could do just that. Sure as hell I wasn't going to dissolve into tears and plead for him to love me.

Feet pounded up behind me. "Hey," he said, his face red. "Sorry. Didn't know you were outside."

I ignored him. He walked alongside me for a few seconds before grabbing my arm. "Come on. I didn't mean for you to see that. I'm sorry."

I shook my arm free, looked him in the eyes, and was too mad to care. I kept walking.

I didn't want his hands on her. I didn't want him doing with her the things he'd done with me. He'd cared about me, but somehow he could transfer all those walks in the dark and swimming trips and everything else from girl to girl, while I was left behind once again, watching someone move on while I was stuck there wishing.

"Dammit, Jackie, just talk to me," he said. "I don't know what to do."

I turned on him. "It looked like you knew exactly what to do."

He crossed his arms, his eyes hard. "You can't be mad at me for this. We can't be together. We agreed we couldn't make it work."

"Don't tell me what we agreed like I don't know." The faintest breeze puffed dust eddies up from the gravel road.

"I am so sick of you getting mad at me for things I can't help. If you're upset, it's because you push people away because you can't stand them thinking something bad about you. Stop letting the world hang on what other people think."

He did not just say that. Like it was such a small thing to tell the world your brain was screwed up enough you couldn't keep your hands off your cousin. "This coming from the guy whose go-to solution for problems is pretending they don't exist." All I wanted was for him to realize he was hurting me, or at least show something, anything, to let me know he missed me.

He uncrossed his arms. "You have no reason to be angry. This is ridiculous. You practically told me to go find someone else."

"I did not. I wanted you to be happy, and since it couldn't be with me—"

"Oh, don't worry about me. I'll be fine." He stared down the road past me like I wasn't there.

"How can you use her to get over me? That's really low. If she doesn't know about us, and she really likes you, and all you're doing is distracting yourself, how is that fair to her?"

His back went ramrod straight and he shoved his hands in his pockets. "That's the thing. I do like her. I'm not just messing around."

My brain stuttered. "You—you what?"

"I'm not using her. I like her."

For the briefest moment, it was hard to breathe. My heart beat once, and I got my air back in a rush. "Well, stellar job picking someone. You know she lied about Ellie? They played on the same volleyball team. She knew her. I found photos of them together. Sylvia knows something about Ellie's murder. She has to."

He stared at me like I was crazy. "Is this about being jealous? Accusing her of being involved in a murder isn't some way for you to get back at me. That's serious."

"I know it's serious, Marcus. That's the point. You barely know her and she's hiding something. We were together for more than a year, and then bam, you're all over her like she's magical."

His eyebrows lowered. "Well, that's the way you wanted it." He turned around and trudged up the hill away from me. He didn't look back.

It wasn't what I wanted. It was what we wanted. I sat down on the side of the road in the knee-high grass and cried.

Chapter Eighteen

My eyes were swollen and bloodshot when I got back to the house. Mom gave me a concerned look and tried to stop me, but I ran to the bathroom and locked the door. I started the tub filling and poured in twice the bubble bath anyone in their right mind would need. By the time the tub was full, the bubbles were piled so high I couldn't even see the water. I sank into it and absentmindedly shaped the fluff into towers.

Marcus didn't love me the way I loved him. If he could move on to Sylvia and kiss her like that so soon, if he could really like someone else already, then he hadn't really loved me. If I hadn't been able to do it, and he could, clearly I'd been less to him than he'd been to me.

I'd almost risked so much for him.

And I was trying to stop pushing people away. But the more I cared about someone, the more I cared about what that person thought. Investing in other people but being my own person was a lot harder than it sounded.

My phone started ringing. I glanced at it, dried off my hands on the towel, and answered it.

"Hey, Jackie Lawrence." Will's low voice came through. "I was going to make myself give it a few days before I called you, but I couldn't help myself. When can I take you out again?"

The smile in his voice lifted the weight on my chest a little. "Whenever, as long as the parents don't need me. I don't have much planned."

"Darn. I'd come get you right now, but I'm headed to work. What are you up to?"

I swished my hands through the bubbles. "Well. Right now I'm in the tub."

The line was silent for a moment. "You had better not be teasing me."

I laughed. "It's true, I swear. I'm taking a bubble bath."

"I'm really trying to not be a perv right now, but I don't think it's going to work."

I laughed again. "Sorry. I wasn't going to tell you, but you asked."

"Cruel thing to do, when I have ten hours of stocking shelves ahead of me."

"Any chance you'll survive?"

He sighed. "I'll have to, if I'm going to get to take you out again. How about tomorrow afternoon? Evenings are hard for me because of this whole job thing."

"Sounds awesome."

I was trying, for me, for Marcus, for our families. Far more than he knew. But it was one thing to be hit by something when both of you were caught in the fallout, and entirely something else to be in it on your own.

When Will pulled up and climbed out of his car the next day, my mom raised her eyebrows. "Cute."

"Ugh. Mom."

"I won't be home when you get back. Carnival planning at the library. Marcus is babysitting while you're gone."

"I—he is?"

His voice drifted down from upstairs, teasing one of the kids. I could hear his grin from where I stood in the kitchen. He hadn't sounded like that around me for a while.

"He said it was fine."

If I had to babysit all four of the kids so he could go out with Sylvia, I wouldn't have been happy. I grabbed my purse and went outside before Will could get to the door.

"Hey," he said. "I thought we'd go bowling."

I hadn't been bowling in a long time. "Sounds great."

As we headed to Harris to the bowling alley, he asked me question after question about my family and the produce stand and Marcus. And he listened. He kept his eyes on the road, but they flicked over to me every few seconds, and he nodded or gave me a half-smile every time I said something. He didn't seem to think any of it was weird.

"It's actually interesting," he said. "It's different. I wish I had a family like that."

It had been a while since I'd thought of differences as interesting. It took me until we got to the bowling alley for me to realize he hadn't told me a single thing about himself. "What about you?" I said. "How many girls have you taken bowling?"

His eyebrows disappeared under his longish dark hair. "Legit taken bowling, or like, taken bowling as a metaphor?"

We walked across the parking lot. "Let's say metaphorically." I didn't care, but I was curious. He'd probably gotten his first girlfriend in third grade.

"Hmm." He looked me over and held the door open. "It's a policy of mine to not tell girls I'm dating how many girlfriends I've had."

"No way," I said. My voice lowered to a whisper. "I told you I'm hung up on my cousin, and you can't tell me how many girls you've gone out with?"

"Not a chance."

"Why?" I gave my shoe size to the guy at the counter and we headed over to our lane. The place wasn't too busy, just a few other afternoon bowlers.

"Because it always makes them angry."

"It can't be that many."

He winked at me and gestured to the lane. "Ladies first."

I chose a ball. "So, you're insecure. That's what you're telling me. You're insecure and afraid of angry women."

"Any wise man is."

I rolled my eyes and stepped up to the lane. He was fun. And interesting. And I liked him so much.

We bowled for almost two hours, after which he offered to take me out for ice cream. "Um," I said. "We can. But I wanted to tell you something." I set my shoes on the counter.

"Shit." His face fell, and he held the door open for me again. "Sounds like I'm going to need the ice cream."

I turned around on the sidewalk. His shoulders were hunched and he shoved his hands in his pockets. "So, what did I do?" he asked. "Honestly. I want to know. Is it too much?"

I put a hand on his arm. "What? No, I just can't do this to you. You're such a nice guy. Like, weirdly nice."

He looked across the nearly empty parking lot. "You're not doing anything to me. You told me what was going on."

"Yeah. But I don't think I'm going to get over Marcus any time soon. We had a fight last night, and—" My voice caught.

"Let's talk about this in the car." He headed over to his Neon. I hurried to catch up to him so he didn't have to open my door.

When he climbed in and shut his door, I turned sideways on the seat. "I just can't think about anything else. And I don't want to use you to get over him."

"Why can't you think about anything else?" he asked, forearm resting on the steering wheel.

"Because everything I do makes him angry, and everything he says to me makes it worse. Maybe he doesn't mean it, but it still hurts, and he lives in my house, and I'm terrified that even when this is over, I'm still going to love him, but I'll hate him, too, and he'll hate me."

Will turned toward me on the seat. "I don't understand why you decided to end it with him. I mean, it's not my business, but if I was that miserable, I'd fix it."

"I can't fix it." I played with my thumbnail. I couldn't change the way the world worked.

"What would happen that's so bad it's worth being miserable? It's legal, you love him, and once you're eighteen, your parents don't have a say in it."

I'd once thought it was to save my friendship with him. But I was losing that, too, just like Claire had said. If we kept this up, before long we'd have hurt each other too much to fix. Even ten years from now, after college, when we were involved with other people, this would hang over us.

And regardless of what it did to us, it would wreck our families. My hand tightened around the seatbelt. "Family stuff, I guess. And we couldn't tell anyone."

"You could." He rolled down the car window.

Technically, yes. I could tell people. Claire had thought it was weird, but she hadn't made fun of me or shut me out because of it. But who knew what Kelsey and Hannah would do.

But if I didn't care what it did to my friends and family, I'd want Marcus back. It wasn't fair, it really wasn't, for the world to see differences between people as gaps keeping them apart.

"He told me yesterday that he likes Sylvia."

He lit a cigarette. "Rebounding."

I watched him blow the smoke out the window. "He doesn't want me back."

"Sure he does. Make him realize it."

I didn't know how to do that. How to get him back. I shouldn't even want it. "I don't know. But I'm not ready to date someone else."

"Well." He held the cigarette out the window, resting his arm on the door. "I'll make you a deal."

Strange. "Okay."

"What made you realize you wanted him back?"

I'd always wanted that, I just hadn't been able to accept it. "Seeing what being apart did to us, I guess. And seeing him with Sylvia." I couldn't be with Marcus, but I did want him to miss me, to not be able to replace me so fast.

"So keep going out with me."

"What? Why?" This guy made no sense.

"I like you. Are you okay with that?"

"It's actually really nice." I played with my fingernail again. "You've been great."

He looked out the windshield, not at me. "Then I'll stick around. Marcus will realize the same thing you did, and that will be that."

"I can't be your girlfriend." As much as I'd like for that to be the way things were going, they just weren't.

"You don't have to be my anything. I'll come hang out and take you out sometimes and be your boyfriend or whatever, and you can just work on making him jealous. As long as you keep me updated on what's going on with you and him, I'm okay with it."

I didn't want to make Marcus jealous. I wanted him to miss me. "That doesn't sound fair to you. I seriously don't think I'll be dating anyone for a long time."

Now he grinned for real. "Don't worry about my feelings, okay? Let me decide what's fair to me. This is a win-win. You get the guy you want, and I get to hang out with you until he gets his head on straight."

"But if you genuinely like me—" I'd end up hurting him. And I couldn't do that to someone else.

He flicked the cigarette onto the cracked pavement and rolled up his window. "I'm a pro at not falling in love, Jackie. For real, don't worry about me." He started the car and spun the steering wheel as he backed the car out of the parking space. "I guess I can tell you now. I've had eleven girlfriends. And I haven't been in love once. I'll be fine."

We didn't talk much on the drive home. Will toned down the flirting, which was okay. He told me a little about his job and I watched the hills go by. When we pulled into the driveway, I saw Marcus through the kitchen window. He was sitting at the table, mug in hand. Hot chocolate, probably.

Will saw him, too. He parked and I climbed out, but so did he, and he came around to my side of the car. "Thank you," I said. "I had fun. For real." And I'd needed it.

He leaned against the car. "Anytime, babe. You think your parents are home?"

"Dad's probably in his office, and Mom will be watching the news in the living room if she's back."

"Good." He turned toward me and took a step closer.

"What are you doing?" I asked. "Marcus is right there. He can see us."

"That's the point," he said. He took another step, and I leaned back against the car. "Get his attention, right? That's what you want?"

I nodded. My heart sped up.

"Okay, then." He put a hand on the car by my shoulder and leaned against me, pinning me to the car with his body. He moved his mouth next to my ear and whispered, "How far can I go?"

His breath was warm on my skin. I couldn't stop the words before they came out of my mouth. "What, you want to have sex on the driveway?"

He laughed. "I mean, it's your call."

Now I laughed, but nervously. "That might be overkill."

"I just meant, I don't think a sweet little first-date kiss is going to get his attention as much as . . . maybe a third-date kiss."

I glanced up at the window. Marcus was still sitting right there, and even through the glare from the sun on the window, I could tell he was staring at us. Probably trying to annoy me. Screw it. "Fine. Third date. Tenth date. Make him notice."

Will moved closer, but he waited, watching me. I wondered why until I felt myself relax. My glance couldn't help but fall to his lips. I breathed in, out. He slid a hand up to the nape of my neck, under my hair, and his lips met mine. I tipped my head back and he kissed me harder. My hands slid around his neck and I kissed him the way I used to kiss Marcus. Focusing on the heat and the closeness, letting it make me feel my whole body the way he did. I almost couldn't breathe, but oh, it felt good. His hands slid into my back pockets and he pulled my body up against his. His whole body was warm and hard and kissing him this way did something to my confidence. He had to know that.

He pulled away and stepped back, and I took a deep breath, not daring to look at the window.

"I'll see you later," he said, and winked at me.

"Bye," I said quietly, as he got back in his car. He lifted a hand to wave before backing down the driveway. I walked up to the door. Another deep breath, and I opened it.

The television played the news in the living room. Someone was interviewing a neighbor of Ellie's family. A murder investigation was underway.

Marcus was still in the kitchen, so there was no way he hadn't seen me and Will.

"Hi," I said.

His eyebrows went up. "What was that?"

"What was what?"

"The making out in the driveway. All the laughing and whispering." His voice was flat, emotionless. He only sounded that way when he was trying to control his temper, which meant it did indeed get his attention.

"Oh. Will and I went bowling." I walked over to the coffee pot. I didn't really want any, but it was an excuse to stay in the kitchen.

"Looked like he wanted to do more than go bowling." Marcus pushed back his chair and brought his mug over to the sink.

"What's that supposed to mean?" I poured coffee into a mug.

"You know what it means."

"Oh, whatever." I went to the fridge and pulled out the half-and-half.

Marcus put his hand on my arm. "You don't have to do this, you know."

His grip was so familiar. I shook myself free. "Do what?"

"Do you actually like him?" he demanded.

I wasn't going to lie. I lowered my voice as I stirred my coffee. "All I did was kiss him. We did our share of kissing, if you remember."

"Yes, I remember," he snapped. "I'm going out to mow." He banged the kitchen door on his way out.

I'd forgotten to put sugar in my coffee. I drank it bitter and barely noticed.

Marcus started the riding mower and worked through the front yard while I watched him out the window. The set of his shoulders and the tension in his arm as he turned the steering wheel told me just how upset he was.

It was a total double standard. He'd told me I had no right to be angry when I saw him and Sylvia making out, and here he was, pissed off about me kissing Will. I turned away from the window.

My thoughts sounded so simple laid out in sentences. I hit key after key, typing out the long chain of ideas that held *Roman Holiday*, *The Fox and the Hound*, *The King and I*, and *My Fair Lady* together. The references to *Rent* and *Brokeback Mountain* worked, too.

I'd been thinking about it for a few days, since my last date with Will, and I'd worked out some answers to my post from several weeks ago. It wasn't selfish, because it wasn't just about those people; it was about the people who came after them. Us.

Marcus was refusing to make eye contact across the living room when I closed my laptop. Awesome. Apparently a few other things weren't going to change, either.

I stood up when Will knocked on the door. His one night off, and he wanted to come over. I opened the door and blocked the doorway. Dusk was falling, and the end of his cigarette glowed red. "You can't bring that in here, pal. We have a healthy lungs household."

He grinned and shoved his lighter in his pocket. "Come stand out here with me."

I stepped barefoot onto the porch and he handed me a little white box. "What's this?"

"Don't sound so suspicious. Open it."

I watched the wisp of smoke curling up from his cigarette and tried to keep from smiling. "You shouldn't buy me things."

"Just open it." He leaned against the door.

I pushed the lid up, and then narrowed my eyes. "Fake boyfriends do not buy their fake girlfriends nice jewelry."

He winked at me. "This one does."

No guy had ever bought me jewelry before. I touched the fine silver chain, the delicate yin-and-yang symbol. "Thank you. But why?"

"Because you deserve it. And I want you to have a reminder that we need opposites and weirdness and people who don't think like we do." He exhaled white smoke. "Don't you like it?"

"I love it." I lifted it from the box. The silver glinted in the dusk. If he knew nothing could happen with us, why was he buying me gifts?

"Here." He put out his cigarette, then took the necklace and helped me clasp it behind my neck while I held up my hair. He nodded, looking proud of himself. "I like it. Let's go show it to Marcus."

"You're horrible." He followed me inside, and Marcus was making hot chocolate in the kitchen. He'd been in the living room when I went outside, but from the kitchen, he would have been able to see us on the step.

Sylvia was leaning against the counter, chatting about how school was starting soon. She glanced at Will, and instantly blushed. I resisted the urge to glare at her. Of course she'd want both of my guys.

Marcus looked up at us, and Will stopped right behind me and whispered in my ear. His hand moving my hair aside, his breath on my neck, his voice lowered just for me—it was surprisingly intimate, and goose bumps chased down my neck. "Touch your necklace, then let's go to your room," he whispered.

My hand automatically went to the silver symbol. Marcus's eyes followed my hand. Oh. That was why. I lowered my hand when his face fell, and he turned back to the pan on the stove.

I suddenly wanted to tell him I wanted to work things out, with Sylvia and Will right there, with all of my cousins in the house. The words paused on my lips, but I couldn't get them out.

He'd said no, too. He'd said we couldn't do that to our families. And it was half his decision.

I walked into the living room, Will following me. He shoved his hands in his back pockets when we got to my room. "Hmm. Nice and tidy, as I suspected."

"Not if you look in the closet." I shut the bedroom door. My parents had never told me I had to leave my door open when I had guys over. Not that it had ever occurred to them, since the only guys who'd ever been in my room were related to me.

And if Marcus misinterpreted my closed door, maybe he'd rethink how I felt about finding him making out with Sylvia.

Will eyed the door and spun the desk chair around to sit on it. "Should I be worried?"

"Why would you be worried?"

He slouched in the chair, feet stretched out in front of him, and clasped his hands behind his head. "I always heard if a girl takes you to her room and closes the door, she wants to take advantage of you."

I laughed. "I'll try to control myself." I sat cross-legged on the edge of my bed and ran my finger along the chain around my neck. "Why did you really buy me this?"

"I told you."

"But you know—as much I wish I did, I can't—"

He pushed on the desk and rolled the chair over to the bed. Our knees touched. "I didn't give it to you as some sneaky way of making you like me. Promise. I gave it to you because I think you're awesome. You said you didn't have a ton of friends and I wouldn't mind having an actual friend, either. Okay?"

I couldn't stop the smile from spreading over my face. "You have lots of friends. You don't need the girl who turned you down three times."

He crossed his arms and leaned back. "I mean, I'm the beer dealer for Chris and his buddies. And I get along with the guys at work. But I work sixty hours a week. Doesn't leave much time for other things."

I had no idea how someone like Will could be lonely, but I was in no place to question that. "So, then, friends?" Without even noticing what was happening, I'd made a friend. One I really liked. And it hadn't been that hard at all.

"Of course, friends. At least, until Marcus realizes what he's missing."

"What?" If I wasn't dating Will, it shouldn't make a difference.

"If you two get back together, he won't want me around. Guaranteed." He spun the chair halfway around.

"Too bad for him. You're stuck with me." And we weren't getting back together; I was just trying to make him miss me a little, make him realize he was rebounding and I had mattered to him.

The front door closed and Mom's voice drifted back to me.

Will sighed. "Stuck with you, huh? Damn these women and their sneaky plans."

If anyone had the sneaky plan in this situation, it was him. "I'm supposed to be babysitting," I said. Marcus was out there, but I shouldn't bail for too long.

"Then let's do it," he said, standing up. "I've never had siblings. Is it weird?"

I shook my head and opened the door. "I like it. Hectic, sometimes, but it's really cool to watch them growing up."

"I think I'd like it, but I'm not sure I want my stepmother to reproduce."

I laughed again. To her credit, Mom didn't even blink when I walked out of my room with a boy in tow. Marcus, however, looked less than thrilled.

Sylvia had left, and he was putting away the twins' toys while Mom herded Nate and Gage toward the bath.

Will sat next to me on the couch, and Marcus went upstairs. "He won't even look at me," I whispered.

"He doesn't seem like the jealous type." Will matched my quiet tone and leaned back against the cushion.

"He's not." I slumped back beside him. "He's pretty quiet. He'll just deal with it."

"What if." He paused. "What if we go on a double date?"

"That will just make him mad."

"We'll go on a double date with him and Sylvia, and I'll make sure it gets his attention."

The idea was tempting. If we were out together, he'd have to look at me. Talk to me. He couldn't keep going to the next room.

He might be done being careful, but so was I.

Chapter Nineteen

Once Will left, I intended to go right to bed, since everything about managing Will and Marcus in the same place was exhausting. But instead I stood in my doorway, staring at the box on my desk. It hadn't been there earlier, so she must have brought it in while I was saying goodnight to Will outside.

Condoms.

Subtle, Mom. I turned around and walked through the house to my parents' room. The door was open, but I tapped on the doorframe anyway. Better safe than sorry.

She leaned around the corner of the master bath, washing her face. "Hello, there."

I crossed my arms.

"You found my gift, I see."

"I did."

She lifted a shoulder in a shrug. "It can be embarrassing to buy them for yourself or to ask the guy if he has one, and I don't want that to keep you from making smart choices."

I rolled my eyes. "Ugh. Mom. Please."

She pointed a finger at me. "It's not a joke. You had your door shut."

I knew that was a mistake. "We're not that serious. At all."

"He seems perfectly nice." She pulled the tie off her braid and worked her hair loose with her fingers.

I didn't want perfectly nice. I wanted Marcus. Standing there in my mother's room felt so normal and safe I took a deep breath and let it out slowly. "Yeah, he is."

She narrowed her eyes and looked me over. "Are you okay? You've been so quiet lately. I heard you laughing in your room with Will, and I haven't heard you doing that much lately."

I wanted to tell her. My mother, of all people, was the one I wanted to talk to most about me and Marcus. But it was half his secret, and so I couldn't. But there was something I could tell her. "Ellie. I miss her. And it makes me sick."

"Oh, honey." She crossed the room and hugged me.

I should have talked to her earlier about that. We sat on her bed and she listened while I said a lot of things that didn't mean very much and I played with the bracelet Ellie had given me. When Dad came in, I slid off the bed. "I'll be fine. I just hate seeing it on the news." I hated it, and I needed to know what was happening, and each one made the other worse.

I headed back to my room, checking my e-mail on my phone, and nearly ran right into Marcus. He stopped in front of me in the hall outside my room, his face pale. He shoved his hands in his pockets, pulled them out again, crossed his arms. His eyes were wide, and he looked like someone had just slapped him.

"I—I was going to—" he said. His voice broke, the silence stretched tight between us.

And then I knew why. As soon as I opened my mouth, he uncrossed his arms and pushed past me.

"Marcus, don't—come back here." I ran after him. What had he been doing outside my room to begin with? Looking for me? Why?

He was already halfway up the stairs. I took them two at a time, but he strode down the hall, his shoulders rigid, and slammed his door. "Marcus, come on. Open the door."

Something crashed against the wall inside. I tried the handle, but he'd locked it. I knocked, and kept knocking. Something else crashed, and I heard the shatter of glass.

I couldn't just start yelling about this in the hall. I pulled out my phone and my fingers hit the keys.

I'm not having sex with Will. I swear. Mom gave them to me like 5 minutes ago.

He didn't reply. Music beat from behind his door, and he cranked it louder.

I scrubbed my hands over my face and then hit his door with my open hand as hard as I could. Pain split through my palm and it hurt so badly I gripped my hand, leaned against the wall, and slid down until I was sitting on the carpet.

So this was why exes couldn't be friends. Not because they couldn't, but because they wouldn't. I dug my fingers into the carpet.

This was what I'd done to him out on the road when he came after me. Except he was wrong. I wasn't with Will. He was with Sylvia. And he liked her.

The music cut out in the room behind me. I sat there on the carpet, my head against the wall, the night silence of the house absolute and nothing inside me except the echo of what we used to be.

If I couldn't have Marcus, then I wouldn't have anyone. Not everyone fell in love or married the love of her life or even got married at all. I didn't need that. And I wasn't going to fill the space with something only good enough when what I wanted couldn't be had.

Some things, some people, felt so much like fate had meant them so specifically for you that finding another one just wasn't going to happen. Us breaking up had left me with jagged edges, and trying to fit with anyone else would always hurt.

Now that his room was quiet, I knocked on the door again. He didn't answer.

I was reaching out, I was trying to make it better, and he wasn't showing up.

He was hurt, too, but somehow he could still move on without me. He could touch Sylvia and not be reminded of me. He did not love me the way I loved him.

Bitterness surged through me and for a moment I hated him as much as I loved him. I'd never felt both at once before, and I thought I would choke on it.

All we had left of us was an angry, bitter silence.

Paraphernalia for the library carnival that coming weekend crowded the house. Mom had me and the cousins package up and label boxes for each of the games while she drove around the county borrowing things and picking up rentals.

Marcus loaded soap, a garden hose, the plastic for the makeshift Slip'n Slide, and the spray nozzle into a box.

He was always mad now. Mad about the curfew, mad that I sat in the living room any time Sylvia was around, and mad at me for being mad at him.

I'd e-mailed Travis back and went on a minor rant about the whole stupid situation, leaving out my history with Marcus. It helped to come right out and say I was angry at him and he'd hurt me.

Oddly enough, Sylvia herself wasn't so bad. Were it not for Marcus, I might actually like her.

I packed a dozen grocery bags of prizes into a large box. "Could you hand me the tape?" He had it at the other end of the table.

He acted like he didn't hear. I sighed. "Candace, would you hand me the tape?" She and Angie were curling long strands of ribbon to tie to the balloons.

Candace reached for the tape, but Marcus grabbed it and handed it to me. Candace raised an eyebrow. "Hi there, Crabby. Are you fighting with your girlfriend or what?" She sounded like a supersassy dose of Aunt Shelly.

"No, I'm not." Marcus labeled the side of the box.

"I bet you are."

"We're not fighting. She's coming over here right now, so you can see for yourself."

I kept on taping down the flaps of my box. Sylvia could come over. I was getting used to it. My phone buzzed and I glanced down. Will.

How are you?

Between him and Kelsey, I was texting a lot more than I used to.

Rotten. Marcus is being a jerk and now Sylvia is coming over.

He'd probably think I was a needy whiner, but then maybe he'd be glad we were only friends. My phone buzzed again.

Want me to come over? We can pretend to be madly in love.

I rolled my eyes even though Will couldn't see me.

"Who are you texting?" Marcus asked.

I looked up in surprise. I made a point to never ask him who he was texting. "Will."

He frowned and went back to taping his box, but he wasn't being careful and mangled the tape instead of getting it to cut neatly on the serrated edge. "Damn it, whatever. I'm done with this." He threw the tape onto the table and strode across the kitchen and out the door.

Sylvia pulled up the drive. I texted Will back. At least having him over here would keep me from brooding about Marcus. He and Sylvia were standing in the driveway, and she didn't look happy. She was holding something and kept gesturing to her car. Marcus bent to look at the passenger seat. He frowned, and then they both came inside.

"What's in the car?" Candace asked. "Someone put road kill in Dad's truck bed once."

Marcus was still frowning. "It's not road kill."

"Someone left a gift in my car," Sylvia said. "A dress." She held up a length of black cloth. The silky material unfurled to become a lace-backed, short-skirted dress with a low neckline. Not the kind of dress someone would give to a friend.

"That's strange." I touched the slippery fabric. "You don't know who left it?"

"No," Marcus said. "But it's weird. Flowers, a movie, and now a dress."

"A date." I said it without thinking.

"Yeah." Marcus ran his hand through his hair. "Your ex wouldn't do this?"

Sylvia shifted from one foot to another. She looked uncomfortable. "No. He didn't buy me stuff like this when we were dating, and he certainly wouldn't a year after we broke up."

I raised an eyebrow at Marcus. Something wasn't right with Sylvia, and he refused to admit it. He looked away.

A car sounded in the driveway. Will was here. Frustrated as I was, I almost grinned when he got out of the car. His longish hair had just enough gel in it to look intentionally messy, his T-shirt was tight and the same light blue as his eyes, and his jeans were low-hung washed-out things that showed a good inch of striped boxer band. For Will, that was dressing up. I waved him inside before he had a chance to knock.

"Hey, all," he said. "Wow, Sylvia. That dress."

Marcus's eyes turned steely and Sylvia blushed. "I don't know if I like it," she said.

"Just teasing her, babe." Will stepped smoothly over to me and draped an arm around my shoulders. "I'd rather see you in it."

I glared at him. He was too good at pretending. "No one is wearing the dress." I wasn't sure Will had ever felt awkward in his life.

"What's going on here?" He looked over the mess layering the kitchen. "It's like a birthday party orgy." Sylvia giggled and Marcus crossed his arms.

"We're packing up stuff for the carnival." I picked up the marker and labeled my box before I forgot what was in it.

"Oh, your mom does that, doesn't she? It always seems pretty fun, but they made me stop going in eighth grade." Will picked up a stray bag of balloons.

I took them from him and started sorting the giant pile into water balloons and normal balloons. "That's because it's for kids ten and younger. You can help if you want, but it's not that exciting."

Marcus stacked the finished boxes. "I don't know how much more help we need. We were fine last year."

I glared at him. Will didn't seem to care. "I'll just come along for the fun, then."

Marcus carried the boxes outside to load in the truck and Sylvia followed him.

"You're going to make him hate you," I whispered. Candace and Angie still curled ribbon strands.

He shrugged. "He can hate me if he wants."

The balloons didn't need to be in boxes, so I shoved the separated piles into bags and tied them shut. Will was standing right behind me, and when I straightened up I bumped into him. I felt his lean stomach and structured abs on my back. I might not want to go out with him, but I wasn't dead.

He winked at me. Surely I couldn't be that obvious. I turned away so he couldn't see my face.

"So, did you ask Marcus about the double date yet?" he asked.

"No." I hadn't found a good moment, and I wasn't sure there was ever going to be one.

Marcus and Sylvia came back inside, and he was holding her hand and looking less irritated. I went back to tying bags, twisting the ties tighter than necessary.

"Mind if I get a drink or something?" Will asked.

"Go for it." I gestured with the marker. "There's iced tea in the fridge."

"Want any?"

I straightened up again. "Sure. Thanks."

"Sylvia? Any for you?"

Sylvia looked surprised and pleased. "I'd take some."

Will brought us glasses while Candace and Angie argued over whether it was better to make the ribbon into longer curls or short, tight curls.

"So I hear you're from St. Joseph." Will leaned against the counter and kept his attention on Sylvia. I frowned, not sure how him flirting with Marcus's girlfriend was supposed to help me get a double date. She nodded.

"You like it around here so far? You'll be the hot new girl once school starts. I hope you're ready to start breaking hearts."

Marcus's eyebrows lowered and he crossed his arms.

"Not—not really. But I like it, yeah." Sylvia looked flattered but unsettled. She swirled her iced tea in the glass.

Will shoved off the counter and came over to me. "Did you still want to go see a movie this weekend, babe?"

We hadn't talked about going to a movie, but I played along. "Um, sure. I guess so."

Will turned to Sylvia. "You guys want to come? We'll make it a double date."

Sylvia glanced at Marcus, and he didn't look happy. "Sure," she said. "Sunday afternoon?"

"Great. We can do pizza after."

We had our double date. Clever, asking Sylvia instead of Marcus. Will winked at me again and I shook my head.

Candace and Angie were apparently bored with curling ribbon, because they wandered out of the kitchen, arguing about whether Angie's shirt was actually Candace's. For all their bickering, they were rarely more than ten feet from each other.

Marcus gathered up the packaging on the table. I picked up the bags of balloons and set them aside so he could get the rubber bands and other litter from around them. He brushed by me without saying a word, and I couldn't help just watching him.

He walked outside with Sylvia again, and it didn't look like they'd be coming back. I must have looked upset, because Will came up behind me and rested his hands on my shoulders. We stood there for a moment, and I expected him to just let me sulk, but instead he pulled me back against his chest and fake-whispered, "Any chance you want to go make out?"

I laughed in surprise and slapped his arm. "No."

Marcus came back after dinner, heated a bowl of leftovers, and went straight up to his room. He left his phone on the kitchen counter, which wasn't like him. It rang an hour later, but I wasn't going to touch it. Not with the way he'd been acting. Instead, I lounged on the couch and watched the evening news with Mom and Dad.

The reporter was talking with Ellie's father, who looked haggard and exhausted. It had been less than a year since I'd seen Mr. Wallace last, but he looked a lot older. *Viewers are asked to report anything that may be of help in locating Ellie Wallace's killer* scrolled across the bottom of the screen.

Mom shook her head. "That poor family."

Strangled. Dumped in the woods. Her family dealing with not knowing, then finally knowing. And me sitting here, wishing for a few twists of the story to take it any other direction.

No more regrets.

Marcus's phone rang again, and the blinking display told me Sylvia was the caller. Of course she was. I sighed, picked up his phone from the counter, and carried it upstairs.

I walked down the carpeted hallway and stopped at his door. He'd left it open about a foot. I lifted a hand to knock, but stopped. Marcus sat on his bed, his head in his hands. He looked so miserable I stopped with my hand in the air. Fingers in his hair, forehead on his palms, he was oblivious to me.

I lowered my hand. In front of him on the bed lay the photo of us sledding, out of its frame. I could see the white of the snow from the doorway. From here, we were just a blur of color going by.

He was sitting there motionless, staring at the photo. I swallowed. His shoulders were slumped and he didn't move the whole time I stood in the doorway.

Marcus was quiet. So different from his hectic, opinionated family. And he didn't wear muscle shirts or show his boxer band or flirt outrageously. He was moody sometimes and he'd get angry when he was hurt, but last winter, he'd dragged the sled up that hill as many times as I wanted, trudging through a foot and a half of ice-topped snow, his boots punching through the surface with every step.

I reached in, set his phone on the dresser next to the broken frame and shards of glass, and turned away before I could see whether or not he looked up.

The day of the carnival was hot enough to make me glad we had water games. An end-of-summer temperature spike. Marcus, Claire, Sylvia, and I were filling water balloons at the hydrant in the park. Water soaked my tank top. All of us had gotten wet from slipping balloons or the nozzle leaking, but we weren't trying to be particularly careful. Ninety degrees with high humidity was like being in a sauna.

Marcus did not seem okay. He stacked shallow crates and tied off balloons while Claire, Sylvia, and I filled them. He was quiet, only talking to Sylvia. Her shirt was wet, too, and being pale purple, was more than a little see-through, but somehow he didn't seem to notice.

Will drove by and honked, then parked and jogged over. "Hey, ladies. Marcus. What can I do?"

"Hey. Um, can you help Marcus carry those crates over to the space for the water balloon game?" I turned when Claire elbowed me in the ribs. "What?"

"Nothing." She went back to tying off her balloon.

Will lifted a crate and followed Marcus and Claire smacked my arm. "Way to be obvious."

"About what?"

"Will! I'm so jealous. You guys are really dating now?"

Sylvia chimed in. "Yep, they are, so hands off," she said brightly.

I scowled. Sylvia was just being friendly, but that didn't matter. I still hated everything she did. And suspecting she knew something about Ellie's disappearance didn't make me want to be any nicer.

"Is he as awesome as he seems?" Claire asked.

I nodded. "He's pretty great, actually."

"Good kisser, I bet." She still watched him.

I turned off the water before her balloon burst. "What makes you say that?"

She sighed. "I mean, he's just tall enough he'd only have to bend a little. No facial hair. He's got big hands and a strong jaw. It's all there."

"Wow. You're going to jump right on him if we break up, aren't you?" I didn't care, but I had to act like I did.

She managed to shut the water off herself this time. "Of course not. I wouldn't date your ex. Sister power, right? But," she sighed, "too bad I didn't get there first."

If Will and I had really been dating, I would have been irritated, but I just spritzed her with the hose.

Kids were already arriving, lining up at the table by the bandstand to cash in their reading points for carnival tickets. For the third year in a row, I was in charge of the face-painting booth. Claire and Sylvia left to run the water balloon game while Marcus and Chris kept the soap slide going. The librarians and their own hapless teenagers were running everything else.

I handed Will a paintbrush. "Paint what they tell you. Don't get it in their eyes. If they don't know what they want, do a cat."

"Don't worry, I got this." Will flagged down a girl and she gave him a ticket. "What do you want?"

"A lion," she said.

A third-grader ran up and announced he wanted a rat. I dipped my brush and mixed some paint to make a plausible rat color.

Will glanced at me. "Claire's in college, right?"

"Yep. She's a sophomore." I dabbed color patches on the boy's cheeks and painted a black nose and whiskers. Tiny white fangs were about the best I could do toward a rat. He and the girl ran off—hers didn't look much like a lion—and we turned to the next pair of kids. They wanted to be kittens.

"So she's what, twenty?"

"Yep." I curled the tips of the whiskers upward. I couldn't imagine not having siblings. Even before we'd moved to Missouri, I'd had Claire.

Halfway through the afternoon, Marcus came over to our stand. "You don't have my keys, do you?"

I shook my head. "No, why?"

"I can't find them." He was talking to me, but wouldn't even look at Will. "Must have dropped them in the grass somewhere."

"We can help look when we're done here," Will offered.

"Yeah. Thanks. I've got a spare in the glove box, but still." He turned away and headed for Claire and the water balloons.

Claire shook her head, and Marcus went back to the soap slide. He sprayed the flat plastic runner with soap solution, soaked it with the hose, and sent kid after kid running through the spray and belly-flopping onto the slide. Some of them got going fast enough they slid past the end of the slide and into the soggy grass.

Claire came over to switch with me. Glad for a change of pace, I took her place at the water balloon game, much closer to Marcus. I tried not to, but every time I stopped focusing on the game, my attention drifted and I'd find myself watching him.

The water balloon game was for the older kids. Teams of two had a towel stretched between them, trying to launch a water balloon from their towel to another team's towel without bursting the balloon. Sylvia was tallying points. I placed a balloon in each towel and scurried out of the way before they started launching the balloons.

"How's it going?" Sylvia asked.

"Good." The carnival was fun, but it was always exhausting. I glanced over to the face-painting booth, where Claire was painting Will's face and laughing. I shook my head. My sister should have come with a warning label.

A truck rumbled by. I turned and Sylvia looked up from her points tally. A red Dodge. I blew out a breath and went back to keeping an eye on the game, but Sylvia had frozen. I looked up again. The red truck kept going, but she was staring at a white one, parked at the end of the block. The white truck that had run Marcus and me off the road. From here, I could see the empty cab.

Sylvia paled. She looked at me, then at the kids playing the balloon game. A cheer went up; one of the teams had broken their balloon. She jotted down points for the wrong team on her clipboard. I ran over to replace the water balloon and the game picked up again.

When I turned, I stopped, my feet rooted to the grass. Beyond the band shell stood the driver of the white truck. Short. Skinny. He stood motionlessly, watching the carnival.

Sylvia looked up. She dropped her pen, then dropped her clipboard when she bent to pick up the pen. "I—can you take these—Sorry—I can't—" She thrust the clipboard at me and ran to Marcus. She grabbed his arm and he stared at her in confusion, then he handed the hose to Chris. He said something to the kids in line, then pulled out his phone and went with Sylvia to his truck, already talking to someone on his cell.

The man walked to the bouncy castle and watched. All he was doing was watching, and there was nothing illegal about him being in the park. I glanced at the clipboard and declared a winning team while trying to keep an eye on Marcus and Sylvia.

He was talking to her, but didn't seem to be getting much of an answer. She just kept shaking her head. After a minute, Marcus climbed into his truck and they left. Him calling the sheriff might help, since he could be charged with a hit-and-run, but there was no evidence to prove he'd done anything else, and they might not even be able to prove he'd wrecked Uncle Ward's truck.

When I looked back to the bouncy castle, the man was gone.

Chapter Twenty

Marcus didn't come home until late that night, way past his curfew. The parents waited up for him in the kitchen, Mom and Dad sorting and unpacking things from the carnival at the table. Chris was still up on one of the computers upstairs, but everyone else had gone to bed. I sat in the dark living room, pretending to be texting whenever one of the parents looked in on me.

Aunt Shelly's voice rose when he came in. Marcus tried to explain why he was late, and his voice filtered into the living room, sounding exhausted.

A few months ago, if he had sounded like that, I would have made him sit down next to me. I would have run my fingers through his hair, and not moved until he'd told me what was wrong.

Maybe I'd let him go, but I was never going to love anyone else like that.

Marcus appeared in the doorway, his shoulders sagging and his eyes tired. The parents talked in hushed voices in the kitchen behind him, Aunt Shelly still sounding angry.

I looked up. "Everything okay?"

For once, he talked to me. "Sylvia won't tell me what's wrong. She wanted me to stay until her dad got home."

I stood up and moved closer. "I saw her run off."

He leaned against the wall. "I have no idea what happened, and she's pretty shaken up. She won't say anything about it except she saw someone she knew."

My brain was spinning. "The guy she saw was the driver of the white truck. He was parked down the block. She saw him right before she ran over to you."

He pushed off the wall. "The guy who wrecked Dad's truck? Are you serious?"

"Yeah. She got really pale and kept dropping stuff, then ran off. Maybe it's not about Ellie, but she's hiding something."

He shook his head and exhaled. "Don't. Just stop accusing my girlfriend of being involved with a murder. It's petty and ridiculous. I'm going to bed." He walked up the stairs, lifting each foot like it weighed a ton.

This time, I kept myself from saying something mean in response. My shoulders slumped and I leaned against the wall for a moment.

I wasn't accusing her. For once, this had nothing to do with jealousy. Warning Marcus was only backfiring, but I couldn't not tell him when something was obviously wrong.

He knew me better than that. He should know being jealous wouldn't make me go that far.

For Marcus to be this worried, Sylvia must have had a major freak-out. I walked back to my room, the house quiet and the carpet soft on my bare feet. Claire was asleep in her bed, home for the rest of the weekend. Not liking the stillness, I turned on my television and slid in *The King and I.* My movies never woke her up, but I turned the volume down a little anyway.

I woke up in the middle of the night to the scene where Tuptim was being dragged off, swearing and crying over Lun Tha's death.

In the morning, I woke up to more screaming, but this time it was the twins. The wailing of two-year-olds penetrated my bedroom door and my sanity. I crawled out of bed, pulled on a hoodie and my jean shorts, and stumbled into the living room.

Nate and Gage bawled on the living room floor. Candace and Angie were offering them toys and looking frustrated, but the twins just cried louder. Aunt Shelly came running down the stairs and hovered over them. "What's going on down here?"

Marcus shrugged. "They've been crabby since they woke up." He was in the kitchen making hot chocolate. He glanced at me and then went back to the stove.

Whether or not we could be together, this was not the way things were going to go for the rest of our lives.

Aunt Shelly picked up the twins and carried them upstairs, both still crying, and I shut the door to the stairs. The quiet was a relief. I went over to Marcus. "You've never shown me how to do that," I said. He might not want to talk to me, but he didn't have a choice.

"You never paid attention," he said.

"I know," I said.

He looked at me like he wasn't sure what I was doing while he poured milk into the pan. "It's not hard."

"I'm not accusing Sylvia of anything, okay? But it's weird, and I don't want you to get hurt. That's all."

He didn't reply, so I tried again. "You heat the milk first, right?"

"Yeah." He hesitated, and then doubled the milk in the sauce pan.

"Then what?"

"Cocoa. Two spoons, once it's hot." He handed me the cocoa powder and my fingers brushed his. "Want to do it?"

"Sure." I whisked the milk so it wouldn't scorch.

"Hey, did you ever find your keys?" Chris asked from the table. He was eating a monstrous sandwich. For breakfast.

Marcus shook his head. "I have my spare truck key, but that's it. They'll turn up somewhere dumb. They probably got packed into one of the game boxes. Okay, add the cocoa."

I sifted the dark silky powder into the steaming milk. Color spread through the white. I turned down the burner and kept stirring. The bittersweet smell of warming chocolate always made me wish for fall.

Partially because it was a relief from the humidity of summer, and partially because the leaves of the hardwoods turned red and orange, fall was my favorite season. Marcus and I always made giant leaf piles for Candace and Angie and went to haunted corn mazes with Chris.

"Don't overcook it. Just add the sugar and it's done." Marcus poured in a tablespoon of sugar.

"That's all?" Maybe I didn't like my coffee supersweet, but this was hot chocolate.

"That's all." He took the whisk from me and stirred, then poured the dark liquid into two mugs. He sipped from one, then stirred in an extra spoon of sugar into the other and handed it to me.

His fingers touched mine again when I took the mug. Hoping adding extra sugar just for me meant he wasn't so upset anymore, I leaned against the counter, holding the mug. He took his hot chocolate into the living room and paused by the stairs. "When did we say for going to the movie?"

"Two," I said, and rounded the corner so Chris wouldn't hear. "Marcus?"

"Yeah?"

My voice was barely a whisper. "It's still me."

He nodded and started up the stairs, and I stood by myself in the kitchen.

Out the window, sunlight flooded the yard. Sparrows hopped through the lawn, picking bugs out of the ridges of mowed grass already dried from the late-summer heat.

Dressing up a little for this date might be a good idea. If I shaved my legs, I could wear that skirt Marcus liked. No one was in the bathroom, so the shower was mine for once.

Thirty minutes later and I had showered, shaved, and tamed my red fly-aways with a little mousse. I'd even gotten some curl into my hair. I stood in my room wrapped in a towel, sorting through my closet. Half the stuff was Claire's. I decided on a soft black V-neck and my green plaid skirt.

When Will showed up, I put on the necklace he'd given me, added tiny pearl earrings, and figured that was the best I could do. He smiled. "Hey, look at you."

I shrugged. "Marcus said he'd meet us there. You ready?"

Will opened the car door for me. "I hope you're ready."

That didn't sound good. "Ready for what?"

He just winked.

I sighed. "I don't want to keep hurting him, Will. He's not getting jealous, he's getting more distant. I don't think he even likes me anymore."

He touched my shoulder. "That's only what you can see right now."

By the time we got to the theater, I was nervous, fiddling with my bracelet and repeatedly checking my texts. Nothing, except Kelsey wanting to hang out. Will parked the car and turned sideways in his seat. "Stop worrying."

"I'm trying."

"There's no reason to worry. You look great, and I love the skirt. Sylvia doesn't stand a chance."

Yeah, right. Sylvia, with her blonde hair and big eyes. Sylvia, with her high cheekbones and long legs and cute shoes.

Will smiled. He had such an easy grin. "I can see you thinking that," he said.

I frowned and unbuckled my seatbelt. "I'm pretty sure I've royally screwed this thing up."

He reached for the door handle but paused. "Hey. I want to kiss you before we go in."

"What?" I stared at him in surprise. We'd been over that.

"Just as friends." He was serious.

"You know that's not something friends do, right?"

"Please? It's for good luck."

He was such a giant dork. "Why would I kiss you?"

He flipped up the armrest between our seats and scooted closer. "Just trust me, okay? If you want Marcus to come to his senses, keep looking at me. Now kiss me."

Oh. That was why.

Will leaned toward me, invading my space. "Besides. You know you want to, one last time."

I rolled my eyes. "You're ridiculous." I grinned before leaning over and brushing my lips against his. He ran a finger along my jaw. Because it tickled, and because the kiss was a little weird, I giggled, and then he started tickling my side and I couldn't help laughing. He kept right on kissing me, his lips touching my neck and nose and cheek.

Eventually, he pulled back. "Hey, looks like they're waiting." He nodded toward the windshield.

Marcus and Sylvia stood in the parking lot, waiting for us. Sylvia wasn't paying attention, but Marcus was looking right at us. "We shouldn't have done that," I said.

Will grinned and opened his door. "Let's go watch a movie."

I should have had Will for my cousin and Marcus should have been the guy from town. That would have made so much more sense.

We walked toward Marcus and Sylvia. She seemed to have recovered from her scare last night, and was hanging onto his hand like they were

Siamese twins, chatting about which movie we should watch. Marcus met my eyes for a moment and how empty he looked startled me.

We walked toward the theater without saying much. Only two movies were starting right then—a thriller and a romantic comedy. We chose the thriller and filed into the dark theater. Sylvia went in first, which meant I was between Marcus and Will when we sat down.

I loved the dark and quiet of theaters. The giant screens usually meant I was able to focus on the film to the exclusion of everything else, but this time I was too aware of Marcus beside me. Our elbows shared the same armrest. Our shoulders nearly touched.

The credits rolled in over a misty lake as I settled back. Water lapped at the screen. Fantastic. Someone was going to end up drowning.

The movie was about a girl being stalked by a spirit-monster of some kind who lived in the lake. Her chances of survival didn't seem high. Will kept whispering to me what he thought was going to happen, but he was almost always wrong. Sylvia jumped and covered her eyes every fifteen minutes, but I couldn't blame her too much. The movie was tense. I was having trouble following it, though, because every time Marcus shifted, I forgot what was happening onscreen and wanted to lean my shoulder toward his. I could feel his body heat and his shirt smelled like fabric softener. If we could only talk to each other, if he would just be honest with me, we could get past this.

No. We couldn't. Nothing had changed except I'd realized that if our families weren't an issue, I'd be okay with us.

Will shifted and put his arm around me, and after a second I felt his hand move to my hair and idly start playing with the lengths. Marcus glanced at us. The dark theater shadowed the planes of his face and made his eyes unreadable. When the girl screamed onscreen, he looked away.

Will kept whispering to me, usually nothing important, but every time he did, Marcus's eyes flicked away from the screen and toward us.

Even though the girl was murdered and her love interest died killing the monster, I couldn't make myself care.

When we left the empty theater, Marcus still barely talked to me. But he was watching. Will, to my surprise, wasn't kissing me, flirting with me, or saying things meant to provoke Marcus. Instead, he held the door for me, rested his hand on my lower back as we walked, asked me what I thought about the movie, and made eye contact while I talked. Everything I did made him smile.

The pizza place in Harris was a hole in the wall with two rows of booths and three tables. The place was nearly empty, since it was before the dinner rush, although nothing ever really rushed in Harris. We ordered two supreme stuffed crusts because there was no point to any other kind of pizza, and I drank a soda and a half while we waited.

Will kept the conversation going, making Sylvia laugh and turning toward me a bit anytime I said something. He asked questions, teased me, said he liked me wearing the necklace. Everything he did made my face turn pink, just because his attention, even though I didn't want it, was so much I didn't know what to do with it.

When our pizzas came, Will picked the olives off his slice and gave them to me. Sylvia chatted on about how scary the movie was—"oh my god, I nearly *died* when that thing rose out of the lake"—and her dad's teaching conference the next weekend. She kept emphasizing that he'd be gone Friday and Saturday, though it was a local conference, so he'd be home at night. She sounded a bit too disappointed about him coming home, and her glance at Marcus was a bit too long, so I leaned toward Will and he obligingly put an arm around me and ate my pizza crust.

Marcus paid attention to Sylvia and spoke anytime someone asked him a question, but he only ate two slices of pizza and sat too straight, too stiffly, all evening.

Will paid for my food, even though I hissed at him that he shouldn't. He winked at me. "No worries. You can pay me back later."

I rolled my eyes. "My fourth of the bill is less than eight dollars. What do you think you're going to get for that?"

He looked me up and down. "If you smile at me, we can call it even."

I huffed and let him pay while Marcus watched us.

Chapter Twenty-One

The double date hadn't changed much, except that Marcus no longer looked like he was angry all the time. He looked worn out. The evenings were cooler now, the garden producing like crazy, and sometimes we did evening chores together, with the evening sunlight lighting up the grass blades on one side and tipping shadows from them on the other. Marcus would throw himself into the work, and even though I knew why, I didn't know how to help.

When he'd come home from wherever he'd been with Sylvia all day, he'd have shadows under his eyes. I'd hear him up walking around at night, or else completely disregarding his curfew and coming in at two A.M.

But he always got up on time, still helped with the kids, still did his share of the chores. When I found him making scrambled eggs one morning, I tapped him on the shoulder. He turned around like I'd startled him.

I said nothing, just looked at him. His eyes were bloodshot.

"It's okay," he said. The kids waited at the table. He served the scrambled eggs onto plastic plates for the twins and carried them over. I divided up the rest and followed him with our plates, but he wouldn't say anything else to me. He ate half his food and left to go start his chores.

I stopped trying to make him talk to me. He didn't want to, and if he wanted to get over me, then I was only making it worse. But maybe, if he wasn't angry anymore, we were making progress. Maybe later on we could be friends, and he'd be happy with Sylvia, and I'd go off to college and start my career.

I went to the pool a few more times the last weeks of August with Kelsey and Hannah, and they teased me about Will. It was fun, and I liked that they liked him and my parents liked him. But their teasing landed in an empty place because it wasn't at all what I wanted.

I buried myself in college applications, blogging, and hanging out with my friends. I bought a stack of books on cinematography and posted what I was learning about light and shadow and the shapes they created between the actors. Space, I was discovering, was incredibly important on set. The width of a room could be an unconquerable distance.

Marcus, too, was around less and less the closer it got to the start of school. I never saw him in the mornings anymore, and sometimes I didn't see him all day. Chris asked me a few times if I thought he was alright, and I honestly didn't know what to say.

The first day of school I saw his truck parked in the lot; instead of riding in with him like I'd done for the last two years, I'd gone with Kelsey. She caught me staring at his truck. "Something's weird with you two," she said.

I lifted my bag to my shoulder. "Yeah."

"What happened?" We walked across the grass and through the doors.

I almost wanted to tell her. "It's not really mine to tell. Maybe soon."

Senior year. We'd made it here, but we couldn't make it across our own house to talk to each other. The longer he stayed away from me, the harder it was to talk to him.

Instead of letting myself drown in it, I focused. I took notes I didn't need to take all through the first week, trying not to watch Marcus out the corner of my eye. With a small school and smaller classes, it was hard to not see him everywhere.

Marcus, too, kept his head down. But by Friday, he looked worse than ever, and he didn't show up for the rest of his classes after lunch.

I walked up to Sylvia at her locker. She probably knew why he went home. She was digging around in her bag and didn't hear me, and I stopped behind her and froze when I saw what was taped inside her locker. "Why do you have a photo of Ellie?" The photo, dog-eared and hidden in the back of the locker, was of both of them, arms around each other's shoulders.

Sylvia whirled around and dropped her chemistry book. She slammed her locker door. "She was on my volleyball team. It's a reminder." Her eyes were red, and she looked tired, too.

I picked up her book and handed it back to her. "You said you barely knew her. You look like friends in that picture."

"We weren't that close."

"But you were friends."

She tried to move away but I stepped in front of her. "You know something about Ellie."

She gripped my arm. "I know why you were looking at me that way and asking me all those questions this summer, okay? But I don't know anything. I'm sad she died. That's it."

I shoved her hand off me. "She was murdered. And whoever did it is getting away with it."

"The police can handle it. Leave me alone." She pushed past me.

If there was one thing I wasn't going to do, it was leave her alone. I had Kelsey follow her after school, but Sylvia went straight home and Kelsey gave me a weird look.

But I was certain now.

I hadn't seen the white truck around for a few weeks. I scanned town and the back roads for it every time we drove to or from school, and I watched Sylvia as often as I could. We drove past her house to get back to mine each day, and every day, she'd be pulling into her drive when we went past.

Claire came home that weekend to hang out with me, and she, Will, and I went for ice cream in Manson. A little green car I didn't recognize crossed the street a block down. I sat between them on the picnic table while Claire talked about her new classes for the semester and her social psychology professor. The car headed along the street parallel to Main; I saw the flash of green in between the houses. It stopped two blocks up, at the park, and someone climbed out the passenger side. Blonde hair. She walked across the park toward her house, and the green car kept going.

Marcus wasn't at dinner that night, and he didn't come home before bed, so when Mom turned off the light in the hall, I stopped her. "Is Marcus still out with Sylvia?"

She shook her head. "She's sick, apparently. Has the flu or something. And Marcus is at work."

I stopped in my doorway. "At work?"

She peered at me, her hair unbraided over her shoulder. "His job. At the bowling alley."

"He got a job at the bowling alley?"

"Money for college, Shelly said. He's been working there for a couple weeks now."

I'd assumed he was out all that time with Sylvia. I told her goodnight and closed my door, but lay awake in bed for an hour.

Marcus was working. That's why he was coming home late. And Sylvia was not sick.

I didn't even know what time Marcus came home, or if he even did, because he wasn't there in the morning, either.

That became the pattern. He left before I got up, leaving lunches for Candace and Angie lined up on the counter, talked to me if I talked to him at school, went straight to work when the final bell rang, and I wouldn't see him again for the rest of the day. Days he didn't work, he got out snacks for the twins and Candace and Angie as soon as he got home, sat the girls down at the table with their homework, and did his next to them until dinner, after which he'd go see Sylvia and not be home until after I went to bed.

Sometimes when I couldn't sleep and I got up in the middle of the night, I'd see a light and hear him doing homework by the computers upstairs. This time when I heard his footsteps up there, I got out of bed and crept up the stairs.

The desk lamp by the computers was on. His English homework lay scattered on the desk. "Marcus?"

He turned to look at me. Maybe it was just the light, but he looked thinner.

"Why are you up?" I asked. "It's two-thirty."

He folded down the page of his book. "The test for English."

I walked over to him and sat down in the chair by the second computer. "I'm worried about you." It wasn't the light; he had lost weight. The hollows on his face were sharper. It looked like it had been a few days since he shaved last, and he had black shadows under his eyes.

"I'm fine," he said. "I'm holding down a job. I have As in all my classes. I have a girlfriend. It's working."

He no longer looked seventeen. Somehow in the last month, he'd aged two or three years. "What's working?" I so badly wanted to move my chair closer and brush the hair off his forehead.

"Will's a good guy for you. I have Sylvia. We're making it work."

"Why are you doing all this?" I whispered. "You're going to make yourself sick."

"No, I won't. I'm dealing with the problem."

At least he was talking to me and we were having a real conversation. "Which problem?"

"That I—we—" He glanced around the silent upstairs. "Us. I'm dealing with it. It's working."

I shouldn't have, but I did it anyway. I reached across and touched his hair, brushed it out of his eyes. His eyes met mine, and then he looked down to the carpet. "I should keep working. That test is tomorrow and I'm only half done."

I lowered my hand to my lap. "You can't keep not sleeping like this."

"Yes, I can." He turned back to his books. "See you tomorrow."

Except I probably wouldn't. I never should have agreed to our new rules.

I stood up and walked down the stairs, and the lamp lit up his brown hair and his pale skin as he bent over a giant volume of Shakespeare's collected works.

When I got back to my room, I pulled out my phone and texted him.

I miss you.

He hadn't replied to my texts in two months. I had no reason to think he would, but I stared at the clock anyway. Five minutes later, he replied.

I miss you, too.

The white truck seemed to have disappeared. The parents all lost the worry lines that had been gathering on their faces, and it had been a while since anyone had bothered Marcus.

But ever since I saw that photo in Sylvia's locker, I was convinced that she had something to do with Ellie's death. I still had a few details to work out, but everything pointed back to St. Joseph. Something had happened there, and for Ellie's sake, I had to know what. I draped my legs over the side of the armchair in the living room. I had several tabs open online—a few articles with dates covering the timespan of her disappearance, the school website, a mention of the volleyball team in one of the city's newspapers. My college-ruled notebook had a page nearly filled with notes and addresses.

Sylvia giggled so I looked up. They were always here, now. Never at her place. She was whispering to him, again. But she still looked tired and her laughter seemed forced. She'd been sick enough she'd skipped school a few times already. Was the entire town not sleeping?

I hadn't replied to Travis in a few days, so I opened his last e-mail and clicked "reply." He'd apologized for not getting back to me for a while, saying the start of the semester had been busy.

No worries. It's been busy here, too. School starting always does that, plus my cousin is always bringing his girlfriend over, and the garden is producing like crazy now, so we're all working with produce almost every spare minute.

We'd started chatting more about things besides film, just normal life things, and I was surprised once I started how easy it was to tell people about myself. It was pretty great having Kelsey and Will and now Travis.

Marcus and Sylvia were whispering. I couldn't tell what they were saying, but their voices were tense. Sylvia seemed okay, though, and laughed once or twice while they watched videos on his phone. But until lately, Marcus had never sat straight up like that, and his attention kept drifting to other things in the room. Usually, he focused. He paid attention.

I closed my laptop. He wouldn't be happy if he knew what I was doing, even though he knew something wasn't right with Sylvia.

Sylvia and Ellie having known each other was too much of a coincidence for me to believe it was one. Sylvia was a nice girl. I'd looked hard and found no legitimate reason to dislike her. Sometimes oblivious, sometimes messy, but she reminded me a little bit of Ellie.

Except Ellie wouldn't have hidden something like this. And as I sat there, watching Sylvia whispering to my ex in my own living room, a thought struck me that made me turn cold.

Maybe she wasn't hiding something. She could just as easily be hiding *from* something.

When a crash came from the kitchen after midnight, I was still awake. Since Marcus hadn't been there for dinner, the parents had talked all about him and young love and how overdue this was. They'd solemnly agreed, with much head nodding, what a lovely girl—just a lovely girl— Sylvia was, while I stabbed my rosemary potatoes. Chris had raised his eyebrows at me, but other than that no one seemed to notice.

I slid out of bed and opened my door a crack. A light was on in the kitchen, and I heard Marcus swear. I pulled a cardigan over my pajamas and went out to see what was going on.

Marcus stood in the middle of the kitchen, setting a chair upright. His eyes were bloodshot and he wore his shoes on the wrong feet. "Are you drunk?" I asked.

He shook his head. "No." He paused and closed his eyes. "Yes."

He didn't look tipsy drunk; he looked sick drunk. He tried to walk forward and ran into the chair again, so I hurried over and helped him set it up. He gripped the rail along the chair back and wouldn't let go.

"Why are you drunk?"

His knuckles were turning white.

"What happened? Are you okay?" Maybe I should take him to the hospital. I could wake Uncle Ward, but they'd freak out if they saw him like this.

"I don't know." He was breathing too fast, but I couldn't see anything actually wrong with him.

I stepped closer to him and touched the back of my hand to his face. He jumped when I touched him and his skin was hot. "You didn't drive like this, did you?"

"They drove me."

"Did something happen? Tell me what's wrong." I touched his hands, trying to get him to let go of the chair, but he pulled away from me and stumbled backward.

"Hey," I said. "Calm down. It's okay."

"No, it's not. I didn't avoid it, I did everything, and it's not okay." The dim kitchen light only lit up half his face.

I took a step toward him. "Let's go sit on the couch. Then you can tell me what's going on."

He turned away, looking out the big windows that let in the night. "You used me, didn't you?"

Now I was the one who felt like stumbling backward. "What?"

He talked to the window, his arms crossed and his shoulders set. "You knew. You had to know I loved you. That I—how I couldn't—but you didn't stop. And you let me. You let me think it was both of us, and you teased me and led me along and then took it away. I never would have done that to you. Ever." He swung around, his eyes red. "You did this to me. You came here when I was fourteen and shy and you were the prettiest girl I'd ever seen. You kissed me, and you talked to me, and you made me love you. And then you said I couldn't, and you didn't, and you were embarrassed to be with me. You said it meant nothing."

"We," I said slowly. "We said. We talked about it." I had not made him love me. Whatever he'd done wasn't my fault.

"Because that was what you wanted." His voice fell flat. "You didn't want me, so there was nothing I could do about it." He walked toward me. "Just tell me. I have to know. I can't stand not knowing."

He stopped inches from me, and it took everything I had to not touch him again.

"Anything," I said. "I'll tell you whatever you want to know."

"Tell me the truth. Just tell me, okay?"

"Okay. I promise."

He ran both hands through his hair, then backed up, like he couldn't be too close to me when I answered. "Did you love me? Did you ever really love me?"

That night at the creek, I'd told him I did. But the boy standing in front of me didn't know it, thought it wasn't true, thought he hadn't meant enough to matter. My throat went tight. "Of course I did. I told you I did."

"No." His voice was a hoarse whisper. "You kept saying you didn't, before."

I couldn't stand him sounding this way, looking at me like that. "I didn't know, at first. I didn't want to." The kitchen floor was cold on my bare feet as I walked toward him. "But I did love you, Marcus. You have to believe me. I didn't know you'd loved me all that time, and I never would have kept up with it if I'd thought you did."

He looked down at my feet on the hardwood floor. "You said it, that time at the creek. But later I figured I was wrong and you didn't really. Once you'd gotten away from it, you changed your mind." His jaw clenched and unclenched. "I was right, wasn't I? You—you cared about me. You loved me like your cousin. But you never loved me like that."

"I did. I loved you!" I wanted to yell at him that I still did; I wanted to shake him until he looked me in the face and told me what the hell had happened tonight. But if I did that—

"I'll be fine, okay? I know—compared to Will, and he's not your cousin. But I have to know if it was just me or if it was you, too, and somehow I lost—" He stepped forward and gripped my shoulders. "I can handle it and I'll be fine. Don't lie to me." His grip trembled, and he shook me.

I put my hands on his arms and tried to push them away. "Stop it. Marcus, let go." But he didn't. His hands didn't hurt, but he was so much bigger, so much stronger than me. I gripped his wrists and shoved. "Let go. Damn it, let go of me!"

He dropped me like I'd burned him. He looked horrified, and stared at his hands for a minute. "I'll move out," he said. "I'm almost eighteen. I'll move out."

I pulled my cardigan tight around me. "Stop it. Stop whatever this is. Don't move out, just believe me, Marcus. I wasn't using you, and I'm so, so bitterly sorry I hurt you. But it wasn't ever just you. Please, believe me."

He looked up from his hands. "You loved me."

"Yes."

"It wasn't just me. You weren't using me."

"No."

His face fell. "God, Jackie. I'm sorry. I'm so sorry." His eyes flicked over every part of my face. He reached out to touch me, but then didn't. "Did I—Did I hurt you?"

I swallowed hard. "You just scared me," I whispered.

"I scared you. Me." He looked dazed. He walked into the living room and sank onto the couch.

I went over to him and sat facing him, cross-legged on the cushion.

"It's not working," he said. "I'm not fine."

"Tell me." I knew, but if I didn't find out what was going on in his head, this would be it for us. We were falling already, and if this kept up, we'd keep on falling until we hit the bottom and broke.

"I can't do it," he said. "I'm dating someone else. I'm working every spare minute. I never even see you anymore. That night you came upstairs, I told you it was working, but it's not working." He gripped the edge of the couch, his fingers digging into the fabric. "And I can tell from the way he treats you. Will actually cares about you. And that's great. I don't care if you're sleeping with him. No, shit, I do, but what I mean is, you have the right. You have the right to, okay? But I can't stop thinking about it, about you and him, and even Sylvia can tell." He rubbed his hands over his face.

I could barely see him in the light coming from the kitchen. We were only two feet away from each other, but it felt like miles.

"Marcus." I waited for a moment, because I wanted him to hear me, believe me. He lifted his head and he went back to gripping the edge of the couch. His eyes were black holes in the dark, and he was looking somewhere across the room, but he was listening. "I am not dating Will."

His hands let go of the couch.

"And I didn't sleep with him, either. We went out a few times, and I tried to make it work because of what you and I said. But he wasn't what I wanted. We're friends. That's it."

"You're not dating Will." He said it like an echo, like he didn't know what it meant. "But you are. In your room, and going out to the movie. And whatever."

"We've just been hanging out."

"Oh." He took a deep breath. He held one hand in the other and rubbed a thumb across his palm. "I've been going back and forth.

Thinking you used me and didn't care about me, and it was just me, and everything that had been so good about the last year I'd never actually had, or else that it wasn't just me, and I did have it, which was almost worse, because it meant I'd lost it."

I took a second to sort through his words. "If you lost something, I did, too."

His breathing slowed as he stared at the carpet. "So if"—He cleared his throat. "If I wasn't me, if I wasn't your cousin, would you still want to be with me?"

Now I touched him. I rested my hand on his shoulder, traced my fingers over his cotton shirt and down his arm. His shoulder was thinner than it had been. "Yes. If you were just you, and I was me, and we weren't cousins, there'd be no question."

He froze. His slow breathing sounded loud in the darkness of the room, and so did mine.

The things we shouldn't say lay there between us, all the things we wanted and regretted. But then Marcus reached for me.

He'd only kissed me that first time on a dare, and it had taken him months to bring it up again. I'd told him to kiss me a second time, and after that, I'd been the one to find him, tease him, push him, until we'd both admitted what we wanted.

But this time, it was his hands that touched my skin, his lips that crushed mine, his body that tipped mine backward onto the couch. I didn't move for a moment, because I didn't want him to know, but he had a right to the truth and I was done pretending. I put a hand on either side of his face and kissed him.

His lips parted mine, hot and impatient. He tasted like whiskey, and the way he kissed me threatened to make me drunk with it. He fumbled with the sleeves of my cardigan and tore it off me so I was in my pajama shirt and shorts. His hands came back to my face, though, and to my hair. He touched my eyebrow, and my ear, and my eyelashes. Ran his hand through my hair and kissed me and I kissed him until we were nothing but shape and shadow and motion in a dark, silent house.

All we did was kiss, but it was so much, and it was everything. For hours we lay there, hearing the clock tick but thinking it must be for other people, seeing the dark but still able to see each other. And if someone came downstairs, all they'd find was the truth.

Chapter Twenty-Two

I woke Marcus at four A.M. He'd fallen asleep on his side with his arm around me, and I'd stayed there on the couch with him. At night, the house was another world where we could be like this. I turned toward him and traced my fingertips down his chest. He stirred. I touched his nose. He blinked at me, then sat up.

"Oh my god," he said. "Sylvia."

"I know," I said.

"What do I—we still can't—"

"I know." Everything had changed, but at the same time, nothing had changed.

He bit his lip, touched my knee, then put his head in his hands. His words were so quiet I had to lean closer.

"I cheated on her," he said again.

That stung. I was not the other girl; she was.

But she was his girlfriend, and she would not want him kissing me, especially not like that.

He stumbled up the stairs to bed, and I went to my room.

I got a horrible two hours of sleep before I had to get up for school, and my shower took twice as long as it should have. Marcus was gone by the time I got out.

When Kelsey and I got to school, the sky hung low and thick like a gray tundra. End-of-summer storms were predicted for the entire week. Even though the sun was hidden, the heat kept building. At least it was Friday.

Sylvia was in all of her classes that day, but she looked as tired as Marcus and I did. Even though the humidity was suffocating outside, she wore a long-sleeved shirt.

I stopped her at her locker after class again, and she whirled around, her eyes angry.

"Listen," I said, before she could say anything. "If you're being harassed, you have to tell someone."

Her eyes widened. "I—I have to meet with the guidance counselor," she said, and then just left me there, her books and backpack on the floor and her locker hanging open.

I had no way to make her show me, but I was pretty sure if I did, I'd see bruises on her arms. I had to go to St. Joseph.

I didn't try to talk to Marcus about the night before even after school. He came home, helped Candace and Angie with their homework, and then washed produce in the yard after dinner. He'd eaten, though, instead of picking at his food and then leaving.

When I went out to check on him, he and Chris were washing tomatoes in the industrial sinks. I rolled up my sleeves and plunged my hands into the cold water. When Chris carried a crate of green onions to the cold cases in the garage, Marcus stared at the road as a little green car drove by. "Are you okay?" he said.

"I think so." The clouds had turned darker, twilight falling much too early. Knowing hadn't made it worse this time. It had helped a little.

"Me, too," he said. "At least, better in some ways."

I knew what he meant, and we left it at that.

Saturday morning, the rumble and clang of the truck and trailer being loaded woke me. Marcus would be helping the parents load the produce.

I didn't want to go to St. Joseph by myself, but I couldn't take Marcus to go investigate his own girlfriend. Will would be sleeping still, since he worked nights, and it was too much to explain to Kelsey.

The parents wouldn't let me go if I asked, but I had to. I couldn't go to the police with suspicions about a girl who had a photo in her locker and had worn long sleeves. I couldn't do anything more about the white truck, and the police were already doing what they could to find Ellie's killer. Today, the parents would be gone til almost noon. I'd packed the night before, and as soon as Marcus went back upstairs, I'd leave.

I rolled over and dozed until someone knocked on my door. Marcus poked his head in. "Your dad said we should go do chores now if we don't want to do them in the storm."

Dang it. I hadn't planned on the rain. Leaving while all the kids were in bed would have been easiest. I sat up. "Okay. Coming."

"I'm going to try to get Chris out of bed." He disappeared and feet pounded up the stairs.

I put on jeans and my boots in case it did start to rain while we were out. Out the kitchen window, the sky looked like a heavy iron lid set over the world. Updrafts and swirls in the clouds threatened a storm instead of just rain.

Marcus came back downstairs. "Chris will probably be a few minutes. We should just go."

"Mom and Dad went to St. Joseph in this weather? There won't even be a farmers' market."

He shrugged. "It's clear there. Moving north."

I texted Claire. Tornadoes were always a risk with temperature changes like this.

Hey, check the weather before you drive. Looks stormy here.

We went outside and Marcus opened the garage door to let Heidi out. The humidity made walking around feel almost like swimming. Thunder sounded off toward Manson. Heidi ran around us in circles, jumping and whining. Storms always upset her.

The streaks on the horizon meant rain was falling a few miles off. Chris showed up fifteen minutes later, lugging two bottles of milk replacer for the calves and followed by a sleepy-looking Angie. I was surprised she'd gotten out of bed, but Angie was loyal to her animals.

An hour later, a chill came through on the wind, starkly different from the water-laden heat. I filled Heidi's bowls and left the garage door open for her. Marcus came up from feeding the chickens when I headed for the house, but he stopped in the driveway, staring in his truck window. "Jackie."

I came back, feeling the hairs on my neck prickle. "What?"

"Look."

The driver's seat was ripped open from top to bottom. Foam swelled out of the gash, the edges a ragged zigzag. He tried the door, but it was locked. He straightened up and looked at me just as thunder cracked overhead and rain fell.

Usually a warning sprinkle would come first, but water fell like someone had upended a bucket, pounding on the cement and bouncing back up. We were drenched in the seconds it took us to run for the garage. Angie and Chris burst in behind us. We peeled off as many layers as we could and left our shoes in the garage so we didn't track mud into the kitchen.

That maniac had been in our driveway. It was definitely time to go. It only took me a few minutes to get everything ready, and I even grabbed a hoodie so I'd have something dry to change into. After pulling on dry jeans and toweling off my hair, I came back to see Angie sitting at the kitchen table. The temperature had plummeted. She was still soaked and shivering, watching the rain out the big window.

I just had to get out of the house without anyone noticing.

"Go change, silly." I sank onto the chair beside her.

"She's waiting on hot chocolate." Marcus was over at the stove, stirring a pan.

Angie nodded. "You can have some too if you want."

"I'm okay." I watched Marcus from the table. His face was tense.

"The truck is still locked," he said.

And someone had gotten into it. "Your keys." That was why I had to leave. This wasn't only about Ellie and Sylvia. This was Marcus, too.

"I thought I'd lost them. I don't know. Maybe I dropped them at the carnival and someone picked them up."

I walked over to him and leaned on the counter. "It couldn't have been just anyone. Someone knifed your seat and relocked the door. Who does that?"

"Yeah." He tapped the whisk on the edge of the pan and turned off the burner. He faced me, his eyes worried. "If someone has my keys, we need to get the locks changed."

"Marcus, this is serious." I was scared. Really scared. "It has to be the guy Sylvia saw at the carnival. Maybe she doesn't know anything about Ellie, but this guy is after you for some reason."

"I know." He crossed his arms.

"She didn't tell you anything else about him?" Sylvia had never said why she'd gotten upset when she saw the man in the white truck, not even to Marcus.

"She says she's only dated one other guy and it wasn't him. I don't know. She's being weird about it. Maybe I should start keeping Dad's gun in the truck."

"Uncle Ward has a gun?" My eyebrows went up.

"Yeah. Locked in the top of his closet."

Thunder cracked outside and a shiver trickled across my skin. Marcus handed Angie her hot chocolate as lightning ruptured the sky. My phone buzzed with a text from Claire.

Yeah, I'm not coming. Starting to look stormy here and Will says it's nasty there.

Claire had been talking to Will. That didn't surprise me.

"Call the parents and tell them. They need to know. Maybe with this, they can convince the police to do something."

My sheet of notes was tucked into my purse, and both it and an extra bag were hidden in the car in the driveway. The keys were in the pocket of my jacket. All I had to do was get away from my cousins.

"Marcus." I paused. "Tell the parents, and call Sheriff Whitley, and ask Sylvia what's going on. Make her tell you. Really."

Marcus looked up from his phone, already calling the parents. He could work on that, and I'd work on my list. He nodded, and when the parents answered, he started telling them about the truck. I could hear him talking as I walked through the living room and back to the hall. My door was closed, and it would stay that way. I went into Dad's office, closed the door behind me, and hit the thumb lock on the doorknob. My jacket was waiting on his chair. I slid it on and used the elastic on my wrist to pull my hair back in a ponytail. I climbed up on his desk.

Since he worked in here all day, his office had a window dug out of the side of the hill. The window didn't slide up, but it did have a hand crank that would open it far enough. I popped the screen off and cranked the window open.

Getting enough leverage to pull myself up and out was difficult, but I did it.

The unnaturally dark morning meant I could sneak around to the car easily. I kept the lights off and put the car in neutral. Since our driveway had an incline, the car rolled backward to the gravel road. I backed it down the road as far as I could, and when it came to a stop, I waited for a rumble of thunder to start the car. With the lights still off, I made a cautious three-point turn in the narrow gravel road. Heading away from the house, without ever having to drive past it, I finally turned on the lights.

For months, I'd told Ellie I'd come visit again. Now, almost a year too late, I was finally going.

The rain would slow me down, but I'd be driving out of the storm. Really, I'd be in no danger. I could stay with Claire if the storm got worse before I came back.

Rain beat on my windshield. My headlights lit up the whirls of rain being whipped by the wind. The wipers sloshed water off the windshield, and I tried to tune in to the steady swish-slap to keep my heart from racing.

I had a hard time believing Sylvia had anything to do with Ellie's death. After getting to know her a little, it didn't make sense. Ellie had been killed, and one of her friends was being harassed. It made the most sense that both girls had gotten involved in something bad.

But what? And if both girls had seen something, why would someone kill Ellie, but only scare Sylvia?

And why would someone be after Marcus? Sure, he was dating her, but this had started before Marcus asked her out, and making violent threats like this seemed more likely to draw attention than cover tracks.

None of the articles I read on Ellie's disappearance, nothing I found on the Internet or saw on the news, mentioned Sylvia. She hadn't been interviewed or given a statement of any kind.

Maybe Sylvia was what the police were missing.

Thirty miles out, the rain lessened and I could finally drive the speed limit. The rain was only a steady dripping there, the storm mostly wind. The hour drive to St. Joseph took me an hour and a half.

By the time I got off the highway, my hands hurt from gripping the steering wheel. I pulled into the driveway of the address from my sheet of notes, but couldn't get out of the car.

She'd lived here. I sat in the driveway of Ellie's parents' home, the house I should have visited more often, and my throat went tight. I touched my charm bracelet. The edge of the bird's wing pressed into my finger.

The windows of the house were dark, the shades still pulled. It was barely eight-thirty on a Saturday morning. I'd come back after my other errands were done and convince her parents to let me in. Search her room for a journal, find out if they'd kept her car.

The school was my next stop. I just had to hope it was open. I parked on a side of the school away from the street and had to try three doors before I found one open. Ducking inside, I glanced around. The muted roar of the giant floor cleaners whirred from somewhere down the hallway to the left.

I went right. Only a few lights were on. From the staff listing on the school website, I'd found the office number, and from the school PR photos, I thought I could figure out where it was. Coach Stevenson, Ellie's e-mails had said.

My footsteps echoed down the long halls. This place was much, much bigger than Manson High. It smelled cool and clean in the way only an empty school could smell. I found the gym, but was on the wrong side of it. It was locked, so I had to circle around through the halls.

G104. That was the office number I was looking for. I passed a trophy case and stopped. Inside was a framed photo of the volleyball team with the coach; it wasn't a great photo, but I could make out Sylvia and Ellie. It had to have been taken at the beginning of the fall semester last year.

Ellie looked happy. I stared at her for a minute; seeing her in such an unfamiliar place was strange. I pressed the heels of my palms into my eyes and took a deep breath.

Both girls had played volleyball. I couldn't get past that. I kept walking down the hall, suspicion turning into dread in my stomach.

There.

G104. Coach Stevenson's office.

Locked, of course.

This was why I'd come. It had to be the connection. They could have just met because of volleyball and become friends and gotten into something bad later. But if Sylvia had been telling the truth and they weren't very close, then volleyball was the connection.

I tried the door again. I'd figured it would be locked, and part of the reason I'd come today was because Saturday seemed like one of the least likely days for him to be here. I peered through the tiny window in the door but couldn't see anything. Too dark.

I thumped the door with my fist and backed up, thinking.

The trophy cases and the locked door told me nothing. I kept walking. Maybe I could convince the janitor I was a student here and I'd left a bag in his office. It was a long shot, but the worst that could happen was I'd be told no and asked to leave.

If this didn't work, I still had Ellie's parents to talk to, and if I still found nothing, I had the address of one of the teammates who had shown up most often in the photos of Sylvia and Ellie.

Halfway down the hall, near the office for the football coach, I stopped. Hanging in a row with the photos of the two other coaches was a clear, crisp headshot of Sylvia's stalker. Skinny. Shaved head. The driver of the white truck.

Blurry newspaper photos of him with hair looked nothing like this one of him without hair. *Mitch Stevenson*, the label under the photo read.

I sprinted down the hall. My shoes squeaked on the floors.

The coach was Sylvia's stalker. I hit the door still running and it flew open. Someone yelled behind me, but I didn't stop to see who. I flung open my door, started the car, and pulled out of the parking lot.

Getting to Sylvia and asking her why her coach had followed her when she moved should give me a good idea of what was going on here. She'd have to tell me.

The wind had picked up and the sky had darkened; the storm might be moving north, but it looked like St. Joseph was going to get hit, too.

I could go to the police with this, but what would they do? I knew the name of the guy who had wrecked Marcus's truck now, but they wouldn't arrest him for that tonight. Sylvia obviously hadn't reported him for harassing her, and if she wasn't pressing charges, he couldn't be arrested for that, either. Fear crawled through me.

If I could convince Sylvia to tell me what was going on, we could go to the police together. That was best thing to do.

My phone vibrated in my hand and I nearly dropped it. Marcus. They must have figured out I wasn't in the house. I put the phone on speaker.

"Jackie—where are you? Why did you leave? The power is out here and the storm is getting really bad. I can't get ahold of the parents—"

"Marcus, stop yelling at me. Listen—"

"—Water ran all over your dad's office floor—"

"Stop it! Listen! It's the coach, Marcus. Sylvia's volleyball coach is the man who forced us off the road and he's the guy she saw in the park."

"What?" He stopped interrupting.

"I'm in St. Joseph. I went to his office at Ellie's school and I'm headed back now. It's the coach, so Sylvia must have seen something."

"Holy shit," Marcus said. Lightning flooded the road with ghostly light.

I gripped the steering wheel. Silence fell over the line. "Have you heard from Sylvia?"

The twins started crying in the background. "She didn't answer. I called twice."

Not good. Rain pounded the roof of my car. I turned the windshield wipers up a notch. "Maybe it's the reception. You couldn't reach the parents, either. I'm heading home. We have to talk to Sylvia, so keep calling her."

"Don't speed, okay? The last thing we need is you going in the ditch. The roads have to be bad."

They weren't great. My tires plowed up water and the car swerved. "Yeah. I should go. Call me if anything happens. I'll be home as soon as I can."

I hadn't been truly afraid in a while. People around Manson didn't lock their cars or their houses, and the worst that happened was minor vandalism or petty theft. Sometimes there were stories of a house being broken into, but that was usually in Harris and it never happened to anyone I knew.

I could take a wild guess that this guy had something to do with Ellie disappearing, and if Sylvia had seen something about that, it made sense that he'd threaten her. But why not kidnap her, too? Why let her move away, why just follow her around, and not put an end to a witness?

A sinking feeling in my gut told me the answer wouldn't be good.

For another thirty minutes, my hands gripped the steering wheel and my eyes squinted to see through the rain. The sky was so dark it looked like late evening instead of mid-morning.

I glanced at my sheet of notes to double-check Sylvia's house number. It was one of the houses that barely made it inside the Manson city limits.

All the lights in the house were on, so at least she was home. I parked on the side of the road and ran up to the porch.

The front door hung open. I pounded up the steps. "Sylvia?"

No answer. I nearly stepped on a square of white by the doormat, something folded up like a gift. A blue number eight shone up at me. Before I could think better of it, I picked it up. A volleyball jersey unfolded.

I dropped it. Ellie's number had been eight. I'd seen it in the photos of her and Sylvia and in the photo in the trophy case at the school.

My best friend's killer had been here. I could report this. I could report finding a murdered girl's clothing.

He'd come here while I was in St. Joseph, and now he had Sylvia. I dialed 911 and ran into the house.

Looking through the living room and bedrooms was probably the dumbest thing I could do, but I couldn't stand the thought that maybe she was inside somewhere with him. I gave the address on the phone and the license plate of Mitch's truck—neatly copied onto my sheet of notes—while I ran up the stairs and looked in the kitchen.

A plate was smashed on the kitchen floor. The only thing out of place in the entire house, as far as I could tell, was a broken plate.

The woman on the line told me to get out of the house. She said to leave the jersey there, and to stay on the line until I got in my car, and to go home immediately; the police were on their way to the address. I told her which way I figured Mitch must have gone.

I ran out to the porch and paused; streams of water poured in free-fall off the roof as the gutters overflowed. Lightning spidered across the sky, whole chains of it flaring up like cracks in glass.

If he'd taken Sylvia, it must have been only minutes before I pulled up. The porch wasn't a deep one; the whole porch had been soaked by the rain but the living room rug was barely damp. The door couldn't have been open for long.

I dashed for my car, but when my tires spun through the water and bit gravel, I knew I couldn't go home.

One girl dead, one girl missing, and one free.

I hadn't passed him coming into town, and unless he'd taken one of the dead-end gravel roads here in town, he'd headed out north on the highway.

The police would be coming from Harris. They'd take twenty minutes minimum to get here, longer because of the storm. By the time they searched the house, the coach would have nearly an hour's head start.

I hadn't been there for Ellie, but I wasn't leaving Sylvia.

Something cracked against the window. A drumming started up, low beats in the pounding of the rain on the roof. Hail.

I wiped my jacket sleeve across my face to stop the water dripping in my eyes. Turning up the heat would help; my fingertips were going numb from cold or nerves or both.

The road ahead of me was dark. My headlights burned a tunnel through the storm. I found Marcus in my recent calls and hit "call."

Marcus. The coach could be heading there. He could be there already. He answered before the first ring even finished.

"He isn't there, is he?" I blurted out. "Or Sylvia? She's not there?"

"No, no one's here but me and the kids. Why? Are you okay? Where are you?"

"I'm past Manson, but I'm not coming home. I wanted to tell you where I am in case something happens. Did you get ahold of the parents?"

"I got through to Mom. I told them everything and Dad was trying to get ahold of the sheriff and your dad was yelling on the phone too, last I heard. They're coming back."

I'd made it back, but they had a trailer. The wind was forcing the car around on the road; driving the truck with the trailer would be even worse.

"Wait, you're not coming home? What's going on?"

I passed the turnoff for my house; the house was dark, so the power must still be out. Branches were down on either side of the road, rolling in the wind like giant tumbleweeds.

"Ellie's volleyball jersey was folded up on Sylvia's porch. Sylvia's gone. I think the coach—he—" I took a breath and started over. "He was there right before me. I called 911, and I'm driving along the blacktop to see if I can find him."

"What? No! Come home—are you crazy? You're going to get killed. Sylvia's gone?"

I explained as best as I could. Going home, though, wasn't the plan. Scanning the fields on either side of the road for lights, I was suddenly grateful for the darkness.

Something banged or fell over the phone line. "What was that?"

"Nothing. Seriously, Jackie. Dammit. Dammit! Come home, please; come back and let the police do their job."

"I can't. They'd be almost an hour behind me before they even started looking for him. He could kill her, too."

"You don't know that. Oh, no, Sylvia. Shit, shit." More banging.

"What is going on there?"

"It's the kids. They're scared of the dark. Where are you? At least tell me where you are and where you're going. Keep me on the line so I know if anything happens."

That was a good idea. My hands trembled, but my mind was clear. I couldn't panic. I'd have one chance to do this right.

"I passed the house three minutes ago, heading north. He must have gone this way if he's going far."

His voice was strained. "Jackie, please. You can't do this. You can't chase this guy in a storm by yourself. Turn around and come back. If he has her, you won't be able to help and dying won't help anyone. This is stupid, really stupid."

"Sorry." Hail smacked my windshield and bounced up from the asphalt.

"Dammit, Jackie, just dammit. Chris!" The phone silenced and came back after thirty seconds.

Static sounded. "Are you there?" I asked.

"Yeah. Keep talking to me." It sounded like Marcus was fumbling with something. "You found Ellie's clothes?"

I talked him through the whole thing, everything since I'd left the house that morning. He didn't say much, just asked questions or said, "That makes sense. Where are you now?"

Having him on the phone helped. I was a little less terrified than I would have been, and the small element of company kept me from freaking out at the hail and the dark and the fact I was chasing my best friend's killer.

My headlights reflected on a road sign. I looked down the turnoff but couldn't see anything. I might have passed him already; any one of these tiny gravel roads would take him far away from towns and people.

All I could do was keep going.

Sylvia. Why hadn't she gone to the police earlier? Why hadn't she told someone if he was threatening her?

"Are you still there?" He said it quietly. His voice had lost some of the strain.

"Yeah."

"Good."

Driving through the rain and the dark talking to Marcus healed some small part of me. After that night, we were okay. Not great, not fixed, not together. But we were okay.

I kept my eyes focused on the road. "Say something," I said. "Talk to me."

He was silent for a while. "I don't think I remember everything we said that night."

"You were a little drunk."

A tense, short laugh came over the line. "I went out with the guys from the bowling alley after it closed. They—uh—know people."

We hadn't talked this much in weeks, and now we had no choice but to talk. "What happened? Why did you get so drunk?"

The line was quiet for a moment again. "Well, you."

The problem we couldn't solve. "I wish I'd thought of that solution. Did getting drunk help?"

He laughed again. "No."

Lights. I killed my headlights immediately. The pinprick glow of a vehicle descended over a hill ahead of me. I wasn't going to tell Marcus yet. He'd go crazy.

I sped up. If I could get close enough to follow him, I might be able to keep my lights off. The lights made a right turn, going east and leaving the northbound highway. The lights were low, though. Too low to be a truck. It might not even be him. I told Marcus about the turn so he'd know where I was going, and promised him I'd hang back.

"I don't remember," he said, "if you said a specific thing that night." His voice was calm and even.

"Which thing?" I asked.

"Whether all the times you said you loved me were in past tense." He paused. "Or, if some of them weren't."

I'd very specifically stuck to past tense. Loved, instead of love.

The driver was heading east now. If he went far enough, he'd hit a small college town, but between here and there it was mostly tiny towns built around grain elevators or highway intersections. This direction did take us closer to St. Joseph, though, by a little.

"Jackie?"

This was not the conversation to be having right now. But it was the only thing I knew to talk about with Marcus right then.

"I'm here. But it's pointless."

"You said before you weren't okay with us being together, for yourself."

"I wasn't."

"And you still think that?"

I could be following the wrong person. Mitch could be far away by now. If that was the case, I'd done my best. I'd tried everything. "No."

His voice went up a bit. "Then—what do you think?"

If I'd told Will, and Claire, and thought about telling Kelsey, I could certainly tell Marcus. "I don't really care anymore if people don't like it. People at school can talk about me all they want. We're us, and if they don't like it, that's their problem. But I do care what our families think. I don't want the kids getting bullied. I don't want our families to split up."

I swerved a little on the road. Driving without my lights was terrifying. My tires kept hitting the shoulder, spinning and jerking on wet gravel, so I drove down the middle of the road. I'd see lights from any oncoming traffic. Hopefully.

"Same. I don't know what to do about that."

"Me either." I topped a hill and had to brake hard. The car fishtailed. The vehicle ahead had slowed down and was only maybe two blocks ahead of me. He didn't use a turn signal but pulled off the road. A flash of lightning lit up the vehicle.

Not a white truck. "Marcus, it's not the truck. It's a green car." I'd seen it before, dropping Sylvia off in the park. Driving past our house yesterday. "It's turning onto a gravel road."

"Does the road have a marker of any kind?" He sounded panicked again. I must have, too.

"No. Unmarked. I don't even see—wait, yeah, those little reflectors marking the ditch on either side. That's it."

"Okay, if it's a gravel road, then he's probably stopping soon. Park the car on the side of the road, keep the doors locked, and don't go any farther."

I'd tell him I was sorry for lying later. "I should go. I need to call in the location."

"Okay. Stay in the car. Someone should be there soon."

It wouldn't be soon. The police could still be in Manson. "Yeah. Talk to you later. Bye."

He hesitated before saying, "Bye."

I zipped up my jacket and, after calling to report the location and telling the woman that yes, I was actually going home now, I slid my phone into my pocket. Lights still off, I turned the car down the gravel road and crept along. I could go slower now; I'd see him again eventually. Unless he knew the area, and this road connected to the highway farther down. I sped up a little.

Two miles. Three. I watched the odometer climbing and the glowing clock on the dashboard changing as the minutes ticked past. Finally, I saw the car's lights wavering ahead of me.

I honestly didn't know what I was going to do. I couldn't save Sylvia—I wasn't dumb enough to think I could rescue her or stop him.

But I couldn't leave. Knowing all this and being right behind him meant I had to do something.

He turned off the gravel road onto a muddy lane. His headlights lit up a building; from here I couldn't see what it was. An old barn, maybe.

I pulled over to the soggy edge of the road and felt the grass and dirt give beneath the tires. He would see me if I drove up the lane. He wouldn't be able to miss it. I had to leave the car. A fringe of trees hid this part of the road from view of the building, so for right then I was safe.

With the car parked, I rested my head on the steering wheel for a moment. I couldn't screw this up.

My jacket was soaked, so I took it off and grabbed my hoodie from my shoulder bag.

I dug through my purse to see if I had anything useful. Gum, my wallet, a handful of crumpled receipts, loose change, a nail file, a notepad, lip gloss, spare eyeliner, and three pens. When had I started carrying around so much useless crap?

The trunk kits. Another one of Aunt Shelly's Internet ideas. Each of the family vehicles had a storm kit, an emergency kit, and a first-aid kit in the trunk. Excessive, as always.

Bless Aunt Shelly and her constant over-preparing.

I scrambled over the seats and onto the bench in the back. The middle section of the seat pulled down as an interior access to the trunk. I had to crawl halfway in to reach one of the waterproof plastic containers that had slid, but I found all three and pulled them out onto the bench. I pulled the lids off and dug through them. An all-weather radio, card games, glow sticks, a flashlight and batteries, a small, tightly rolled tarp, and a laminated sheet of instructions detailing what to do in case of a tornado were in the storm kit; the first-aid kit held gauze and scissors, antiseptic, Band-Aids, antibiotic salve, a first-aid guide, pain reliever, and hand sanitizer. I grabbed the scissors, gauze, glow sticks, and the flashlight, then dug through the emergency kit and pulled out duct tape and the survival knife. I put everything but the scissors and the knife in my shoulder bag; those I slid into the front pocket of my hoodie. My keys and cell phone were in the front pocket of my jeans where they couldn't fall out.

I cinched the strap all the way down on my shoulder bag and slid it over my neck and one arm, with the strap across my chest.

I put my cell phone on vibrate, pulled up my hood, covered the flashlight with my hand before turning it on, and stepped out of the car.

Chapter Twenty-Three

My high-topped sneakers squished into the roadside mud. Rain pierced my hoodie and I closed the car door quietly. Tree branches whipped back and forth. I cracked two of the pencil-sized glow sticks so they'd start glowing, and wedged them straight up against the rear windshield. A confirmation this was the place.

Walking up the lane, no matter how dark it was, wouldn't be a good idea. I stepped through the wet grass to the line of trees that would, on a sunny day, shade the lane.

Maybe if I'd been able to see Sylvia was just a scared teenager, I would have been able to figure this out sooner.

I'd already lost too much time. I walked as fast as I could, following the line of trees. The long grass soaked my shoes and whipped the legs of my jeans.

The building ahead of me was an abandoned farmhouse. Lightning illuminated it every few minutes. Part of the porch roof had fallen in. An enormous tree grew to the side of the house, its swaying branches spreading over the peak of the roof. Behind the house stood a giant barn. The doors hung open. A vehicle was parked inside, and I'd bet it was a white truck.

A pale light flickered in the house. Maybe this was where he'd taken Ellie. An abandoned farmhouse forty-five miles from St. Joseph.

Places like this weren't that rare. A family farm with the grandparents gone. The land around it turned to crops, no one wanting to tear down or sell the old house. Instead, it decayed.

I stuffed my hands in the pocket of my hoodie to keep them from shaking. I gripped the knife, then pulled it out and unsnapped the strap of the little sheath.

The house was huge. Two stories, a big cellar door on the side I could see, and a yawning front porch with three windows and six pillars. This might have been the last place Ellie had ever seen. It wasn't going to be the last place Sylvia saw.

The little green car was pulled around the side of the house, away from the road.

I hadn't planned on getting out of the car. I hadn't planned on going up to the house. But the police still had half an hour before they would be here.

But they could be earlier. Some random cop could be closer than I thought when the call went out. I had no idea how things like that worked. Getting myself killed wouldn't help Sylvia at all, and my little knife and my determination wouldn't take down Mitch Stevenson.

Another light went on in the house. The shades were pulled but light still shone through.

All I had to do was make sure he didn't kill her in the next half hour. If things got bad, I'd cause a distraction. Stall for time.

If she even was here. He'd driven down this lane, but what if Sylvia wasn't with him? Maybe she'd run out of her house and gotten away. Maybe I was doing this for no good reason.

A flower pot tumbled across the yard, a big, bucket-like thing that sailed in the wind. A dozen steps and I'd be at the porch. Thunder pounded directly overhead.

The light from the windows flickered. My clothes were completely soaked now, and if I weren't already shivering from fear, I'd be shivering from the cold.

The steps looked solid, even though the roof had collapsed at the end of the porch. A giant limb from the tree that spread over the house had speared the rotting roof, dangling by the branches caught on the frame. I crept up the steps and knelt on the porch by one of the windows. The shades were old pull-downs that didn't fit the windows. A gap next to the frame showed me an empty yellow-carpeted living room, but I couldn't see Sylvia. The light came from the kitchen.

I circled the house and found the rickety back door—an ornate screen door that had long ago rusted. Holes had been torn in the screen. The wooden door was open. I stayed away from it and crouched by a window to the side. These blinds had slats, and through them I could see a table and chairs right next to the window.

Sylvia sat in one of the chairs not two feet from me. Her hands were in her lap, probably tied.

On the table was a lit candle. An oil lamp rested on the counter, its light flickering over the kitchen. The electricity had probably been turned off here years ago, if the power wasn't out from the storm.

Sylvia was dripping wet. I could only see the side of her face, but her whole body was tense, not moving at all. Her leg was tied to the chair.

The short, skinny man I'd seen so many times walked from the living room into the kitchen.

Sylvia started crying. I tensed, my grip tight on the knife. If I had to do something in a split second, I had no idea what I'd do.

"Don't cry," he said. "We'll go away and you'll be happy."

His voice was muffled some by the rain and the window, but I could hear his words. He reached for something draped over one of the chair backs and held it up. Black cloth. The dress Sylvia had brought to our place. "I wanted you to wear this."

Sobs tore from her throat.

"You can't keep telling me no," he said. "You lied to me. It's not right. I said I'd leave that boy alone."

"I'm sorry," Sylvia sobbed. "I'm sorry, I'm sorry."

I wanted to get her attention, to let her know I was here, but I couldn't risk it. Thunder pounded and lightning tore through the sky.

Something cracked. A branch from the tree hanging over the house hit the roof and scraped across the shingles before crashing to the ground behind me. Branches smacked into my back, but the limb itself missed me. I scrambled out of the way.

He glanced out the window. Maybe he saw something in a flash of lightning or maybe he'd suspected he was being followed. He moved toward the door.

I turned and ran.

Footsteps pounded down the steps. I sank back in the shadow of the house, around the corner. My hands trembled so I gripped the knife harder. If I made no noise at all, he might think it was only the falling branch and go back inside. I didn't think he'd actually seen me. He couldn't have gotten outside in the time it took me to run around the side of the house.

If I ran, I risked him seeing the motion. If I stayed here—

"Hello, Jackie."

I screamed.

He'd stepped around the corner of the house, not ten feet from me. I could barely make out his features in the dim light. I ran, sliding on the wet grass, and he pounded after me.

I couldn't outrun this guy. Within a few yards, he grabbed my arm and flung me up against him. "Give me the knife." I swung my arm but he caught it and twisted the knife away from me. He threw it into the yard and I couldn't see where it fell.

The pressure of his hands on my neck made me hold still. "Don't worry, I won't hurt you," he said. My heart beat funny, skipping beats.

He pushed me back toward the house. I tried to jerk away, but he kept his hand clamped on my neck. He was impossibly strong.

I should have stayed in the car. I never should have gotten out of it. His grip on the back of my neck made my whole body hurt. I stumbled on the steps and he forced me inside. The wind caught the screen door and it banged open, held flat against the house. He left it.

Sylvia's eyes widened when she saw me. Her face was streaked with black trails of mascara. "Jackie."

I got my first good look at him close up, in the light. The dim light illuminated his shaved head.

He was soaking wet, but he didn't seem to notice. Water ran off him and pooled on the kitchen floor. He couldn't be more than ten years older than me, and he wasn't as skinny as he looked. His wet biceps clenched and corded muscles stood out of his neck.

"Jackie knows what this is like," he said. "She knows what you're doing to me."

Rainwater blew in from the open doorway, soaking the floor. Sylvia stared at me, her face white and her lips parted. She'd had no idea someone was following her or anyone even knew where she was.

So far it wasn't doing her much good.

If I told him the police were coming, he might panic and leave us, or he might take us with him. Or he could kill us both and then himself. I hadn't seen a gun, but he might have one somewhere. He jerked my shoulder bag away from me and pulled my cell phone and keys from my pocket, then his hand closed around my arm and he pushed me into the living room. Sylvia started crying again.

The living room was empty. Him separating us wasn't good. I twisted in his grasp, tried to kick him, but he clamped down on my neck and shoved me into the bedroom near the living room. I saw a brief flash of the room in the moment when he opened the door, but then he slammed it and the room went dark. I heard the door lock.

I could have fallen over in relief that he stayed on the other side of the door.

The bed had been made, and I'd seen a blanket. If this was his room, there might be a light. I felt around until I found the legs of a dresser. Nothing on top of it except what felt like paper trash. I kept going and nearly fell over a nightstand. Something clunked to the floor and then rolled under the dresser. A flashlight.

I grabbed it and turned it on. Light pierced the room. I paused for a moment on the floor and leaned against the dresser, trying to get air back into my body.

The quiet was shattered by Sylvia screaming. He started yelling, both of them so loud I couldn't hear what he was saying. I wanted to cover my ears to block out her terror.

We'd be okay. We had to be okay. I hadn't planned on getting caught, but the police would be here before long. They had to be.

I had to get out of here. Shag carpet ran to the walls, and the windows were boarded up. I tugged on the edges of the boards, but they were solid wood, not plywood, and they'd been screwed to the window frames.

Maybe they weren't even coming. I'd told them about Ellie's jersey, and it was still on Sylvia's porch, but what if they didn't think it was hers? The only thing out of place in the house was a broken plate. If Sylvia hadn't reported problems with Mitch before, they'd have no reason to believe me. My panicked call about following a car out of town and that jersey was the only evidence they had that anything was wrong. Maybe they'd think it was a prank call. Maybe they'd think it was an ordinary volleyball jersey.

I couldn't leave that to chance.

Maybe the dresser drawers had something. I jerked open the top three, but they had a few changes of clothes and that was it. The bottom drawer, though, had two giant scrapbooks. I shone the light into the drawer and opened the cover of the first. I froze.

Sylvia's face stared back at me.

I pulled the book out. Photos in neat rows of her playing volleyball. The next page was more photos. Photo after photo. Some in the winter, some in the fall. Some of her at the pool, from a ways away. One of her with Ellie after a game. In almost none of them was she looking toward the camera. Several were of her with Marcus.

The pictures were lined up neatly, trimmed to fit the page. Mixed in with them were receipts, notes, small pieces of paper she'd written on. The last half of the book was filled with tiny, neat handwriting, marked with dates and times. Places she'd gone. Things she'd eaten. Who she'd talked to. Sometimes what she'd said. It went back for months.

I didn't have time to do anything but skim it, but this would put him in prison. I reached for the second one. This had to be Ellie's, and it might say why he'd killed her.

I opened it and then dropped it. My throat closed up and if it hadn't I would have screamed.

Not Ellie. Me.

I touched the cover, then grabbed the book and opened it. Photos of my house. Of Candace and Angie. Of me at the pool, in my bikini. Me and Claire with ice cream. The house at night, through the big kitchen window, with us sitting at the dinner table. Sylvia's car, sitting in our driveway. One of me searching through his tent that day Marcus's tires had been cut. A blurry shot of me on the bandstand, talking to Will. All of us walking into the pizza place on our double date.

Me and Marcus. So, so many of me and Marcus. I nearly threw up when I saw the one at night, at the creek. I could barely see us, but we were there, a dim shape on our towels.

My book was thinner than Sylvia's. None of the pictures went back more than a few months, to the beginning of the summer when we'd met her.

I turned past the photos because I couldn't look at them anymore. The next section was a long list. *Drinks coffee with cream and sugar. Likes chocolate ice cream. Likes Hitchcock, Audrey Hepburn, Humphrey Bogart. Doesn't like cigarette smoke. One sister. Wears a charm bracelet that matches Ellie Wallace's. Wears shorts most of the time. Owns a green-and-white bikini and a black-and-white checkered one. Doesn't like mornings.* The list went on for whole pages. I kept turning them, looking at the facts of my life over the summer. Chills trickled down my back, settled in my stomach.

The list ended. I turned the page and there in front of me were my blog posts. All of them, printed out and annotated with his handwriting. He'd underlined sentences and scribbled in the margins on every single one. Several of them were in each plastic sleeve. I flipped through them. They went back two years.

The final section made my fingers curl tight around the edges of the book.

My e-mails to Travis. All of them. With his replies. Highlights, underlining, notes in the margins. None of my other e-mails, just the ones to and from Travis. I pressed my hands onto my legs and took several deep breaths, but it didn't help.

The shrill scream of a car alarm punctured the silence. I scrambled to my feet. Something scraped at the lock. Mitch opened the door. His eyes were red. He strode over to me and grabbed my chin, a giant kitchen knife in his hand. "What is that?"

He could break my neck so easily. I looked into his eyes and hoped he couldn't feel me shaking. "I don't know."

"Is that your car?"

I shook my head. There was no way my car alarm would be this loud from this far away, not through the storm. He let go of my chin and my stomach sank. For one second, I'd hoped the sound was a police siren.

"You were e-mailing me," I said. "This whole time."

He looked at the books on the floor, then back to me. "Sylvia doesn't want me anymore," he said. "But you. You understand wanting something you can't have." He touched my face again. "Because of you and your cousin. You know what it's like."

He gripped me by the neck and pushed me out of the room back to the kitchen. The shrieking of the car alarm kept whipping through the air, punctuated by the blare of the horn. He grabbed the last of the nylon rope from the counter, pulled my hands behind my back, and tied them together. The rope slid in tight figure-eights around my wrists.

He forced me down into a chair. The oil lamp flickered in the wind from the open door but stayed lit. The candle guttered.

Mitch shoved my chair back into the corner, away from the table. He jerked the last length of rope around my leg and the leg of the chair.

I pulled against the rope on my hands, but couldn't get it to give. I glanced at Sylvia. Swelling bruises marked her neck and her cheek.

I felt around but couldn't find anything sharp on the back of the chair or the wall to scrape the ropes on.

Sylvia shivered, her eyes wide. He grabbed her hands and hauled her up, but all he did was cut the ropes on her hands. The slit lengths dropped to the floor. She stumbled a bit, her leg still tied to the chair.

"I wasn't going to hurt you," he said. He stepped back and picked up the dress. His breath rasped in and out. "I was going to take care of you."

If Sylvia panicked, things would get worse fast. The storm blew sheets of water against the windows.

She was so pale. She looked like she might pass out. Something smacked the window outside. Hail here too, now. "Sylvia," he said. His voice cracked. He handed her the dress. "I bought this for you. Put it on."

The black fabric trembled as she held it. "Here?"

"Put it on." The alarm kept blaring, echoing against the buildings. Sylvia's leg was still tied to the chair. He pushed her down into it. "I'll be back in less than two minutes, and if one of you is gone, the other one will pay for it."

He ran out the door and into the rain.

It must be his truck alarm. Sylvia put her head down on the table as soon as he left. I jerked my leg against the rope. It was a small piece, not quite long enough to tie as tightly as he had my hands.

She had to pull it together if we were going to get out of this. "Can you get the ropes off your leg?"

She sat up and watched me. "They're cutting into my ankle."

The knot gave and the rope on my leg pulled apart. I stood up and ran over to the counter, looking for anything we could use. "What if you take your shoe off?" Plastic bags, the oil lamp on the counter. Nothing else. I tried opening drawers even though my hands were tied behind my back, looking for something, anything.

"I can try." She reached down and fumbled with her sneaker. It thumped to the floor. "Almost. I can't get them over my heel."

"Can you grab anything to help you pry on the knot? Will the leg pull out of the bottom of the chair?"

She worked at it with her fingers. She gasped and choked out a sob. "He's my coach. My volleyball coach. He left Ellie's uniform on my porch."

My hands were tied, but I could run. He'd catch me, though, and if I was gone, he'd hurt Sylvia. She couldn't leave, tied to that chair. "I know," I said. "It's okay. I called the police and they should be coming."

"Oh, God. Oh, thank God. But I can't get the knot. I can't get it!" Her whole body shook. I'd never seen someone this panicked before. She choked. "I had a thing with him last semester. He seemed nice. He said he liked me." Her words tumbled over themselves and she cried into the sleeve of her shirt. "I had sex with him in his office. Just once. But Ellie saw me with him, after. He kept talking about her, said it was a problem. When she disappeared, I got scared. He kept messaging me online and calling me and wanting me to come over to his house. We were moving, so I deleted all my stuff online, changed my phone, and hoped he'd give up."

The traveling rolls of thunder quieted. The truck alarm abruptly cut out. Sweat pricked my body.

A creak sounded from the living room behind me.

A glow stick rolled into the kitchen. Sylvia didn't notice, still crying and wrestling with the knot. I stared at the little white tube. I edged over to the living room, my heart pounding.

Just the other side of the kitchen wall stood Marcus. I stared at him, stunned. He put a finger to his lips and spun me around in the doorway. I caught a glimpse of Uncle Ward's gun.

He sawed at the ropes around my wrists. His truck had the same kits as mine. I saw Mitch out the door, walking through the rain. "He's coming back, he's coming!" I hissed. "We can't leave Sylvia. She's tied to the chair."

The cords fell off. Mitch climbed the steps. Marcus's hands left me. All Mitch would be able to see was me standing in the living room doorway. I walked into the kitchen, away from Marcus. Water ran toward us from the pool by the open door. Hail bounced on the front step, cracking when it hit the cement.

He was calmer now, and that was more frightening than his labored breathing had been. "Sit down," he said. Hands still behind my back, I moved toward the chair and sat down.

"Did you mess with the truck?" he asked.

I shook my head. "I didn't even see it."

He grabbed Sylvia's arm and pulled her up again. "You didn't put on the dress." He thrust the cloth at her again.

Marcus. Come on. What are you doing?

Mitch was right in front of Sylvia. Marcus would wait until he moved.

Tears ran down Sylvia's face. She'd been shaking for so long, she had to be exhausted. She pulled her shirt over her head. Her black bra made her skin look even whiter in the dim kitchen. Sylvia looked to me.

Mitch followed her glance. He looked from me to the doorway where I'd been standing. The rope lay on the floor. He lunged at me and Marcus stepped into the doorway.

But he wasn't fast enough. I bolted from the chair, but Mitch grabbed me and jerked me up against his body. His blade pricked my throat. "Don't move," he said. I fought down my panic. My whole body was tuned in to the cold steel on my neck. He could stab me and I'd die right here.

"Put the gun down," Mitch demanded. He pushed my chin up with the knife. His forearm tightened across my chest, pinning me to him. He yanked me closer to himself and I felt his heartbeat.

Marcus lowered the gun. My body shuddered as I pulled air into my lungs. The kitchen door still hung open. The sagging floor tilted the water toward us.

"Put it on the counter," Mitch said.

Water trickled past me on the floor and Marcus kept looking at me. His face had gone white. He set the gun down on the counter. Hail cracked against the kitchen windows.

This man had killed Ellie, had watched me all summer, had written my life down in a book. My hand brushed the pocket of my hoodie. The scissors.

We weren't victims yet.

Marcus. Look at me. Be patient. One more moment.

His eyes were frantic, looking from the gun to the windows to Sylvia. He was going to do something rash; he wouldn't let this guy hurt either of us without getting himself killed first. I needed him to look at me. He needed to wait.

He'd had a knife when he cut my hands free; he should still have it. In his back pocket or something. It had to be fast, before Mitch got this anymore under control.

Sylvia still stood in her soaking wet jeans and bra. Mitch looked toward her and I felt his attention shift. His chest and arms tensed. Right then, he wasn't thinking about me. The girl he'd been stalking for months was undressing.

Look at me, Marcus. Please. Notice what I'm doing.

Without moving my upper arm, I slid my hand into my hoodie pocket. Thank God for the rain. I wouldn't be wearing a hoodie otherwise. Finally, Marcus looked at me. I met his eyes, careful not to blink. I pulled out the scissors. They were small but sharp, meant for cutting gauze in the first-aid kit. I could feel where Mitch's jeans stopped on his waist. My fist covered the handle and most of the blades.

Marcus saw it. He looked back to my face. I blinked once.

Moving just my fingers, I turned the scissors around so the blades pointed down and opened the handles just a bit. I blinked again. A slight movement in Marcus's shoulders told me he was ready. He had to go first, but only by a second. He was a few feet away.

I blinked a third time and Marcus dove for us. I plunged the scissors backward into Mitch's stomach.

Mitch screamed and Marcus crashed into us. I flung my arms up and his knife sliced my arm instead of my neck. Pain tore through me. Mitch stumbled and slipped on the wet floor. We fell. His head smacked into the table. Marcus grabbed the knife and grunted as he wrestled it away from him. Mitch thrashed but Marcus knelt on his chest and had his knife at Mitch's throat before I could untangle myself.

"Jackie, get my knife and the scissors and everything else you see and take them out of here. Sylvia, it's okay. Put your shirt back on. Both of you just stay away." His voice was firm and his hands gripped the knife, the blade pressed against Mitch's neck. The blade was bloody.

I stood up, my knees unsteady, and moved anything Mitch could grab, then wound the only dish towel around my arm. It hurt like the devil, but it was better than being dead. I moved over to Sylvia and slit the rope so it unwound from her leg.

Mitch's breathing rasped and he struggled to throw Marcus off him. His voice cracked. "Sylvia. Don't do this to me."

Sylvia sank to the floor and seemed to finally be out of tears. Shock, probably. She closed her eyes and didn't respond.

I didn't know how Marcus was so calm. I'd always gotten the nervous shakes. Had I not put those scissors in my pocket, one of us could be dead.

I wasn't going to stand back while Marcus handled this himself. I grabbed the roll of duct tape from my bag.

"Jackie, stay back. Don't come over here."

I ignored him. The duct tape made ripping sounds as I unrolled it. I grabbed Mitch's feet and wound a figure-eight of tape around them. He kicked when he felt what I was doing but Marcus slammed Mitch's head back to the ground. "I swear to God, if you move again or say one more word, I'm sticking this knife in your neck and then I'll stab you in the balls."

I finished his feet and moved to his hands. Pulling and ripping the tape sent pain burning through my arm.

Marcus's shirt was splashed with red. I did a double take and let the tape fall to the ground. A horizontal rip in his shirt right in the middle of the red patch. I touched him on his shoulder so he'd know what I was doing, then moved the hem of his shirt. Blood stained his jeans, a thick red trail spreading from an inflamed slice above his hip.

Stab wounds could be bad. I gently touched the angry skin above the wound, and he sucked in a breath. "Your hands are cold."

"Sorry." I moved my hand.

"No," he said quietly. "It helps."

I glanced up, but he wouldn't look at me. "We have to get pressure on this. You're bleeding everywhere." My hands had stopped trembling. I unwound the towel from around my arm and carefully pressed it to his side. The knife had cut muscle. He stiffened. The towel grew warm from the blood almost immediately. Out the big kitchen window, headlights pierced the rain. Blood, so much blood.

I'd put gauze from the emergency kit in my bag. I grabbed my bag and pulled out the white roll, folded it into a square, and pressed it carefully to his stomach. The red stain soaked through, so I pressed a little harder.

Marcus jerked. His skin was turning unnaturally pale and clammy. I peered into his eyes, checked his pulse. It was faint and far too fast. I pressed harder on the gauze and kept talking to him. "Hey, Marcus. Keep your eyes open, okay? Hey. Look at me."

Feet pounded up the steps. Three men in blue uniforms. One of them pulled me away from him, tried to look at my arm, but I sent him back to Marcus. The other two men had hauled the coach to his feet. The officer tore open a first-aid kit and pressed a clean dressing to Marcus's side.

I leaned my head back against the base of the counter.

Sylvia hadn't seen something, like I'd thought. Ellie had seen something, she'd been killed for it, and now she was the silent ghost who lived in the threads between Sylvia and me and Marcus.

The cop came back to me and checked my arm while I glanced around the room. This was where Ellie had died; I was sure of it.

If I waited long enough, maybe she'd walk through the doorway to the kitchen and ask me where I'd been.

Chapter Twenty-Four

The doctors kept Marcus overnight at the hospital. We'd both gotten stitches, but he'd lost a lot more blood than I had. I talked to the police four times, said a hundred times that yes it was a dangerous thing to do, and answered every question at least twice. The white truck turned out to be borrowed, and the volleyball jersey was Ellie's. When our parents and Sylvia's dad arrived, everything started all over again and nothing I could say would make Mom stop crying or Uncle Ward stop hovering.

In the hospital, left alone for a moment by both the doctors and the police while they talked to the parents, I turned to Marcus. "You followed me when I called you, didn't you?"

He looked a little less pale now. "You wouldn't come back, so I grabbed the gun from Dad's closet and told Chris to watch the kids. I was maybe three miles behind you, so it wouldn't have taken me so long, but you didn't park your car where you said you did. I missed the turn."

I played with my fingernails. "I couldn't sit there in the car."

A nurse came in to check my stitches, and after she left, I said, "We never finished our conversation."

He moved his arm but winced and stopped. "That's true."

I had to leave, but he'd be home soon. I hated the way he looked in that white bed, hooked up to an IV. "You take getting better seriously, okay? None of this halfway stuff."

His smile was tired, but it was real. "You know me. All or nothing."

Lately, that was me, too.

I slept until ten the next day, but since a guy had attacked me with a knife the day before, I figured no one could complain. I sat up in bed, leaning on my arm before remembering. I sucked in a breath and checked it. The bandage was still fine. It just hurt.

Claire took off work and came home that afternoon, arriving shortly after Will. By the time Aunt Shelly came back from getting Marcus, I'd told the story so many times I'd lost count and I really couldn't handle one more person asking me one more question. When Marcus saw me curled up in the armchair in the corner of the living room, he smiled and was more than happy to take over the storytelling. By the time Angie and Candace were done with him, the story had gained a machete, an M16, and a skateboard. Chris listened skeptically, but only rolled his eyes once.

I walked outside to get away from the chaos. Will and Claire were helping Mom with dinner inside; the clatter of plates and cupboard doors drifted out to where I sat on the front step. The cement had dried after a full day of sun. I was playing with my charm bracelet when the door creaked open and Will came out.

He sat beside me, but didn't say anything. I pulled my knees up to my chest and rested my chin on them. "So, I told Marcus we weren't together."

He nodded. "That's probably good." He nudged me with his shoulder. "But you'll still wear my necklace, right?"

I touched the yin-yang symbol around my neck. "Already am."

He pulled his cigarettes out of his pocket and tapped the pack, but didn't pull one out. "You and Claire get along pretty well, right?"

I shrugged. "We're really different, but I think sometimes that helps."

"So." He paused again. "I have an awkward question for you, and it's going to make me sound like a horrible person."

I glanced sideways at him and waited. He pulled out a cigarette and took a long time lighting it. He looked at me, then down, then played with his lighter.

Because he looked so guilty, I took pity on him. "You know, you should ask Claire out. I'm ninety percent certain she has an enormous crush on you."

For once, he didn't have a comeback. He just blinked. "Well?" I asked.

Relief showed in his blue eyes. "You think she does?"

"Ask and find out." I wasn't sure what I thought when the idea first occurred to me, but it made sense. Will and Claire would be great together.

He grinned. "You're okay with that?"

"I'm definitely okay with that."

He stood up, a giant silly smile on his face. "I'll go inside and see if I can help your mom. I gotta make her like me for real now."

"Dude. If you want her to like you, leave that out here."

He groaned and ground out the cigarette on the step. The screen door banged behind him when he went inside.

Marcus came out, talking on the phone. To Sylvia, it sounded like. He walked past me. She must have been talking a lot, because he wasn't saying much. He climbed into his truck and sat there for a while, drumming his fingers on the steering wheel and occasionally saying something I couldn't hear.

He looked tense when he climbed out of the truck a few minutes later, but I couldn't tell if it was from his wound or the call.

"How's Sylvia?" I asked.

He leaned against the truck. "Her dad's freaking out. He didn't know any of this until last night. He's been in and out of the police station all day. She says they might move again." His dark hair stood on end, and he'd shoved up the sleeves of his long-sleeved T-shirt. He stood awkwardly, leaning his weight on one foot. His side would be hurting for a while yet, and the stitches probably pulled.

"Oh." I stood up and walked over to him.

"She told me her dad's going to have her see a therapist or something."

"That might be a good idea." Seeing my life in a book that way had scarred me for life. I couldn't even imagine what the whole thing must have done to her. "Did you tell her about us?"

He shook his head. "I figured I shouldn't. I think she guessed, though. And . . ." He looked down. His face flushed and his eyebrows drew together. "After that night I came home and we—I told her I cheated on her."

I wanted to step closer to him and take that look off his face, but we were right in front of the kitchen windows. "But it wasn't like that, Marcus. It's not the same—"

"Yes, it is. It's exactly the same. I was with her, and I kissed someone else."

I stared at the bricked driveway. "What did she do?"

He rubbed his hands on the legs of his jeans. "I tried to be as honest as I could about it. I told her there was someone else, and I'd kissed her, but that was all." He shrugged. "She dumped me."

I kept my glance on the bricks. No wonder Sylvia hadn't looked good in school that day. She'd been meeting up with her coach to keep Marcus safe, and then Marcus came and told her he'd kissed someone else. "I'm sorry."

He was quiet until I looked up at him and found his gaze pinned on me. "It's a good thing. She's not who I want."

Now that he'd said it, we had to do something. "Can we go somewhere?"

He followed me down the driveway to the gravel road. I didn't want someone coming outside and interrupting us. "What are we going to do?" I asked.

"What do you want to do?"

"I don't know."

"Tell me what you're thinking." His pace matched mine. His arm brushed me as we walked.

"I'm thinking we're stuck, because we can't do this again and hide it."

His voice was quiet, hesitant. "Would you be okay with not hiding it?"

I put my hand on his arm, and he flinched. I hadn't been thinking about his stitches when I asked to go for a walk.

"Let's sit down."

He looked relieved. "Sure."

We walked off the road to the side of the hill and sat down in the long grass. It was still damp, but I didn't care and he didn't look like he did, either. "I'm not ashamed of us. If my friends can't understand something this important to me, then I don't need them. And I don't care what people would say behind my back." That night he'd kissed me, he'd asked what I'd do if he wasn't my cousin. But if he wasn't my cousin, he wouldn't be Marcus. There was no way to separate the two, and I was done thinking I should. "You're what I want, and the rest of it doesn't matter enough to make a difference." A few months ago, I wouldn't have been able to say that, but it was true.

The tiredness lifted from his eyes. "You still do? You still want me?"

"I still want you."

"I would never cheat on you. I don't want you to be worried because—I wouldn't."

That hadn't even crossed my mind. "I know you wouldn't."

He was quiet for a minute. "We have to make this work. Somehow."

"But our families are different from our friends. We can't—" The way his hand closed over mine stopped me.

"We don't know what they'll think. We haven't told them."

"They'd lose it." Aunt Shelly especially. Mom would try to understand, but I had no idea what Dad or Uncle Ward would say.

"I'm not saying it would go smoothly." He smiled halfheartedly. "All Mom's healthy living, and look how I turned out."

"Maybe if she'd fed you more tofu." I bit my lip to keep from smiling. "You know, though. The twins. They'd grow up knowing about us and thinking it was normal. By the time they're old enough to know it's unusual, they might not care."

"You know this would make you not normal, right?" He was teasing me, but I could see the hesitation in his eyes.

"I'm starting to think being normal is abnormal." Maybe my mother was right about that. Being normal was just a thing in people's minds, and something no one really was.

He took my hand and gripped it. "I missed you like crazy."

Something trickled through me, and it wasn't until I smiled that I realized how happy the thought made me. "So we'll figure it out," I said. "We can think about it, and figure out a way to make it work."

And the thing was, if we could handle our families, we probably could make it work. Being together wasn't illegal. Our parents might not like it, but we were seventeen, almost eighteen. If we both wanted it, if we could handle the complications, then we could.

Lines creased his forehead and his lips made a thin line. "I'd want us to last, Jackie. This would be it for me."

I nodded. No way did I want to go through that again. "Me too."

We didn't have to be a doomed romance. We weren't some cosmic mistake. We were us, and we couldn't be stopped by anything but ourselves. All we had to do was figure out how to make it work. "I want to do it right," I said. "No pretending, no hiding. Everything real and no limits."

He pulled me closer. "I really want to kiss you," he whispered into my hair.

"Then do it," I said.

And he did. His lips were familiar, but kissing him with no guilt and no secrets and him knowing what I wanted was so new.

When he pulled back, we sat there for a few minutes, his hand in mine. A breeze filtered through the hills and teased my hair.

Someone yelled from the yard. It sounded like Chris. I pulled back a little. "It's probably dinner time," I said. He couldn't see us from here, but we should go back anyway.

"Right." Marcus got to his feet, a little stiffly. He brushed the bandage on my arm with a finger and took my hand again.

Dinner was on the table by the time we went inside. Marcus sat in his usual place across from me, and kept bumping my foot under the table as we ate. Everyone was there, but no one noticed how Marcus seemed unable to stop looking at me and I couldn't quit smiling. The parents talked on about the coach and when they thought the trial would be and whether we'd have to testify. Dad kept saying yes, but not for a while, and the twins banged their spoons on their plates.

Will occupied Claire at the other end of the table, and for once, she wasn't the one talking. He turned to look at me, and when I nodded, he winked and went back to Claire.

After dinner, the parents told us they would take care of the chores, saying we could probably use a break after last night. No one argued. I was sore, and still exhausted, and after spending so many hours soaked to the skin, I was permanently cold.

Chris went up to his computer and Will and Claire said they were going outside. Claire gave me a guilty look, but I grinned and texted her.

No worries. Have fun.

Marcus came up behind me in the living room while the parents got the twins down from the table and cleared the dishes. He moved my hair aside, and his breath warmed my neck when he whispered. "I have an idea."

I turned around. "Tell me."

He glanced toward the kitchen. "Not here."

"Take me out." Now that I'd thought of it, I couldn't let it go. "Let's go, right now."

He must have thought it was a good idea because he grabbed his keys and beat me to the door. The parents would know we were leaving together, but that was okay. He opened the door of his truck for me, then jogged around to the driver's side.

He slammed his door and started the truck. A slow smile spread over his face. "So, is this a real date?"

I laughed. Nearly two years after I'd kissed him, a year after I'd loved him, we were going on our first date. "It's totally a real date."

He took me to Todd's in Manson for ice cream, and got us sundaes. We took them over to one of the picnic tables in the corner of the lot and sat on the top of the table, resting our feet on the bench. People milled around us; couples, parents, friends hanging out on a Sunday night. It was a very normal date, and I wouldn't have changed anything about it.

"So what's your idea?" I swirled my spoon through the chocolate sauce.

He watched me, not touching his ice cream. "I figured we could get the parents out of the house. Talk to all four of them at once, both of us. And start with telling them that I'm moving out."

I stopped swirling the sauce. "What? No. You can't—"

"Listen. It makes sense. They're far more likely to be okay with us if we're not living together while they get used to it. And teachers and social workers would have no reason to get involved if it's not a home environment issue."

It sounded like he'd researched this. The living together part did make everything that much more awkward, and my family would have no reason to leave if Marcus wasn't living there. "I could move out. It doesn't have to be you. I could move in with Claire."

A smile tugged at his mouth. "You are your parents' last child. My parents have five more."

Fair point. "Okay," I said. "You'll move out. We'll tell them about us. Then what?"

"Then." He finally took a bite of his ice cream. "I'll transfer for the rest of this year to a different school."

Absolutely not. "You can't leave your senior year."

"I'll still see my friends. But this will be so much easier for both of us if we're not giving people daily opportunities to be weird about it. And after that, we'll go to college where people won't know us and it won't matter. We'll handle it one thing at a time."

I could handle people teasing and gossiping, but it wouldn't be fun. If people weren't seeing us come to school together in the mornings, weren't seeing us in the halls together, it would be easier to adjust. Plus, if it wasn't happening at the school, the grades my other cousins were in might not even hear about it. It might not be an issue for them.

"Besides," he said, "at a new school, I could tell people all about this awesome girl I'm dating."

"Well. You're not dating her yet." I kept my attention on my ice cream.

He set his down. "You're going to make me ask you, aren't you?"

I ignored him and licked my spoon. We weren't normal, whatever that meant, and that was okay. But the traditional crush and first date and first everything that other people got still sounded pretty good.

He sighed, but I heard the smile in it. He slid off the table and stood up. "Hey," he said. "So, I think I've seen you around somewhere."

I shaded my eyes against the evening sun and looked up at him. He stood awkwardly, his hands shoved in his back pockets. I grinned and played along. "You look familiar, I guess."

"You here by yourself?"

I tilted my head. "Not anymore."

"I thought I'd come see if I could convince you to go out with me."

Not the world's greatest pickup line, but I'd give him points for being direct. I raised an eyebrow. "Like, a casual pizza and a movie date?"

"No." He leaned down and put one hand on either side of me on the table. "Like a serious, make-you-my-girlfriend date."

For no reason at all, a shiver ran through my stomach. I leaned back a little. "That sounds pretty intense."

"It would be."

"You'd have to meet my parents. I don't know if you can handle that."

He rested his forehead on mine. "I bet I can."

I smiled. "Then yes. I will go out with you. But I like to get to know a guy first," I said.

We had to try, or we'd lose who we were. The last two years had been a long, hard fall, but some people took the risk because the safe choice would always leave them missing something.

The rest of this year and the start of college and the fallout with our families would probably have many little ending points, a lot of tiny resolutions our lives could hang from, and like in films, maybe one of them would be something people would use later to interpret how we lived the rest of our lives. But a fade to black was only the point where other people stopped looking in. Ilsa's plane went up into the sky before *Casablanca*'s credits rolled, but somewhere, that plane would have to land, and her story would keep going.

Marcus sat down next to me on the picnic table. "What do you want to know about me?" He reached for his ice cream. I'd eaten pretty much all the toppings off mine immediately, but he was working through his evenly across the container.

"Well, where do you want to go to college?"

He shrugged. "I have a few ideas. Someplace with a good engineering program."

I actually hadn't known that about him. "Engineering. Okay."

He pointed his spoon at me. "A couple of them, actually, are in California."

I scraped the last of the fudge off the top of my ice cream. "I think you'd like California," I said. And there on the picnic table, in front of everyone, I reached between us for his hand.

Acknowledgments

On my bookshelf sits a trio: a nursery with a stuffed rabbit who wants to be Real, and a cupboard under the stairs with a boy who lived, and a pair of teens struggling with hamartia and infinity. Their worlds changed mine, so I want to thank them and their creators for stories with so much life.

I'd also like to thank my readers, because stories need to be sent out and heard, and you heard this one, and that's one of the greatest gifts you could give me. You make this possible.

I owe so much to Jesse. Best friend, first reader, inspiration for all the guys I write. Thanks for making it real.

Of course, I owe so much gratitude to my agent, Carlie Webber. Thank you for taking risks, and for believing in me and this book. You challenge and support me, and this wouldn't have happened without you.

Jacquelyn Mitchard and the wonderful team at Merit and F+W Media have turned this story into a book. Your enthusiasm for it amazes me and I'm so grateful for the time, talent, and effort every one of you put into it. Thank you.

To my sisters and brothers—all twelve of you, biological and in-law—thank you for being such a significant part of my childhood, my adult years, and my writing. Each one of you worked your way into this book. Being your sister is a blessing, and my life would be so much lesser without it.

To my parents, and grandparents, aunts and uncles, and my entire family on both sides who read and asked and encouraged. It's meant so much to me to have you involved. And especially to my niece, who at four years old followed me out of my library and asked me how writing my book was going. I hope you always love reading, Emma.

My friends, too, have been the most supportive people a girl could ask for. Lynn, Robin, Jess, Andrea, Alicia and Jonathan, Nick and Bree, Sarah and Micah, and the rest of you—thanks for being the wonderful people that you are.

So many people have pushed me a step further, encouraged me, and made me keep working. Everyone at Entangled Publishing, the Carol Mann Agency, and Month9Books, who has supported my writing career—thank you. So many authors, agents, and editors have shown a lot of love and support for both this book and my writing, and it's made all the difference. Thank you, also, to my college professors, particularly James Schaap, Mary Dengler, Leah Zuidema, Bill Elgersma, and Ed Starkenburg, for doing what you do every day. You changed the way I saw myself and everything else. And to my writing group—one Monday a month, you tell me I'm not crazy. You're probably wrong, but I love you for it.

The writing and reading community is a wonderful place to be. To all of my Twitter friends, blog readers, the Publishing Hub team, and all of you who have read any of my stories—you make a solitary chair in my library and a computer screen the biggest of worlds. My street team, too, has been the greatest group of supporters and fans out there. Thanks for helping make this happen; you're nothing short of wonderful.

So many gracious beta readers helped me by pushing this book and my ideas. Kat Brauer, Amy Sonnichsen, Diana Gallagher, Amanda Burckhard, Jessica Szabo, Stefan Knibbe, Kelly Youngblood, Lynn Edwards, and the rest of you who read for me—thank you. Special thanks to my sister-in-law Hannah Brauning, who has read so much of my writing and has been so supportive over the last several years, and to

Kiersi Burkhart, for all her encouragement and for never failing to type a really long e-mail back. There's a special group of insanely brilliant writers I have left to thank. Nikki Urang—all the way back then, who'd have guessed? Soul sisters! Alex Yuschik—remember that one day, with all the e-mails and all the chapters? I'll never stop saying thank you, so you'd better stick around. Nicole Baart—thank you for so many hours, for so many rants, for all the times you say something and I say "exactly!" Tonya Kuper— if I ever work half as hard or laugh half as much as you do, I'll call it a success. Emery Lord—your enthusiasm is one of my fifteen favorite things about you. Thanks for being awesome on every level. Bethany Robison—you're one of the most generous, most insightful writers I know. Thanks so much for sending it my way. And to all six of you, thank you for the writing retreats and e-mails and hours on Gchat and texts and edits and advice. Thank you for all your genius and all your art and the totally undeserved support and enthusiasm. You're my kind of people.

Finally, thank you to all the artists who created the things that inspired me and this book. The directors and actors and screenwriters who made Jackie's favorite films, the musicians I wrote her story to (Bastille, Sara Bareilles, Birdy, P!nk, Brandi Carlile, The Killers, and The Swell Season), and the writers who wrote the books that made me want to write. Your art inspires mine.

About the Author

Kate Brauning grew up in rural Missouri in a big family, and now lives in Iowa with her husband and Siberian husky. She loves to travel, works in publishing, and is pursuing her lifelong dream of telling stories she'd want to read. This is her first novel. Visit her online at *http://katebrauning.com* or on Twitter @KateBrauning.